CW00701698

DEPARTMENT 9
BOOK THREE OF
CHIMERA COMPANY

Tim C. Taylor

Theogony Books
Coinjock, NC

Chris Kennedy/Theogony Books
1097 Waterlily Rd.
Coinjock, NC 27923
http://chriskennedypublishing.com/

Publisher's Note: This is a work of fiction. Names, characters, places, and incidents are a product of the author's imagination. Locales and public names are sometimes used for atmospheric purposes. Any resemblance to actual people, living or dead, or to businesses, companies, events, institutions, or locales is completely coincidental.

Cover Design by Vincent Sammy

Ordering Information:
Quantity sales. Special discounts are available on quantity purchases by corporations, associations, and others. For details, contact the "Special Sales Department" at the address above.

Department 9/Tim C. Taylor -- 1st ed.
ISBN: 978-1648551550

Chapter One:
Carnolin Indoh

"I
t was waiting for the auto shuttle that led to my downfall. To this…to my slow-motion execution."

I choke, almost weeping like a human, before continuing in a quivering, little-girl voice. I sound tiny in the dank finality of my cell.

"I was a big supporter of In'Nalla's campaign for the introduction of the auto shuttles." I laugh bitterly. "Despite everything, I still love In'Nalla." I speak carefully, guarding my words, even here when it is surely too late for me. "And I still support the auto shuttles, even though they destroyed me."

I grow angry with my jailer's silence. Were they even still there?

I glare at the cell door with its one-way mirrored upper half. From the corridor outside, jailers and paying visitors can view my shame. Even the darkness doesn't shroud me—the mirror has low-light enhancements, so they are unhindered in their enjoyment of my…licensed humiliation.

I stride across the stone floor, advancing to within a few inches. With my bare feet, I toe the mirror's sight lines painted on the floor. Shamelessly, I cross my arms in front of me and demand of the silent jailer, "Shall I go on?"

"Tell me about the shuttles," they respond in a voice that seems stripped of emotion.

Usually, the speaker grill above the door carries leering voices that try to flail me with their gleeful torments. I have, after all, been placed here for the world's education and amusement. After a carefully orchestrated media campaign, I have been so thoroughly de-personed that to enjoy my shame is not only a licensed pleasure, but a social duty.

This jailer is different somehow.

Although I sense no enjoyment of my plight, there's no sympathy for me, either.

Perhaps I'm imagining this, but I think this jailer is the one being in this world who still regards me as a person.

It's not much comfort. But I take it.

I shuffle back to the pile of clean straw that is the nest I have made in the center of my prison—as I was instructed to do when I was first put here. I sit and immediately feel the chill of the cold stone flags shoot up my buttocks.

I consider asking the guard for more straw, but I cannot risk dispelling the moment. They are listening to me. Actually *listening*.

I can't shake the suspicion that this is all an elaborate joke at my expense, but I try to convince myself that they are genuinely interested in my words. My real words—not the words I am made to say for the public recordings.

I am a person. Maybe for one final time.

And that's far more precious to me than warding off the chill of the stones. So I explain about the shuttles.

"We called them buses. When In'Nalla proposed them, EB-Link was deathly quiet for the first day, everyone watching each other, hoping someone else would test the air so we would all learn how we were allowed to react.

"But it seemed this was a genuine example of the jury of public debate. In'Nalla argued that the Metro areas required efficient, universal coverage, and, above all, safe mass transit, but the existing transport system had failed her citizens. It needed a helping hand."

The patchwork of competing transport companies *had* failed, of course. But even here, I don't dare voice that idea because that would sound like I'm proposing a state-run transit system. And to do that would be to declare support for Jacobin socialism, which is a doctrine out of favor with the Revered Leader.

When she proposed the shuttles, nobody dared to openly accuse In'Nalla of ideological wrong-think, of course. The last person to do that did so thirteen years ago, and the poor wretch is still alive, paraded across EB-Link every few days for another bout of inventive degradation.

I shudder at the thought. Nearly clam up. But I can't lose this chance to speak my truth one last time, so I press on, steering away from any criticism of our Revered Leader.

"It wasn't the buses that destroyed me," I point out, "but my speech crime. I could have transgressed anywhere."

I smile, pleased with myself for sidestepping a possibly incriminating statement, and then shake my head at the bitter irony. My trial had been conducted months ago. My guilt a matter of public entertainment. And I'm still worried about committing speech crimes?

I glance nervously at the sight lines painted on the floor. If I move outside them, passers-by can't get a good look at me through the one-way mirror. Can't enjoy the sight of my uncovered hair, bare feet, and form-hugging one-piece garment.

If I move beyond the lines on the floor, I will be denied that clothing.

No matter how bad things get, I think there's always somewhere lower to sink.

"We went to the theater," I say quickly, trying to regain my sense of temporary good fortune. "My best friend and I. Brighid's her name, and I liked to tease her that it made her sound like a Jotun. She was, however, a human, just starting out, like me, in the accountancy division of Allied Insurance Corporation. The theater is not exactly cheap, but Brighid and I bonded the moment we realized we shared a passion for live performances. We'd been saving for that night's performance of Rimward Inward for months."

I think back to that night before it all went wrong for me. Rimward Inward was an exhilarating fusion of different cultures, mostly from the local Federation subsector, but some cultural strands led all the way back to the aliens who'd come from the Orion Spur. The best of these was the Littorane choir, whose singing seemed to part a veil and reveal glimpses of the true warp and weft of the universe.

"It was one of those moments in life that seemed so good that Brighid and I didn't want the evening to end. So, after the performance, we headed over to the Row #37 bar, on Goudini and 42nd, where they specialize in Zhoogene cocktails. The company was effortless. The surroundings exotic. Brighid even persuaded me to dance. It was perfect."

I run my tongue along the top of my mouth, remembering the fiery sweetness of the drinks we downed that night. "Then the mood snapped when Brighid told me she loved me. I don't think she really did. It was the drink and being soaked in an atmosphere rich in Zhoogene pheromones for hours—you know how humans get sometimes—so I told her it was time to go home.

"The moment we left the bar, the chill night air slapped away our fuzzy-edged jauntiness and revealed us to be exhausted, half-drunk, and needing to be at work in five hours' time.

"The District Five-Gamma auto shuttle shelter was only five minutes' walk away. Inside, it was warm and well lit. Although the next service would require a twenty-minute wait, the half-squad of Militia troopers patrolling outside made me feel safe. Maybe *too* safe."

I pause on the threshold of stating dangerous truths, carefully picking through my memories before putting them into words.

I remember the sudden shock of realizing we weren't alone. There were eight of them—young human males in that dangerous state of drunken boisterousness where they dare each other into ever more outrageous behavior. I can still picture the leering faces.

They didn't touch us, but they did everything short of. Brighid and I were their prey. We were just pretty dolly birds to them. One Zhoogene girl and one human. As far as they were concerned, our entire existence to that point had been engineered to provide them with maximum amusement.

'Was I in season?' one had asked.

Had we made sex recordings together?

Would we kiss each other? Just one kiss. And they promised—laughing insincerely—that they wouldn't record our performance.

I had frozen, too scared to react, but Brighid had stood up to them, screaming at them to go to hell, threatening to record them and let the citizenry on EB-Link decide whether their abuse was acceptable, because she was damned sure it would sicken them as much as it did us.

One of the boys advanced to within millimeters of touching her, licking his lips obscenely. His swaggering confidence stilled Brighid's protests.

He told her she wouldn't dare criticize them. Who did she think she was? They were Millionaires, certified descendants of the million Earth children enslaved by the White Knights.

If true, it meant they were legally entrenched. Criticizing them would be perilous indeed.

Brighid paled and sat down beside me on the row of hard seats, our gazes on the floor, not daring to look up at the jeering young humans who surrounded us, barring our way. They said that if we tried to flee, we would have to push through them physically. If we dared to do that, they would accuse us of physical assault and upload a recording of our crime to EB-Link.

The obscene suggestions grew worse, their baiting more inventive. They drank the heady liquor of their power over us, but they stopped just short of committing a crime.

They could have been lying, of course. They might not have been Millionaires.

In which case, they wouldn't have the legal advantages of being an entrenched group.

But we were too frightened to risk it. We had no choice but to let the abuse wash over us, to pretend it was happening to someone else, so the barbs of their spite would not pierce our spirits where the wounds might fester.

And we were right to do so. I later found out they really were Millionaires.

All citizens are created equal, goes the saying. But some are more entrenched than others.

"What happened?" prompts the guard, and I realize I've been re-living that night silently, in the secrecy of my head. I'm not sure where I left off.

"We encountered an unruly group," I say.

It makes me sick to my stomach—all the horror of their attack—and I feel obliged to wrap it up in euphemism and call them 'unruly'.

"They were Millionaires. Entrenched. I…didn't like what they said. It was nasty. Frightening."

I hesitate.

To assign blame to the Millionaires might be construed as a new crime.

The jailer doesn't seem to care, though, and I press on.

"Eventually, the shuttle came, and the Millionaires got on. I was terrified they would make us get on with them, but they told us our presence offended them and, if we boarded, they would report us for intimidation. We watched them pull away in silence, neither of us able to speak for a long while. Then, all the fear and anger I'd pushed under welled up in a single uncontrollable burst."

Fucking colonists!

That's what I yelled at them that awful night.

I gag.

How could I have been so stupid?

The moment I uttered those words, time had slowed down as I watched Brighid open her mouth in an 'o' of horror.

I had pleaded with her not to do what we both knew she had to.

Not one hour before, she'd told me she loved me. Had she forgotten so soon?

Of course, she hadn't.

It took me weeks of solitude and tormented humiliation in this cell before I could tell myself I had forgiven Brighid.

I tell myself that often, but I don't fully believe it yet.

She had had no choice. Obviously.

Yet what she had done was still an act of betrayal.

"What did they do?" asks the guard, and I realize I have once again allowed my mind to race ahead of my spoken words. It is a defense mechanism I'm finding increasingly hard to break. Words are dangerous; it is best not to speak them aloud.

If only I had done the same that night.

"I committed a speech crime," I tell my confidante outside my cell door. "I called them *colonists*. Someone recorded me committing my crime and reported it through EB-Link. I didn't even go home that night. I reported to the police, and I was arrested five minutes later."

"Did they give you a fair...*trial?*"

I hear the distaste in the guard's words, and hope flutters in my spirit. It's an unfamiliar feeling.

The guard could have come from anywhere in the Federation, not just Eiylah-Bremah. Do they believe me?

I snatch at the chance this might be an off-worlder. "Some worlds champion the concept of individual justice," I tell the guard, "but, here, we champion the orderly functioning of the group. I used the word *colonist* to describe those Millionaires, and, in doing so, committed a speech crime against an entrenched group. Had I been lucky, I could have been sentenced with a heavy fine and a citizenship downgrading. Instead, I became part of the Churn."

"I don't understand this Churn. Explain."

"From time to time, those of privileged status who transgress must be be torn down and humiliated for all of society to see. Those, like me, who fall are balanced by others who embody the virtues of society. These lucky ones are rewarded by riches and status. Never mind that I was a low-paid clerical worker, on EB-Link I appeared entitled, rich, and arrogant—after all, I had been to the theater, which isn't cheap. Facts cease to matter with the Churn. I had a role to play. A spectacle to perform. I needed to be crushed. And since I did utter those words I was accused of saying, yes, my trial was fair. At least, it pleased the will of our Revered Leader In'Nalla."

"Don't you resent her?"

I manage a smile and shake my head the human way. "No. The re-educators tell me that, in the end, I must say publicly that I love In'Nalla, and that I must mean my words sincerely, because deceit would be a terrible crime that would be detected. But it's never been a problem for me. I do love In'Nalla. Always have, despite my fall from grace. I could never say I hated her, any more than a sailor could say they hated the sea, even though they might be caught in a great storm and wrecked."

"And your trial?" I hear amazement in their voice. My words are getting a reaction! "Didn't you hate that?"

"It was…" I stop in time. Even if the guard is genuinely sympathetic, I have to assume every word is recorded and analyzed by AIs honed to detect problematic thoughts. So long as I don't criticize a legally defined group, I should be okay. "My trial was a performance of lies. In the jury of civic opinion on EB-Link, the news and opinion leaders emphasized the money and privilege I must surely have enjoyed to be a theater-goer. When I tried to explain that I had saved up for months, they condemned me even more viciously as a liar.

Every word I wrote or spoke was twisted into new meanings and used to attack me. The encounter at the shuttle shelter was also warped so that, now, Brighid and I were drunken, entitled louts, hurling abuse at the poor and honest Millionaire boys. Never mind that Brighid's ancestors came here on the same Exile ships as the Millionaires, she just doesn't have the documentation to prove it. That was the most terrifying thing—the web of lies the world weaved around us was so farcical, so easy to disprove, but EB-Link would believe anything to justify my punishment."

I stop and listen hard. I know I've gone too far.

The guard outside is breathing heavily.

I think they're angry.

I should be boiling with rage at my story, but I'm too weary of it.

If the guard is raging on my behalf, though, then maybe it's something…

I hurry back to the door, up against the sight line. "Do you believe my story?"

"I do."

My heart skips. I can hardly breathe.

"Please. Please, I beg you. Will you help me?"

The guard laughs. "Help? You're a stupid Zhoogene slut who led on a group of human boys out for hijinks. You deserve all that's coming to you. No, I will not help."

I can't move.

I'm rooted to the cold stone floor, so thoroughly un-personed that I might as well be carved from stone myself.

The guard walks off. I listen to the sound of boots receding to silence. Then I am condemned once more to solitude.

* * * * *

Chapter Two:
Lily Hjon

"This planet's seriously fucked up!"

Enthree lifted an antenna Lily's way, but Vetch and Sward showed no sign of noticing.

She stormed through the guardroom, dodging around the stack of barely drained battery packs the warden had advised them not to notice, and planted herself where the other three were playing cards—Pryxian skat by the look of it.

For a moment, she considered tipping over the wooden crate they were using as a table. But even with her hands trembling with rage at the story the prisoner had told, she stopped herself short of committing what she had told her troopers was a cardinal sin.

Instead of interrupting a game with money on the table, she yanked Vetch's beard and yelled into his ear, "Did you hear what I said?"

Vetch flinched at the sonic assault, blinked a bit, and then laid his cards on the table. Face down.

"Did you get our prisoner to talk?" he asked innocently.

"You know I did."

"And I suppose, now, you want us to rescue her."

"Her plight is a dammed disgrace," Lily declared. "An outrage. There's not much we can do to change the Federation in what little time we've got left. We're convicted deserters, only being kept alive

13

for a little longer, so we can take someone else's place in the meat-grinder. But we all swore oaths. The Militia and the Amilxi People. M.A.P. and all that bollocks. The girl in that dungeon is a citizen, and that means we swore to protect her."

She glanced up. Sward was looking for a chance to get a word in. Enthree was so agitated, she was throwing s-curves along her spine.

"This could be the last thing we do," Lily said quickly, throwing a raised eyebrow at Sward and daring him to interrupt. "Make it count. Show the Federation how people *should* act."

She took a short breath, but she'd run out of steam. Why weren't they arguing with her?

Vetch picked up his cards and studied them. "You sure this girl is worth making a stand for?"

"She is."

He played the five of moons. "We figured you'd get her to talk. Thought this would be your reaction too."

Sward tossed a card on the table, leaned back, and gave Lily a stiff Zhoogene smile. "Vetch has been hatching a plan."

Lily looked Vetch clear in the face. Damn that stupid beard. He'd been grinning all this time. Asshole.

He soon lost his grin when Enthree played her card and scooped up the money on the table.

"Nice play, Bug," Vetch said, recalculating the value of his remaining cards after the last play.

"Well," Lily demanded. "What's the plan?"

"For tonight, we act normal. But in the morning, we bring forward the girl's execution."

It took Lily a moment to realize what Vetch was saying.

Then she parted his silly, shaggy hair and planted a kiss on the crown of his head.

"Neat," she said, pulling up a stool to join them at the table. "I knew you'd make a good trooper one day, Vetch Arunsen. Now, stop gloating that you've finally popped a good idea out of your hairy head and finish the round so you can deal me in. I've got a feeling we won't be playing cards again any time soon."

* * * * *

Chapter Three:
Major Lyssin

Militia Major Lyssin heard the knock on the painted wooden door that cut through the high brick walls of his garden paradise. After a few moments' hesitation, the visitor pushed his way inside and took a dozen hesitant steps along the outer path.

Then he halted.

Lyssin didn't open his eyes, preferring to imagine the man's shock as the warm humidity of the garden's microclimate warmed his skin. His gaze would be piercing the concealing outer covering of blooming vines and seeing beneath the high terraces of miniature trees. There he would discover the bubbling streams of nutrient-rich water draining along miniature stone aqueducts, the tinkling water flow already prominent in the man's acute hearing.

If it weren't for its people, Eiylah-Bremah would be a lovely world. Lyssin's hanging garden was, as far as its owner and creator cared, its greatest wonder.

Lyssin opened his eyes and regarded his visitor with sudden curiosity. Lieutenant Deroh Ren Kay was a Zhoogene. He looked immaculate in his smart blue jacket with its silver lieutenant's bars on the epaulettes and the Demon Wolf Brigade insignia on the collar. Combined with the natural upright rigidity of his people, Ren Kay looked so effortlessly martial in his bearing that Lyssin took great pleasure in showing off the junior officer at public functions and private meetings. Yes, Ren Kay was a perfect demonstration of what a fine unit Lyssin commanded.

Zhoogenes were a photosynthesizing race—a concept that had always fascinated Lyssin. Did that mean Ren Kay appreciated these gardens at a deeper level than any human could hope to?

Or, perhaps, the artificial herbal scent carried by the spray mist and the buzz of insects engineered to be stingless struck false notes with him.

The advancing lieutenant ducked beneath a vine rope stretched from one wall to the other. It was the main highway of battle between rival nests of leaf cutter insects.

He came to attention and saluted. "An honor to be here, Major."

Lyssin waved the salute away. "We're off duty now, Deroh. And if it's an honor, it's one you've earned. I've had my eye on you for a while, and I think it's time for you to move on to more *specialized* tasks."

The smile left Lyssin's face. Ren Kay remained at attention, and Lyssin decided that, within the walls of his prized garden, the Zhoogene's martial look did not please him.

He had a sudden fantasy of stripping the man down to his bare green skin, cutting out his vocal cords, and feeding him drugs to keep his hydraulic bands tight, which would lock him rigid in the prison of his own body.

"Sir?"

He could plant him against the east column, with climbers running up the lieutenant's flanks and arms to bloom into flowers over his head. His chest and back would remain bare so he could photosynthesize, thereby keeping himself alive. Lyssin bore no particular malice against his subordinate, but he'd always been fascinated by rumors of the curious things you could do to living Zhoogene flesh. And now that the idea had been planted…

Ren Kay coughed politely.

"Forgive me." Lyssin waved to the vacant force chair beside his. "It suddenly struck me that, as a Zhoogene, you might be able to help me enjoy my garden in ways I had never previously conceived. But…that's not why I invited you here this fine summer's evening."

Ren Kay looked uncertainly at the force chair.

"I know. I know!" said Lyssin. "My apologies. Here I am, in my silly human head, thinking I have created a natural paradise, when I'm reclining against a ladder of force bands. You must think me ridiculous."

"Not at all." Golden eyes like fresh corn husks regarded him coolly. "It is an honor and a privilege to be invited to your home, Major."

"Yes. Yes, it is, Deroh." Lyssin beamed with delight as his visitor settled into the force chair and relaxed his body.

But always, he thought to himself, *a visit here brings obligation.* Lyssin grinned. *Sometimes, pleasure too. My pleasure, at any rate.*

He indicated the marble-topped occasional table that stood between them. "Help yourself, my good man."

Ren Kay looked uneasily at the box of cigars and the bottles and glasses.

Good, good…You're being offered a step up in society. Don't take it for granted because it can be removed just as easily.

The lieutenant poured himself a glass of Bin-37 Melburnians brandy from Halcyon-3. After a long sip of the liquor that cost more than his annual salary, Ren Kay began to relax.

"You're here so we can get to know each other a little better," Lyssin told him. "But first, I'm afraid I have a little matter of business. Those penal troopers I gave you last month…how are you finding them?"

"Less trouble than I had expected, sir. I think they just want to keep their heads down."

"I *bet* they do." Lyssin laughed. "The question is, are you letting them do so?"

Ren Kay licked his lips while he selected his words. "I am aware these troopers are to be considered particularly expendable."

"Well-chosen words, Deroh, but there's no need to be so circumspect here." He took a cigar from the box and used it to indicate the extent of his hanging gardens. "We're so secure, we may as well be in our own private world." He snipped the end off the cigar.

"I want those expendables expended, and soon. But carefully. The one who was such a disgrace to the officer corps still has her supporters, and, strangely enough, one of them might be the sector marshal herself."

"Sir? But they were sent here from JSHC as convicted deserters. Surely the marshal knows this?"

Lyssin ripped off the heating cap and watched the magic as the roll of finest synth-bacc glowed, releasing its riches. "The wealth of this star system derives from its sources of exotic materials. But here on the planet of Eiylah-Bremah, the greatest export market is ritual humiliation. I think it amused the marshal to have your deserters sent here rather than execute them immediately. Where better to demonstrate the fate of those who defy their superiors before eventually contributing to our military campaign's unfortunate attrition statistics?"

"I understand," said Ren Kay. "We don't want to be seen as having deliberately thwarted the sector marshal's...pleasure."

"Quite so." Lyssin puffed his cigar to life. "How have you managed to balance our deserters' lives on an appropriate knife edge?"

"They spend most of their days in the prisons, working the filthiest dungeons. They also provide prisoner escort for lunchtime executions. I dress them in smart uniforms, kept clean for public duty, and they wear Militia berets sporting In'Nalla's red cockade to show their alliance with the dictator."

"What brave troopers they must be to proudly wear what the rebels regard as symbols of oppression. It's almost as if they were daring disgruntled citizens to strike at them."

"Indeed, sir. And acting as lightning rods for dissent is a vital task because it is difficult to draw out the rebels who have infiltrated the city. I have rooftop sharpshooters posted around Execution Square and the approach roads. If anyone were to fire upon the escort troopers, my snipers would take them out. For any lesser signs of defiance, the police will make arrests."

"Do the crowds know of your trap?"

"I'm sure they do, sir. It is good to let the citizens know how powerless they are. Nonetheless, hotheads will inevitably test the system before long and then my expendable penal troopers will start to be expended."

"An admirable approach, Deroh. However, weapons fire into a crowd of civilians can cause panic and confusion. In such moments of chaos, who can say for sure where the shots came from or even their intended targets? Tomorrow lunchtime, I would like to hear of an incident in Execution Square. A heinous assault on authority by the rebels that, regrettably, results in the deaths of five brave troopers, newly arrived on our planet."

Ren Kay opened his mouth in horror.

Lyssin, too, began to feel regret. One of the penal troopers he wanted skragged was another Zhoogene. The others needed to die tomorrow, but if there was a way to abduct the trooper who was half plant, he could help Lyssin conduct an interesting experiment over by the garden's east column.

He sucked in a sharp breath. Suggesting that notion to Ren Kay would be a little too ambitious. Should have thought it through properly before inviting a Zhoogene to be his assassin.

"I'm not sure, sir." Ren Kay didn't *look* unsure. He looked like a Zhoogene with his mind made up, and they could be such stubborn bastards. "To use deserters as bait and plasma fodder is one thing, but to order my troopers to outright murder them…"

He caught Lyssin's raised eyebrow and pivoted his choice of words. "I'm just not sure I can convince them of the legitimacy of that order."

"Then permit me to give you a good reason." Lyssin paused to roll a draw of smoke around his mouth. "Better still, let me give you twenty thousand good reasons."

"Twenty thou?" Ren Kay's head growth trembled. "Bylzak! Somebody sure hates those deserters."

"That's none of our business, Deroh." Lyssin watched the young Zhoogene calculating in his head. How much of the twenty thousand credits would he have to pay his troopers to become murderers? And how much would that leave for him?

And…there you go, Deroh. Lyssin could see the moment, written plain as day across the lieutenant's face, when he suddenly wondered how much money was changing hands. If *he* was being bribed twenty thou, how much was his superior being paid? And how much more could he wring out of this?

Lyssin shrugged and offered the first of a long list of potential sweeteners. "You know, Deroh, you remind me of myself when I was an ambitious young lieutenant. I was in such a hurry for promotion that I developed an antipathy toward a certain Lieutenant Dorothy Peng. She was a fine officer, but she had better connections than me, and a longer length of service. I felt certain I would always be in her shadow throughout my career. Forever second in line for promotion." He topped off Ren Kay's brandy. "It would only be natural for you to feel the same about Lieutenant Atiff. Especially with an opening for senior lieutenant coming up soon."

"Not at all, sir. Atiff is a good officer and would make an excellent senior lieutenant."

"Well said, Deroh. Indeed, Atiff would also be a good choice for the asteroid defense stations, and their CO has been making such an irritating clamor for reinforcements recently, that it would seem churlish not to send her someone. Funny Atiff should come up in our little chat, because I'm conducting his annual review next month." He paused for effect. "Anyway, have you come to a decision about our little matter?"

"I have sir. My troopers will get the job done. You can trust me."

A victory smile slid over Lyssin's face. "I know I can, my boy." He eased deeper into his force chair, the sensors understanding his intent and reclining. *You belong to me now, Deroh.*

Lyssin felt his gaze drawn toward the east column and licked the sweet taste of brandy off his lips. *One way or another.*

* * * * *

Chapter Four:
Lily Hjon

"You're a disgrace!" shouted a man from the balcony bar.

"Cover your head," yelled a woman sitting at the same table, followed by a confusing jumble of jeers, threats, and cries of "Shame!"

The bar was doing a brisk business this lunchtime, as were the stallholders of Restitution Street who lined the broad, tree-studded sidewalk—a miniature plaza on the north side of the road. They sold pastries, holo hits, and the local specialty—spiced cider punch. The stalls formed a kind of proxy security cordon to keep the crowds away from the road where the Militia troopers escorted the condemned to her death.

Execution Square—where the real crowds were already baying their excitement—was still two hundred yards away, and the noise was building by the second.

"Your entertainment hasn't even *begun*," Lily murmured as she marched. She looked out into the crowd beyond the stalls. "Just wait till you see what we've got in store, skraggs."

Vetch thought she had lived a life of cloistered privilege before being busted to the ranks, but she let the cuddly Viking believe a lot of shit that wasn't true. She'd seen scum baying for blood on scores of worlds, but this…this was different.

These weren't cutthroat gang members who were sipping fine wine on balcony seats that cost twice the normal price during 'execution hour.'

And the people below on the sidewalk weren't the impoverished lower classes being fed bread and circuses as the old Earth expression said.

No, *this* bloodthirsty bunch of chod-skraggers wore the half-brimmed hats that were the latest fashion in the capital city of Kaylingen. Their clothes were freshly laundered, and their wrist slates were the latest models. They had plenty of credits to enjoy the street wares hawked at inflated prices.

They were the capital's lunchtime office workers. Kaylingen University lecturers. Tourists.

Except for one person. There, at a cider stall, was the young human woman Lily had been searching for, seemingly weighing her choice of lunchtime drink.

Damn! Vetch had been right, after all. The thief had held up her side of the bargain.

The briefest of glances passed between the two women.

Lily faced forward and tried to catch Vetch's attention.

He was marching at the front, alongside Sward, both looking chunky due to the civilian clothes stuffed under their jackets. His beret wasn't standard Militia wear, but local cultural norms insisted that uncovered heads were immodest for humanoids of all descriptions.

Behind them shuffled the young Zhoogene, Carnolin Indoh. Barefoot, head growth on full display, wearing garments more befitting a marathon runner than a convicted criminal, she walked with wrists crossed in front of her.

They weren't bound, though. Nor were her ankles shackled as was the usual practice. Not for Carnolin. Not today. That would have proved awkward.

Enthree and Darant marched behind her, with Lily taking up the rear.

"Vetch," she said. "Vetch!"

He fingered his polished war hammer. Tense. Alert. But completely oblivious to her.

Typical of the deaf ape.

"Sward," she tried, raising her voice a little. "Tell the big lump next to you that our distraction is here."

The big sniper tapped Vetch on the shoulder and passed on the message. Thank goodness for the wonders of Zhoogene hearing.

Unfortunately, the same sensitive ears meant the girl, Carnolin, heard too. First, she tensed in the jerky way of her kind and then she began trembling like green shoots in a breeze.

Lily found herself trembling as well.

Am I scared?

Over in Execution Square, a drumbeat started.

Don't be stupid.

She'd never considered herself brave, and, if she appeared fearless, it was only because she'd been cruising on borrowed time for so long, each second was an unexpected bonus.

Vetch halted.

The Restitution Street crowd cheered, misjudging the unexpected stop, thinking the condemned was being presented to them for their pleasure.

Poor Carnolin shook like a leaf at the howls of derision hurled at her by the degenerate assholes.

The weird thing was, Lily shook with her.

The arse-skraggs terrifying this poor girl, she said to herself. *Are they so different from others elsewhere in the Federation?*

Many of the condemned who were marched at lunchtime to Execution Square had been set up. The details changed from execution to execution, but the moral example of the Churn never wavered. Facts didn't matter, only the story. And the story chosen for Carnolin was that of a rich fool, smug in her entitlement, who had to be torn down and made to confess her sins. Publicly. Only then would society be at peace with itself.

Stripped of the surface details, Carnolin's story sounded familiar. It was no different than Lily's.

She shuddered, flinching at the jeers aimed at Carnolin.

As far as the sector marshal was concerned, Captain Lily Hjon had committed a heinous transgression against the Militia officer corps. She had dared to honor her vows to serve the people of the Federation.

Rho-Torkis…Eiylah-Bremah…The sector marshal intended them to be Lily's public humbling. Vetch and the others were just unfortunate enough to be caught up as support actors.

That bitch had gotten her convicted as a deserter. How much lower would she have to sink before the marshal decided it was time for the troublesome Lily Hjon to be hanged? Knowing her, the marshal was already lining Lily up to take the fall as a child murderer or some such evil.

The putrid lies people told themselves to justify their actions.

Human.

Zhoogene.

Littorane.

Pryxian.

Gliesan.

Lily had yet to find a humanoid species that operated any differently.

More drums began beating in Execution Square, thundering their message through the ground to be picked up by the crowds thronging the road, stamping their feet in time.

Vetch led the execution party onward.

In the square, civic scolders awaited their chance to read the condemned's crimes. A professionally produced holo-vid would be shown in which actors performed the key moments in the concocted bullshit story.

Which would prove awkward if Carnolin was presented to the baying crowds.

Because, funnily enough, she wasn't actually the condemned.

Not today.

Carnolin wasn't even the right species.

Vetch had a fistful of alternate plans, and all relied on them never making it to Execution Square.

Lily looked behind her.

Vetch's Plan A relied on the girl by the cider stall, walking away and trying to lose herself in the crowd.

She was the one they were supposed to be escorting to the gallows' noose. Not Carnolin.

An explosion ripped through the air, echoing off the four-story buildings to either side of the road and shocking the crowd to instant silence.

Three bangers left by a master thief inside a barrel of hot cider punch will do that.

A plume of hot punch erupted high into the air, blowing chunks of citrus fruit and sweet coco-chili roots like a cloud of shrapnel.

Lily saw no sign of the grateful thief who'd planted the grenades. She had disappeared, her debt to her unlikely rescuers paid in full.

Lily let the crowd worry about the cider bomb. Her attention was on the buildings looking down on the street.

Sward had alerted them to the possibility of snipers. Too much silence, he'd said, after the first of their sorry lunchtime escort duties.

A few days later, Darant had spotted snipers watching over Execution Square.

Militia? Police? Their allegiance was unknown. Sloppy, though, to allow themselves to be seen.

Were there any in the street? And would they shoot?

She scanned the upper levels of the buildings on both sides, her blaster rifle charged, but she was unable to take comfort from that in this hideously exposed position.

Her body itched to dive behind cover, but to go to ground would be fatal. They had to move quickly. The best way to do that was to mingle with the crowd, but Vetch had been adamant they not use the citizens as shields.

Lily hadn't agreed. The sick skraggs lining the road didn't deserve their protection. The Kaylingeners could go to hell for all she cared.

"We're clear," Vetch bellowed. They all knew it was a highly optimistic assessment. "Go. Go. Go."

Eyes still on the phantasm snipers, Lily led the team back the way they'd come.

"Take cover!" yelled Sward.

Damn! Knew it'd been too easy.

Lily threw herself to the ground and rolled beneath a pastry stall, a bullet gouging the street behind her.

On hands and knees, she scrambled beneath the next stall, praying she was hidden from the sniper's sight.

She was.

Four bullets drilled through the stall behind in a spray of splinters and shredded pastry.

"What's going on?" asked a terrified citizen crouching on the ground, blocking her way to the next stall.

Lily grabbed him by the shoulders and stared into his face. "This is it," she told him. "It's the revolution."

He looked at her in horror, but, possibly, it was as much the sight of her tattooed face as anything else. The metamorphic ink had ditched the bleeding roses she'd grown accustomed to and replaced them with geometric antlers erupting from her eyes.

She tore off her beret and pulled up the hood concealed underneath her uniform jacket. It was a risk, but she stuck her head out of cover to check the situation.

Carnolin was cowering on the ground beneath the cider stall, Darant kneeling over her protectively as he threw blaster bolts up at the buildings overlooking the road from the north.

Sheltering behind the cover of a broad carjacker tree, Vetch and Enthree joined in with a volley of their own. Already, they had discarded their Militia jackets and berets.

So too had Sward, who sprinted under the covering fire to join his two comrades behind the tree.

It looked as though the sniper fire had come from the buildings fronting the broad sidewalk on the north side, but where exactly? She didn't want to present her back to the buildings on the south side, but if Sward was ignoring them, so would she.

With her head on the ground, she craned her neck to watch the windows and rooms, looking for a target.

"What do we do now?" asked an angry voice.

She had forgotten the citizen sheltering with her. "You stay under cover and leave it to us," she said vaguely, her mind on the sniper.

"Come on," she hissed at the enemy. "We can't hang around."

Movement!

Fourth story. Third window in from the west end of the street where it entered the square. Slatted wooden shutters were half open, and she saw a Zhoogene with a camera strapped to her head take in the scene below for half a second.

By the time Lily trained her blaster on the window, the sniper was gone.

"We're…we're surrounded!" wailed the man cowering beside Lily.

"Stay under cover."

"And you're only Militia. Not real soldiers."

Furious, Lily turned back and struck the irritating man a bruising blow on the shoulder with the butt of her rifle. "Stay under fucking cover!"

He gawked at her, wide-eyed, then broke away, sprinting for a narrow alley that cut through the row of buildings at the far side of Execution Square.

A rifle shot rang out. The man screamed and stumbled but did not fall.

This time Lily was faster.

She put half a charge pack through the sniper's position. Not the window where she'd seen the Zhoogene, but the next one. Darant fired, and, together, they blasted off the wooden shutters, sending fragments of flaming wood tumbling to the ground, followed by the sniper. The dead man still gripped his PAS-4 sniper rifle, its barrel twisted from the intense heat of their barrage, as he fell into the crowd below.

By then, Lily had put the other half of her pack through the window where the Zhoogene had appeared. An observer, she assumed.

Why wasn't Vetch's group firing?

As she swapped in a fresh charge pack, blaster fire blazed from beneath the tree where Vetch, Sward, and Enthree were sheltering. They weren't aiming at snipers. They were firing in the direction of Execution Square.

They were answered by angry shouts and a few rifle rounds that pinged off the sidewalk nearby.

Shit!

An eerie silence fell upon the street.

But only for a moment.

Someone was barking orders a short distance away in the square.

"Darant! Lily!" Vetch shouted. "Suppress those snipers."

Lily squeezed shots into the sniper positions.

As the screaming bolts of induced plasma lit up the air, Enthree used the cover to run through the cowering crowd, parting it like a laser torch through butter.

When her insectoid comrade had safely reached the base of the buildings, Lily ceased fire and made a quick decision.

"I'm not Vetch," she told a woman ten feet away who was kneeling on the sidewalk with her hands clasped over her head, still clutching a cream-filled pastry.

The woman looked at her, perplexed.

"I don't forgive," Lily explained. "Not how you've treated the condemned like stars in a damned freak show." She sighted along the entire upper story, unleashing bolts through every window, leaving Darant to fire on the known sniper positions. Maybe enemies were lurking behind those other windows. And maybe they weren't. Maybe civilians were sheltering there. No matter. Whoever was in those rooms was learning to keep their heads down. That, or they had been shot. Lily didn't care either way.

Enthree was fully using all six limbs, gripping onto the vertical surface with her hoof-like hands as she climbed. How someone of her bulk could scale surfaces like a fly was a mystery, but she did. Within twenty seconds, Enthree was level with the sniper positions.

From Vetch's tree, her comrades fired another volley west toward Execution Square.

"Take cover!" screamed a Militia officer.

Lily chanced a look at what was heading their way from the west.

Troopers were behind the walls of the archway into the square, risking occasional peeps out of cover to see what was happening in Restitution Street, but not daring to follow up with rifle barrels. Beyond, the citizens were milling about in panic, trying to find a safe route out. Several were climbing ropes hanging down from an upper story.

She expected to see fresh Militia corpses laid out beneath the arch, but there were no obvious casualties.

"Idiot," murmured Lily, aiming her disdain at Vetch who had clearly ordered Sward and Enthree to fire over the heads of their enemy. "We've crossed the line. Do you still think, after this, we'll kiss and make up with the sector marshal over tea and crumpets?"

Meanwhile, high on the wall in front of her, Enthree had drawn short swords from her back and was bunching up to spring into a shattered window a couple of positions over from the sniper's post.

Lily fired three bolts into the room.

Enthree quickly followed.

Lily turned around and scanned the buildings behind to the south.

Something was bothering her, but she wasn't sure what.

Then she heard them. Drones!

They were directed by a Gliesan, kneeling on the roof. He was looking down at her and giving a thumbs up.

Cheeky blighter!

She shouldered her rifle and sighted on the drone operator.

But then she looked again.

The Gliesan was smartly dressed, in local Kaylingen fashion. He was no Militia trooper.

"Press," Lily shouted. "They're press…Don't…*fire.*"

But Sward already had. The finest shot in Raven Company had obliterated both drones.

"I know," he said. "Well done for realizing that with human eyes."

"Clear!" Enthree shouted from the scorched opening the sniper had fired out of. "The entire floor is clear."

The big Muryani was shaking her head from side to side as she did when excited. She waved her gore-coated short swords.

"Bloody little insect, aren't you?" muttered Lily. If it ever came to war with the Muryani, as many insisted it must do one day, the Federation would be utterly screwed.

She hollered at Darant, "Get the girl out of here. Make this count for something."

"Go on!" yelled Vetch. "All of you, follow Darant. I'll cover you."

With Vetch directing fire over the heads of the Execution Square troopers, the others sprinted for the alleyway that threaded through the row of buildings to the north of the street—the exit route they'd planned. Meanwhile, Lily set to work. Fast as she could, she tipped over the sturdiest looking stall tables and turned them ninety degrees, so they faced the attack from the square.

It didn't exactly constitute hard cover. The jumble of stalls was more of a baffle to make it unclear where she was firing from, and that might buy her a few seconds. She wasn't running for the alleyway yet, and when Vetch did, someone needed to cover *him*.

She crawled through her cover and sighted the archway through a narrow gap between the tables.

Looked like the troopers were getting ready to rush them.

An eager young Zhoogene face filled her scope.

She took a calm breath and eased back the trigger.

Damnit!

At the last instant, she'd lifted the barrel, sending the bolt whining over the youngster's head, taking his beret with it.

It wasn't like taking out the snipers who'd fired on them first. The troopers she was engaging now had been pulling the same execution guard duty as Lily and the others.

The fact that she'd fired over their heads would make no difference if Lily were ever caught.

But it mattered to *her*.

Bolts screamed out from the friends behind her, aimed at the archway.

Vetch seized the chance to break for the alley.

Unfortunately, the Execution Square troopers picked the same moment to gather up their courage and assault.

Lily fired rounds over their heads, but they had grown wise to the tactic.

She rolled away and took up a new firing position.

A fusillade of bullets and blaster bolts lashed the street and its broad sidewalk, shredding the stall tables around Lily in clouds of splinters that ripped through her clothes and flesh. She kept shifting position.

Vetch grunted in pain, and a Zhoogene screamed. Sounded like Sward. Human civilians were also screaming, mostly in fear, but some in agony.

"This planet is really pissing me off," Lily bellowed, then loosed a flurry of bolts at the advancing troopers. Single shots. Center mass.

She scrambled back along the line of tables behind her, then popped up from cover to drop two more troopers.

Now that the shit had gotten real, with Militia casualties, her former comrades were stung into action. Some advanced stealthily up the jumble of stalls. Others broke into buildings on either side of the street, seeking decisive firing positions.

Lily had to fight back the gnawing emptiness in her heart. She'd never believed it would come to firing upon other troopers.

There was no coming back from this.

But agonizing wouldn't keep her friends alive.

Bullets flew over her head.

She moved. Fast. Back up the street. But now she was moving away from the alleyway. She dove behind a broad tree, somehow dodging the rounds sent her way, and landed on the ground.

Ahhh! The impact drove in splinters all over her front. Worse, she felt the rumble of gravitics through her belly. Skragg! Something heavy was approaching from the east. Whatever it was, it hadn't yet come into view, but when it did, they would be trapped and slaughtered!

"Hey, Lil'!" called Vetch. He was over in the alleyway, waving at her angrily. "Are you coming or what?"

She could hear the pain in his voice, but his mail shirt must have dissipated the bolt he'd been shot with a few moments earlier.

She shouted back, "Someone has to watch over your hairy ass, I suppose."

"Then get your finely sculpted officer butt over here on the count of...now!"

A covering fusillade of bolts flew from the alley and from a window overlooking the alley, courtesy of Enthree.

Lily ran for her life.

The advancing troopers quieted. They had probably gone to ground, but Lily didn't care.

All that mattered was getting to that alley.

Most of the civilians had already drained through this escape route. Not all. Some were still hugging the ground. Lily jumped over the man who'd hidden with her under the stall. He'd bled out on the sidewalk, just a few feet from safety.

And she made it.

Her friends were waiting for her. Carnolin, too, now clothed in the unremarkable civilian clothes Vetch had hidden over his ample belly. Enthree was scrambling down the outside of a wall toward them, firing her blaster as she moved.

What now?

Vetch produced a palmful of green plastic tokens stamped with the Kaylingen city crest. "There's a tram stop four minutes from here. Let's hope it's on time."

"It will be," said Lily, grabbing a transport token. "If there's one thing I've learned about worlds with nightmare dictatorships, it's that they know how to keep the busses running on time."

"Careful," Carnolin warned as they pushed through the alley, "that's a speech crime. People who overhear you will report you."

"Typical sodding dictator! What does In'Nalla call herself, then? Every citizen's cuddly friend?"

"The Revered Leader is proud to call herself a dictator. What will get you reported is the implication that centrally planned transport is preferable to a liberal market solution."

Lily slowed as they began to press into the panicked crowds backing up on the other side of the alley. "Your planet's seriously nuts. You know that, don't you?"

"Let's keep our opinions to ourselves," said Vetch. "No wisecracks."

"Halt!" called a voice behind them.

Lily turned, trying to act like a scared civilian, many of whom had also turned around to see what new disaster was unfolding.

They were confronted by a young Zhoogene Militia lieutenant in a pristine uniform. Behind him was a column of troopers and, behind them, a light grav tank.

"Nobody move!" commanded the lieutenant.

Two small cylinders dropped onto the paving slabs in front of the officer. They rolled between his legs and into the mass of troopers.

"Grenades!"

The warning shouts seemed to come from everywhere, not just from Vetch and the others further ahead in the scrum.

Then the grenades went off, and the shouts turned to screams. Pushing. Panic. Elbows and kicks and a surge of bodies blindly fleeing. And they *were* blind for the most part. Even though Lily had known the bangers were coming and had closed her eyes, the effect was total confusion for a few moments.

The plan. Keep to the plan!

Despite Eiylah-Bremah's permissive personal weapons' laws, she obeyed the instructions Vetch had issued earlier and let her rifle fall to the ground. Pretending to scream in panic, she pushed through the crowd, shoving people to either side in her desperation to keep up with the big, bearded oaf.

She would follow him anywhere, even to board a tram in a messed-up, nightmare world where saying a single dangerous word could turn you instantly into an enemy of the people.

Sheesh!

Life as a trooper had never been boring.

But Lily couldn't be a trooper again. Not after this.

What did her future hold?

* * * * *

Chapter Five:
Lily Hjon

They sat in silence on the gently rolling hillside of red rye, waiting for Sward to die.

Back when they'd been running for the alley in Restitution Street, a Militia bullet had pierced his lung. A near miss from a blaster bolt had melted the back of his head.

The silly skragg had simply stolen a civilian's cap and pulled it down over his head wound. He hadn't said a word as they'd taken the tram to the last stop before commandeering a brace of fast food delivery vehicles parked in a depot.

They'd abandoned their stolen transport in a managed forest five klicks away. Only then did Sward let on that he'd been badly hurt.

Dammed stupid man.

In the field of almost-ripe rye that reached to their shoulders, Sward had insisted in a burbling wet voice that he could go no further.

His body had locked rigid. He told them in a stuttering voice to remain silent and still, so he could properly enjoy his surroundings. Then he beckoned to the Zhoogene girl he had given his life to save.

She seemed to know what he needed, and she sat behind him, lowering the undamaged side of his head into her lap and humming him to his rest with a quiet melody.

Rynter.

Deep Tone.

Meatbolt.

And now Sward.

Lily didn't think it would be long before she joined her friends.

It had been a long time coming.

When Carnolin lifted her face, streaming with tears, and told them Sward had died, they used their knives, blaster sidearms, and the shaft of Vetch's war hammer to dig a grave.

Lily decided not to ask Vetch why he had asked them to discard their rifles to blend into the crowd when he still carried his hammer.

In fact, no one spoke, and that didn't suit Lily at all.

It meant she was left to fester in her thoughts.

Years of endless running had soured them.

Losing her friends had scarred them even more, and she had lost many before she'd thrown in her lot with Vetch Arunsen.

She watched her best friend's face as he worked. Sweat beaded in his beard from the gentle heat of the afternoon sun. He'd been her project for the past few years. She'd steered him away from being prison scum to become the leader she knew he could be. Now, she tired of that too.

Strangely, with Vetch prominent in her mind, she found herself thinking about his jack equivalent, Sybutu.

The two sergeants—now that would be a good name for a pub! Vetch and Sybutu had been hilarious together. An odd couple pushing each other because neither wanted to look weak in front of the other.

Much as she adored Vetch, Sybutu had the sweeter body. Maybe, one day, she'd get the chance to make up for burning it when they'd first met.

And then the grave was dug, and Lily was back in the awfulness of the moment, moving to help lift Sward into his final resting place.

Vetch gently pushed the others away and lifted Sward alone, planting him in his grave.

Carnolin looked down at the man who'd died in her arms. "Sward followed you, Vetch Arunsen. My life belongs to you now."

"No!" Vetch loomed over Carnolin, his face red with emotion. For a moment, Lily thought he was going to grab her by the shoulders and shake her like a rag. "You do not belong to us. Sward was a Militia trooper. A good one, as we all aspire to be. M.A.P. The Militia and the Amilxi People. Many of our kind sour their oaths, but many more do not. I thank you Carnolin Indoh, but you owe us nothing. We were just doing our duty."

Carnolin looked down.

"Although," Enthree told the Zhoogene, "I want you to commit to the decade watch for Sward. That was his death custom. Are you familiar with it?"

She nodded. "A day of quiet remembrance on each anniversary of his death. On the tenth, all grave markings should be removed to make way for the future. Yes, it shall be done."

Receiving that duty put the sap back into Carnolin. She straightened up and asked Vetch, "What will you do now?"

"I don't know."

"What?" Darant clenched his fists.

"We were sent to Rho-Torkis to die," Lily reminded him. "That didn't work, except for poor Meatbolt, of course. So, they sent us to Eiylah-Bremah to finish the job. Typical, bloody Militia. Always fanny-arseing around just to save themselves the hassle of executing us."

"We're deserters!" Darant groaned. "Traitors. Murderers. I mean, they'd convicted us of desertion before, but now we really *are* deserters."

Lily punched Darant in the gut. The pain in her knuckles told her he was wearing mail under his hooded jacket, so she stood on tiptoes to make her point directly to his face. "Call me deserter again, fuckwit, and I'll cut you deep. What we're doing here is clearing our names. Nothing less."

"We are?" asked Vetch.

Oh, not you too, Arunsen. Grow a pair!

He stumbled on in his attempt to articulate his thoughts, such as they were. "I just wanted to do the right thing one more time. It wasn't right what they did to you, Carnolin. I meant it when I said we were sent to this planet to die and die quickly. But…now I've made real deserters of us all."

Lily drew her knife. "Same goes for you, Vetch. I'm not bluffing. Call me, you, Darant or Enthree a deserter again, and I'll cut off your beard and shove it so hard up your arse that it comes out your mouth."

Vetch almost grinned. It was a start.

"Listen up, all of you," Lily commanded. "A deserter is someone who shirks their duty." She pointed back at the city. "It's those frakkworters back there who were shirking their duty. We've always done ours. M.A.P. The Militia and the Amilxi People. We never forget that. Those scum who call themselves officers on this planet, they're the ones who have neglected it."

"A fine speech," said Darant. "But the nights are cold here, and I don't plan on freezing my ass off on a hillside while we argue over our purpose in life. Where do we go now, Sergeant?"

"We find a secure, hidden, and defensible position," he answered. "Then we lie low for a few weeks while reconnoitering our situation and developing a strategic plan."

Darant rolled his eyes. "So, basically, we are going to dive into the nearest rat hole, wait around for a bit, and then make things up as we go along?"

"Is that not precisely what I just said?" Vetch grinned. The cheer suddenly fled his face, and he addressed Carnolin. "But first, let's get you home."

"I can't *go* home; I can never return to my old life. We might be able to hide out in the country."

"There is no *we*, dear," Lily informed her. "People will come after us to make sure we're dead. You need to go to ground without us."

"The countryside is filled with dispersed communities," Carnolin continued, oblivious. "People spread themselves out like oil on water, minimizing contact with their fellow citizens, so their friends can't report them for illegal thoughts and words. We can find a space to hide."

"Is there someone there you can go to in safety?" Enthree asked. "Family perhaps?"

"Close family will be watched. But I have a distant cousin who lives about thirty miles from here. I've never met her, but she'll take me in."

"If you don't know her, how can you be sure?" Vetch asked.

"Because she'll be grateful I brought you with me. She's a recruiter for the Revolutionary Forces of Reconciliation."

"Oh, mercy!" whispered Lily. "What have I brought them to?"

"What's wrong?" The Zhoogene looked in confusion at the stunned Militia troopers. "Don't you want to join the rebellion?"

* * * * *

Chapter Six:
Yat Darant

"Join the Militia and experience the galaxy. That's what the recruitment pod told me. Never said nothing about being a goddamned milkmaid."

It also hadn't mentioned to the young Yat Darant that he would spend so much time talking to himself.

"Only way I'll get a sensible fucking conversation on this goddamned stupid planet," he shouted at the stack of refrigerated canisters filled with fresh basten milk.

When the canisters didn't answer back, he grunted and returned his attention to the dirt track along which a trading truck might be rolling today.

Or might not.

Today was the day for trading along this route. In the widely dispersed barter bays that lined the narrow road, farmers, artisans, brewers, gun traders, information brokers, and all sorts could set up shop and trade to whoever passed. Farmhouse Control had even told him slavers traded on this route in bays such as the one he'd claimed. Except they didn't use that word. Indentured servitude they called it here, but Darant knew a euphemism when he heard it. He also knew Farmhouse Control would spin any old lie to drum up support against In'Nalla's regime, but it just so happened he believed the one about slavers.

That pretty Zhoogene girl—the one who'd led them into this mess—had said the next stage of her prison journey would have been to publicly beg either for her execution or for servitude. In'Nalla's jailers were excellent at making every alternative worse.

"Makes me irritable," Darant informed the stupid planet. And it did. The idea that a few hundred yards up the road, in a leafy bay, there could be damned slavers...He shifted his butt in the folding canvas chair but couldn't get comfortable.

He fingered the bulges in his jacket that outlined his pistol and knife and took comfort from them.

What if there really *were* slavers close by? He could kill them, free the captives, and be back before anyone realized he'd gone.

At least it would be something to do.

He spat at the dusty ground. "Why me?" he groaned.

The answer was obvious.

In the circus freakshow that was all that remained of Raven Company, and latterly of Chimera Company, he presented as the normal one.

Darant laughed at the notion. It was ridiculous, but true.

Even if he could be parted from his damned war hammer, a hulking, hairy beast like Vetch would always attract unwelcome notice.

And as the only Muryani Darant had seen on Eiylah-Bremah, their talking insect had to stay hidden too.

Lil' could charm the wheels off any truck that passed if she chose to, but those morphing tattoos wouldn't be easy to forget. They made her look like a goddamned space sorceress. Lil' swore her tattoos changed according to the whims of her subconscious, and he believed it. Under her smartass exterior, Lily Hjon was batshit frakking crazy.

And with everyone else too dead to help—except, hopefully, Green Fish, who was lying forgotten in a JSHC hospital bed, last he knew—it left good old Yat Darant, the one chosen by Farmhouse Control to pass the first test set to the Raven fugitives, by the side of the dusty road.

He scowled at the canisters.

The test was to pass as goddamned milkmaids.

"I'm *not* a milkmaid," he shouted at the empty road along which no trading trucks were driving. "I'm a murderer."

He stormed out of his chair and walked up the road.

The high hedges that lined the road made it impossible to see beyond the bend a hundred yards ahead. They kept the road cool, too, except for a narrow sunlit strip along its center that he followed, basking in its warmth like a sodding Littorane.

Four hours he'd been here, stewing in his own juices, and not a single vehicle of any description had passed. Even though the route was open for business, that didn't mean any trucks would come. According to the Farmhouse—whose pronouncements were as trustworthy as a federal senator's—it was 200 klicks to the nearest region the rebels claimed to control. The year before it had been 350. The steady advance of the rebels was beginning to disrupt trade in the capital zones, encouraging worried citizens to relocate to the loyalist island strongholds off the Dicadian Peninsular.

He rounded the bend. From there he had a good view along several hundred yards of road, but still no fleet of trucks.

"Murderer," he murmured.

Vetch had done the right thing in surrendering their futures in return for giving one back to that Zhoogene girl. And since they hadn't died fleeing the city, life of sorts went on. But he could never go back to being a trooper now, not after killing a few of the poor bastards in blue and cream in Execution Square.

Darant had originally signed on to the Militia in return for a pardon of his sentence as a convicted murderer. He'd had to confess his guilt first. He had told them the men he'd killed had it coming and that he enjoyed killing. Then he asked if it would be useful for him to direct his passion at the Federation's enemies instead.

Now that he was a deserter and mutineer, the pardon would be annulled.

It made no practical difference. The Militia didn't need legal records to want to kill him.

But it mattered to him.

Because now that he couldn't call himself trooper anymore, murderer was the only title that remained.

He chortled. "The milkmaid murderer. A fellow could grow into a name like that."

A sudden noise startled him out of his inward thoughts. A truck was coming around the bend.

Shite!

Darant raced back toward his trading bay, but he wasn't going to make it in time.

Halfway there, he turned, planted himself in the center of the road, and flagged down the truck.

It was a four wheeler—twin lateral engines by the sound of her—finished in plain brushed metal without color, marking, or any adornment.

He shrugged at the driver hidden behind the polarized windshield. "Milk?" he asked hopefully, pointing toward his trading bay.

Darant walked back, sat down in his canvas chair, and watched the truck.

It didn't follow. It sat there with its engines idling.

"That's right," he said quietly. "Check me out. Take as long as you like; I've got all fucking day."

Luckily, it didn't take that long.

The truck pulled up alongside the bay and parked, and a man jumped down from the driver's seat.

He stood beside his vehicle and regarded Darant and his wares with a vacant, but vaguely pleasant, expression.

"This here's your finest basten milk," Darant told him. "Squeezed it out of the little lovelies myself not far from here."

The trader's expression remained fixed.

Darant felt his pistol pushing against him from the concealed inner pocket of his jacket. He didn't like the way this was going down.

A breath of dusty wind blew up the hedge-lined road, causing the trader's lower face to tremble and Darant to understand. Beneath the man's plain, mesh cap, he wore a face flap. It was essentially a specialized viewscreen, shaped and colored to match the lower half of the man's face which was set into a neutral and inoffensive expression.

People wanted these high-tech veils to hide behind, because in this crazy-as-shit world, you kept your thoughts and feelings as secret as you could.

A camera and microphone were attached to the lapel of the man's faux wool jacket.

It was what everybody hid from.

Darant felt convinced this reticent guy must have seen the outline of his weapons. Technically, light firearms weren't illegal, but the Farmhouse had told him to keep them hidden in case he spooked any traders.

Well, sod the Farmhouse, because the man didn't seem bothered by them. Darant reckoned it was his lack of a recording device that was making the guy frown. The whole planet was insane.

The man seemed to realize his thoughts were leaking, and he pulled the peak of his cap down to cover his frown. For a moment, his face flap's illusion of his lower face failed. Then the pixels swiped away, and his mask was perfectly realigned. Neat that.

The trader folded up a side panel on his truck to reveal tiered banks of goods for sale or barter.

Food, entertainment, booze, medical and cleaning supplies. Power.

Darant was careful to ignore the battery banks that were his principle trading objective, instead inspecting leafy purple balls that he decided were a local form of cabbage.

He tapped metal cannisters like those he was offering for trade. "Basten?"

"Yes," the trader replied after a tiny hesitation just long enough for Darant to know what the man really wanted to say was, "Of course, it's sodding basten milk, you moronic skragg. What else could it be? Cow's milk?"

"Dumb question," Darant admitted in response to the pause, which was a giveaway he wasn't fluent at this. Humans and the other Orion Spur exiles had been foot soldiers and worker slave races in a pre-jump tech alien empire. To be of practical use to their masters, their guts had been reengineered to eat food from pretty much anywhere, including the Perseus Arm. Zhoogenes, on the other hand, were Perseid natives. They couldn't digest much unless it originally came from their home world, like the cute six-legged basten goats.

With a shrug, Darant moved from the milk to the stack of battery banks which were in desperately short supply in the hideout he shared with his fellow deserters.

Without lingering on the power banks, he quickly toured the available goods before making his offer.

He pointed at the large bags of universal rice. "Twelve of these."

Then at the battery banks. "Ten."

Finally, he asked for one pack of water purification tabs, a couple of cheap viewscreen rolls pre-loaded with books, and sanitary gel for Lily. For laughs, he added moustache wax for the bearded monster.

The man said nothing.

He inspected Darant's milk and took a metal cup from the cab of his truck to test a sample. For privacy, he turned his back on Darant before removing his face flap.

Stupid planet.

The trader indicated his wares on the side of the truck. "Your choices in exchange for all your milk. Agreed. Except…" He pointed to the power banks. "Only five of these."

"Ten!" Darant insisted. He guessed ten was a high number, but he'd never liked bartering. He considered drawing his knife and adding a sharp blade to the throat to the trading balance. It was more his style.

He turned his back on the man, suddenly shy about the lust for violence that must be written on his face.

Farmhouse Central had sent Darant here as a test. If he couldn't do this, they weren't any use to the rebellion in these parts. Darant couldn't give two turds for the rebels, but Vetch and Lily seemed to think they were their best route off this world.

Siding with rebels didn't sit well with him, but he'd do almost anything to be shot of Eiylah-Bremah.

He faced the trader. "All right, mate. You drive a hard bargain. I'll settle for eight of those power banks."

The trader remained impassive behind his false face.

"I'm not shifting lower," Darant told him. "Take it or sod off."

"Six. Final offer."

The trader's words were as dry as an airless planetoid.

Six batteries. They would last for weeks. It would have to do.

"Six," Darant agreed, but quickly tapped four transparent plastic bottles bearing the handwritten label 'whiskey-scotch.' "And these too. And you'll bring my milk cans back clean next week, yeah?"

"Deal."

Without thinking, Darant advanced on the man, hand outstretched to seal the transaction with a shake.

Naturally, given how messed up this senseless planet was, the man refused his hand, backing away.

"Sorry, friend," said Darant. "Here, let me help you load up."

Before taking the goods he'd bartered for, he helped the trader stack his cannisters of milk on the back of the truck.

The gesture seemed to impress the man, and when they were done, the trader hesitated.

What's your problem now, mate?

The trader stared pointedly at the bulging outlines of Darant's weapons. "Saw police up the road. Coming this way. Here soon. Maybe in an hour."

"Police? What's their business? Is it a raid? Is this a shakedown? A corrupt cop looking for a payoff? What's the deal?"

The man panicked under the barrage of questions and fled back to his driver's cab. Without folding up the side of his truck, he sped away, spilling cabbages out of the open side, onto the road.

"Strange fellow," Darant muttered as he picked up the fallen cabbages.

He stowed them under a thorny bush a short distance from the barter bay, along with the rest of his haul.

Then he ran to Farmhouse Control.

* * * * *

Chapter Seven:
Lily Hjon

When Lily finally found him, Darant was observing the farmhouse from behind the low stone wall of a pig enclosure. Police trucks were parked on the driveway, and heavily armed officers in body armor and helmets had secured the area.

"Yat. Yat. Yat! I hope you know what you're doing," she muttered to herself. But he usually did, so she crept over to his position, keeping behind cover all the way.

She got within twenty feet of him before a badly placed boot squelched in the sucking mud that lined their side of the wall, making him whip around and aim his pistol at her.

"Easy, old man," she whispered.

"Damn it, Lil'. I could've shot you."

She closed the gap between them before replying, "You could have shot *at* me. You left your shooting spectacles back at the hideout."

"Vetch and Enthree with you?"

"No. They're holding down the fort, looking after the goats. Don't worry, they'll take good care of them. Especially your favorite."

"I don't have a favorite sodding goat."

She opened her mouth as if in shock. "I'll have to tell Hubert, you know. I'm not sure he'll understand."

"Hubert's a fucking goat. He can take it." He shrugged and placed his attention on the farmhouse entrance where Carnolin's distant cousin—Farmhouse Control as she called herself—emerged in conversation with the police commander, who was also a Zhoogene woman.

"Hubert's cute, though," Darant admitted. "And I find I like a little basten milk in my coffee. A man can have his pleasures, can't he? Now, relax for five minutes, Lil', and let's see whether this is a friendly visit from the local guardians of the peace or whether we're gonna have to shoot our way out."

Lily grinned at the eagerness written all over Darant's face. There was no doubting which outcome he would prefer.

That was why Lily had been dispatched to locate the ever-grumbling, book-reading trooper and bring him in. Of all of them, he was the most stir crazy, the one most likely to crack violently and spectacularly. Lily was the one best able to talk him out of doing anything dumb, and she had no desire to go out in a blaze of weapons fire that achieved nothing.

Without much to occupy her mind, she was still struggling to absorb the pain of losing Sward. She wasn't ready to lose another comrade.

Sward's sharp eyesight and acute hearing would have been invaluable right now. Lily observed the proceedings at the front of the farmhouse through a gap in the dry stone wall, but she couldn't hear what they were saying.

The police commander and the farmer, who claimed to be a rebel controller in her spare time, were both Zhoogenes. If they had been human, Lily would have classfied what she was seeing as a cordial conversation between friends. But they weren't. She'd served alongside Zhoogenes—had friends and lovers too—and she'd learned never to make assumptions about aliens she didn't know personally.

The conversation stretched on.

"What the hell are they talking about?"

When Darant didn't reply, she added, "That was an actual question. Darant?"

But Darant had gone, leaving a trail of boot prints in the feces-strewn mud that led to the driveway.

She risked popping her head over the wall and swiveling it around to spot the mad frakker.

No sign of him.

Don't you dare get me killed, Yat Darant.

She slung silent curses at the trail he'd left in the mud. Then she pulled herself together and put her eye, once again, to the crack in the wall.

* * *

"They were just doing the rounds," said the farm woman after the police left. "Checking I'm not billeting a rebel battalion in my pig sheds."

While Lily hid beneath a nearby trailer, Farmhouse Control spoke into the air as she topped off the pigs' feed trays.

"You appeared to be on very good terms with them," Lily whispered.

"I was speaking with Sub-Commander Rea Konestogga. She is a good person. Most of the police personnel are. It is when they arrive with Militia troopers that you know you are about to be plundered. Nonetheless, she defends a repressive dictatorship and must be destroyed."

This distant cousin of Carnolin Idoh said nothing more to her, preferring to speak comforting nonsense to her pigs instead. Lily couldn't remember the woman's real name. Carnolin had mentioned it once, before she was smuggled away to a safer place.

"The sub-commander was worried about me."

"Oh, we're talking again, are we?"

"She said desperadoes were in the area. Militia deserters. She gave me a description of a bearded giant, a Muryani, and a tattooed human female."

"You see the circus I'm forced to travel around with?" asked Darant, choosing that moment to open the gate and walk bold as an emperor into the pig enclosure.

"Where the hell have…?" Lily started but saw the two boxy items Darant was carrying under his arms and pivoted her question. "What are they?"

"High power fuel cells." He stopped beside Lily's trailer, looking pleased with himself.

"But you already got power banks. I found them under a bush."

"Can't hurt to have more." He squatted down to give Lily a quizzical look. "I took them out of the police trucks. Relax, they weren't using them. Just spares."

Idiot!

They were supposed to be laying low and learning to blend in.

All through his performance, Darant had ignored the Zhoogene. Lily didn't know what was between them, but they hadn't gotten along from the start.

Farmhouse Control took four steps toward the human with the stolen police equipment. For a moment, she looked impassively at him out of her green, alien face. Then she blinked her yellow eyes.

That was all. But coming from someone on this messed up world of cagey paranoia, her reaction was like shrieking in rage and tearing out the shoots on her head.

"It is time you moved on," said the Zhoogene. "Shepherd will be making his rounds about now; he often comes in the wake of the police."

When she didn't offer any elaboration, Lily crawled out from under the trailer and dusted herself down. "Shepherd?" she asked. "Who's that?"

The alien blinked. "You'll see."

* * * * *

Chapter Eight:
Vetch Arunsen

The man strode the paths at the edge of the fields, keeping to the most visible routes and taking care not to damage the crops, even when that meant backtracking and taking a detour when the path he was following was blocked by purple-stemmed rows of young bragdy beans. He wasn't headed directly to the hideout, but his path passed less than a klick to the north, which didn't feel like a coincidence.

Vetch tracked his movement through the scope he'd detached from his PPR3 before abandoning his rifle to flee the city. Beneath a brown traveling cloak, the guy wore tough green camo gear, stout boots, and gaiters. The wide-brimmed, leather, relic-hunter hat topped off the man's ensemble, making him look like a tourist.

Reconnect with your soul on a 12-Planets walking vacation.

It's all about the journey…

Yeah, Vetch remembered the dumb adverts that had been shut down when too many people had tried reconnecting with life by traipsing through combat zones and promptly wound up dead.

Vetch laughed when the scope overlaid a targeting reticle on the man. Connecting with a blaster bolt would be just about right for a 12-Planets vacation walker.

Could he be a genuine backpacker, though?

Vetch flicked off the targeting overlay and took a closer look at the man's face. He was in his fifties, perhaps, with a neat white beard that followed his lower jawline, partially concealing a red-and-white knotted neckerchief. Red and white were the colors of the Panhandlers, the Federation-wide rebels. His lips curled up ever so slightly.

This was a man caught with a permanent half-sneer on his face. Someone who looked upon his fellow citizens of the galaxy and knew he was the one with the right answers. Vetch hated his guts already.

Yeah, this could be a rebel recruiter all right. He looked more convincing than the Zhoogene farm girl, but maybe that was just Vetch relating more easily to another human.

Vetch flicked the targeting overlay back on and wished he had the rest of his rifle with it. But what good would it do to take out one more rebel? The only future Vetch could offer his people was to hide out like frustrated rats until they were eventually captured and tested against the fabled torturers of Eiylah-Bremah. They needed to get off-world quickly to look for Green Fish and then team up with the rest of those Chimera Company assholes. Maybe this smug bastard in the brimmed hat could help them do it—unwillingly, of course.

Still…siding with the rebels…

He tugged at his beard.

For years, he'd made allowances for the failures of the Militia and of the Federation as a whole. He rarely admitted that, even to himself, but he wasn't a total fool. He *knew* what a hot mess Far Reach had become. Thank goodness the original Exiles were long since dead. He wouldn't have wanted them to see how badly their descendants had failed them.

This man in the fields…Despite what he probably thought, he wasn't going to solve any of the galaxy's problems. But he might lead them to someone who could.

Vetch broke cover and jogged off to intercept him.

* * * * *

Chapter Nine:
Yat Darant

"Eugh!"

Hubert froze, the cute alien goat startled by Lily spitting out her whiskey-scotch.

"What's the matter, Lil'? Not used to a drink with bite?"

Lily shot Darant a ten-megawatt glare that lit up the hideout they'd dug into the side of a wooded hill. "Whatever the hell kind of putrid rocket fuel you made us drink, it's not sodding whiskey. What's wrong with you?"

Shepherd laughed that condescending fake laugh that made Darant want to ram the plastic whiskey bottle down the man's throat and watch his eyes go wide as he suffocated. "It *is* rather an acquired taste, isn't it? But quite agreeable if you stick with it."

Vetch growled into his beard.

"No, really." Shepherd poured another tot of the orange liquid Darant had bartered from the roadside trader—allegedly a form of whiskey—into his tiny metal cup. He held the dented thing in a pinch grip, wafted its aroma into his nose like an ancient Littorane high priest divining the hidden paths of the universe, and knocked it back.

However, Shepherd was too cultured to do anything so coarse as to drink the stuff. Not immediately, at any rate. First came the noisy business of slurping whiskey through his teeth and lapping it up against the roof of his mouth. Only then did he gulp it down.

"Like a ripe cheese," he declared. "Yes, I'm definitely getting cheesy carboxylic from the breakdown of the high-protein rye."

Lily shook her head. "The only cheese I'm smelling is the stink from Darant. Dirty frakk-bucket hasn't washed since we were sent to this planet."

"What the…" Darant dried up instead of snapping back that he was the most fastidiously clean of all three humans. Must be the whiskey muzzing his head. Only then did he realize Lily hadn't just been acting weird since Vetch brought Shepherd in that afternoon. She was acting weird for a *reason*.

"What the hell makes you think it's a good use of my time to wash between my toes every day?" He shot a warning look at En-three. "My feet don't rot, and I've got better things to do with my valuable time."

Enthree tilted her head, puzzled, but leveled it again when she figured out the humans were lying on purpose again and would probably explain why in good time.

Join the back of the line, mused Darant. *Why the hell are we acting dumb today, Lil'?*

Enthree resisted the powerful temptation to point out that she and Darant were strong advocates for foot hygiene and allowed Shepherd to stew in his own smugness.

"Shut up the pair of you," Vetch snapped. "We need to fit in to local culture and customs. Hence, you *will* drink the local liquor, and you will damned well enjoy it."

"Yes, sir, General Arunsen, sir." Darant gave Vetch a Legion-style salute.

"Asshole," said the Viking.

"Bite me," Darant replied and then whistled.

Hubert knew that sound. The basten goat turned and raced across the dirt floor to his favorite human friend, using the stiff-legged turtle gait that made Darant chuckle. Hubert leaped into the human's arms, pressed a hot nose to his cheek, and licked the underside of his jaw.

"I know you love me, pal. I like you too. That's why Uncle Vetch said I have to give you a present."

"I think the little fellow likes to lick the salt from your skin rather than enjoying your company," said Shepherd. "Nonetheless, I find it fascinating to see a bond of trust between an animal native to Zhooge in the Perseus Arm—"

"And an animal native to the dockside gutters of Earth," said Lily. She mussed Hubert's furry head. "Hey, fella. Didn't your mother warn you about mixing with bad sorts like Darant?"

"The little guy is learning to live a little is all," Darant retorted. He grabbed a bunch of fresh feed stalks, soaked them in the whiskey, and offered them to the animal. "Compliments of General Arunsen. Even the company mascot needs to enjoy the local hooch."

Hubert took one sniff, gave a high-pitched sneeze, then tucked in.

"That's my boy," Darant cooed.

"You ignorant fool!" yelled Shepherd, leaping up and snatching away Hubert's treat. Or he tried to, at any rate. The basten goat laid his floppy ears flat along his head and gave the nasty human a warning growl while clamping the booze-soaked food between his teeth.

Shepherd gave up and pointed a finger at Darant instead. "You need educating about animal cruelty."

"Who, sir?" Darant replied innocently. "Me, sir?"

"Yes, you. You little shit. Animals have rights. They are not toys and playthings."

"We're just borrowing them as cover," Darant replied, his voice calm, but his eyes shooting daggers at the rebel. "Their fate is down to the farmhouse. Tomorrow, Hubert might find himself inside a pie, so he may as well enjoy today to the fullest." He gave Shepherd a glare laced with the threat of violence. "I can relate to that."

"Excuse me, Shepherd." Enthree waved a forelimb in front of her, the Muryani gesture for dispelling tension. "Am I reading this correctly? You value the animal more than the humans?"

"Of course, I do. That goat is an innocent creature, native to this sector. He's worth more than all of you." He glared before adding in a small voice. "More than all of us."

Suddenly, the recruiter seemed unsure of himself and glanced nervously at Vetch.

The big Viking, though, merely glowered silently behind his beard. Confidence, arrogance—whatever it was called—wrapped snugly back around Shepherd like a thick, protective coat. He took a few steps back so he could address the space like an orator, but he banged his head on the low ceiling of the dugout, shaking loose a sprinkle of dirt from the tree roots that bound the earth together.

Shepherd sat down instead. "Farmhouse Control tells me you're Militia deserters."

"Is that really what you call the girl?" asked Vetch. "Farmhouse?"

"It is her code name, yes. I don't know her real one."

It seemed to Darant that the other humans shrank back into the shadows of the gloomy hideout, a half-concealed pause in which to consider their next move. He ignored them, scratching behind Hubert's ears and whispering, "Stick with Yat, mate. I'll make sure you don't wind up in a pie."

"You're right that we were Militia once," Lily told Shepherd. "And now, we're looking for a new home. Might as well be your outfit. If we are ever captured, they would torture us and string us up to encourage others to toe the line. Fighting for the rebels wouldn't make our deaths any worse."

"Quite so." Shepherd gave Lily the half smile that meant he thought she'd said something stupid. The man used that smile a lot. "However," he pointed out, "I suspect your end would not be as quick as a hanging. It would be prolonged. The full Eiylah-Bremah treatment. They would make you see the error of your ways, and they would make you betray everyone you loved. You would choke on guilt so intense you would beg for execution, not just for the release from your torment, but because you truly believed that was what you deserved."

Vetch rubbed his beard and grunted an affirmative. "That's what…that girl said. We rescued someone guilty of speech crimes. She said they would make her beg for execution or slavery in the end, but I didn't buy it. No one's gonna make *me* beg for the noose."

"And yet, like so many others who also believed they were impervious to the demands of the re-educators, you *would* crack in the end. Her case is a little different. You refer to Carnolin Idoh, yes? She fell victim to the Churn. This, my friends, is a planet of confabulists, and the cynical dictator, In'Nalla, exploits this to her own ends. The Churn was already in place before her rise to power, but she has made it her greatest weapon. Even if, tomorrow, she were to disappear forever, Eiylah-Bremah society is so dysfunctional, it would take generations to calm down their evil nonsense."

Darant slid his gaze along his friends, wanting one of them to explain what the hell a confabulist was or ask the smug skragg in the red and white neckerchief. None of them looked eager to be the one.

No matter. I'll ask Enthree later.

Lily said, "We saw only a jail cell with a viewing window for the public to mock the convicted inmate. There has to be more than that. So, what is it? Drugs? Torture?"

"Yes, all of those, plus plenty of patience. The process takes years in many cases. Yet they nearly always succeed, and the public knows they will eventually see the transgressor recant. It is not enough to merely humiliate a criminal and make them confess to a crime they did not commit. On Eiylah-Bremah, they don't stop until they have *convinced* you of your own guilt. Those confessions are always genuine, even though the alleged crime is often an enormous distortion of the truth. Federal and planetary authorities across the Federation bring their high-profile prisoners to Eiylah-Bremah to be broken until they beg to publicly confess. Being able to make prisoners believe that two plus two equals five is a major part of the planetary economy."

"I thought that was mining."

"Ahhh…" Shepherd gave Lily a condescending smile as a reward for her naïve comment. "The outer asteroid belt is indeed rich in rare minerals and degenerate condensates. It is the great natural bounty of this star system, and its wealth should be fairly distributed among all deserving citizens. Instead, the tyrant, In'Nalla, has leased the mining rights to her federal senate backers in return for Militia military support. The asteroids that should make this world rich instead pay for the Militia jackboots that press down upon the throats of the people so In'Nalla can force her political ideology upon them."

"Man!" Darant shook his head angrily. "That shits."

"Yes, that, as you say, shits."

"Tell me again about those jackboots, Shepherd. They sound neat, but I don't remember being issued any footwear in my career as a trooper. Damned thieving commissary goblins."

"The system is corrupt," declared Shepherd, rising above Darant's quip. "That is why the Pan-Human Progressive Alliance is here to change things to a better way. Eiylah-Bremah is the galaxy in microcosm. Across the Federation, there are disgraces such as the theft of natural wealth and monsters such as In'Nalla. The rebellion will redistribute wealth to those who are deserving. Power will be seized from the corrupt elite and their cronies and reserved for those whose values are worthwhile."

"We get it," said Vetch. "Enough of the speeches already. How do we join?"

"Not so fast, my friend." Shepherd tutted. "You have all parted ways with the Militia. I accept that, but that makes you desperate; it doesn't make you one of us. I shall interview each of you in turn and in isolation. Starting with…" He swung out his finger. "Starting with you, Darant."

* * * * *

Chapter Ten:
Lily Hjon

Enthree was Shepherd's last interview and, by far, his longest.

Lily had figured that was the way it would play out. She'd scattered a few clues that indicated she was ill-educated scum, and she grinned when he had cast horrified glances at her tattooed face. His prejudice had done the rest.

After all, Militia troopers were all murderers and thieves. And Lily's party were deserters from the Militia, which made them an even lower form of underclass.

Luckily Darant and Vetch had picked up on her lead to play dumb. Literally, in Vetch's case, he had clammed up completely.

Shepherd had quickly dismissed the humans as worthless plasma fodder. His interview with Lily had been a halfhearted series of probes, checking for problematic beliefs. But a Muryani was another matter, and Enthree loved to debate humanoid political philosophy.

While Shepherd was quizzing Enthree—and probably the other way around, knowing her favorite bug—Vetch and Darant pressed Lily to explain what she was playing at.

"I recognize his sort," she explained.

"He's a skragging rebel," Darant pointed out helpfully. "He's the sort we killed until we came to this damned planet. Now, we don't have a home, so we change sides. We've been through this, Lily. Why are you being unreliable?"

"It's still a smart move. But it would never work with the likes of Shepherd. I hoped it might, but we'd never fit in with his lot, and that would get us killed before we got off-world. I used to know people like him. In his head, he's a hero in his own story of liberation and justice. The truth is that he wants to replace a corrupt elite with a new one based on moral and political purity."

"And based on knowing the right people."

"Precisely. And if they win, they'll split into factions based on ideological differences and fight each other. It's how Cora's World started out. The original Cora convinced herself that she was establishing a refuge of ideological decency. Her political descendants are a human-supremacist death cult who have long since denounced their world's founder as a xeno-apologist."

"So, he's an arrogant pile of drent," said Vetch. "I've wanted to tickle him with Lucerne since the moment I clapped eyes on him. I brought him in anyway because we need him. No one's signing up for the cause. We're just exploiting the local situation to get ourselves transport off-system. If not with him and his damned Panhandlers, how do you propose we do it, Lil'?"

Yes, how? Lily's idea was a gamble based on guesswork. They hadn't been given Militia intel on anything, just tasked with jobs day by day. But Lily had asked, listened, and read between the lines. The official line was that the rebellion on this world was part of the Panhandler insurrection flaring up across the Federation, but too much of what Lily had overheard hadn't added up.

"Shepherd's not a fighter," she explained. "He's an intellectual starring in his own heroic adventure. The Panhandlers have expanded so fast, they can only be doing so by allying with local malcontents. Maybe recruiting mercs too. He'll be part of a hardcore cadre that's put in place to ensure the locals don't stray from the right politics. Our best bet is to make him despise us so much, he doesn't want us in with the Panhandlers, but will redirect us to allied groups instead. Darant figured it out. Yat, you did brilliantly in feeding that goat whiskey."

"I did? I just wanted to see what Hubert would do."

Lily shushed him, because Shepherd had emerged topside to gather them like a schoolteacher herding errant children.

* * *

"I'll come straight to the point," Shepherd announced once they were back underground. "The role of the PHPA in regions like this—ones still under legacy regime control—is to prepare the way for the forces to come. We need leaders. Articulate advocates who can communicate the robust political arguments that underpin our cause. I regret to say that we cannot use you in such a capacity."

Lily felt her heart pounding. *Steady…*

"However…"

Jackpot! Lily looked down at the dirt floor to hide the grin on her face.

"We do have a role for you. The rebellion has armed and organized local civilian groups. Our political advisers are embedded within, but the organizations are largely able to run themselves for simple everyday tasks."

I bet they're capable of more than that, you arrogant bastard.

"I'm sorry to disappoint you. Not everyone can be a leader, and we must all make our contribution, each according to our abilities." Shepherd gave his condescending laugh. "For gasbags like me to be able to wander the planet, claiming to be intellectual badasses to those who will listen, we need many more brave individuals to do the actual hard work of revolution."

Darant scowled. "Plasma fodder. That's what you want us to be."

"Careful, Yat Darant. You use an objectionable term. Foot soldier is preferable."

"And Farmhouse Control," said Vetch. "Is she a foot soldier, or is she a leader like you?"

"That is not for the likes of you to know. Our local affiliate organization calls themself the Revolutionary Forces of Reconciliation, and their forward base is in Zone-41, two hundred klicks east of here. It's quite a trek through government-controlled territory, but with your Militia background, one I'm confident you can make. Within a year or two, you'll be back here as part of a military unit with guns in your hands and the glory of victory in your blood. Pass me your wrist slates, and I'll key in the coordinates. Tell them Shepherd sent you, and all will be okay."

"Shepherd," muttered Darant. "Guess that makes us sheep. Sheep that you're leading to—"

"To a purposeful destiny," the Panhandler insisted. "As I explained, we all have our contributions to make to the cause—"

"And ours is to fall under the enemy's guns as…foot soldiers."

"Perhaps. It's a matter of perspective, Darant. Everything in life is a matter of perspective because our minds see the universe as *stories*. In'Nalla is a narcissist and a brutal authoritarian, but she's right that we're all confabulists in the end. So, stop using objectionable terms like plasma fodder, and tell yourself a story in which you star as the heroic rebel soldier. The Zhoogenes are no different. Stories are the machine language of their brains too. Even you, my Muryani friend, are the same. Am I right?"

"You are correct," Enthree agreed.

Lily could see Darant mouthing, 'W*hat the fuck?*'

Shepherd could too. He took in the sea of blank human faces— and one inscrutable intelligent giant ant—and shrugged. "Who am I kidding?" he said. "There's three and a half bottles of whiskey-scotch need finishing off. Ten credits say we can't finish it by midnight."

For the first time, a fulsome cheer filled the hollow under the hill.

* * * * *

Chapter Eleven:
Vetch Arunsen

"**D**on't curse me too hard, or it will become a habit," Shepherd advised as he bade them farewell. He smiled, but it was a forced gesture from a man whose head was obviously pounding from Eiylah-Bremah whiskey.

"Tell me again why that's a problem," said Darant, with the cheery smile and booming voice of a man who knows he's the only one in the room with the constitution of a hazardous waste reprocessing plant.

"Because I feel sure we will meet again." Shepherd looked about to elaborate but thought better of speaking. Or making any kind of sound.

Darant slapped the rebel heartily on the back. "Cheery-bye," he said. Loudly.

Shepherd groaned and walked away.

Sitting beneath the cover of the trees, they watched him go in silence, those with aching heads enjoying the cooling breeze rolling up the hill from the fields below.

"In case there's any doubt on the matter," said Vetch once Shepherd had disappeared, "this unit ain't a democracy. I'm in charge." He paused in case any wished to dissent, but it didn't suit any of them to disagree, not even Darant. "However, if anyone thinks we shouldn't go find these Revolutionary Forces of Reconciliation, speak now."

"Good," said Enthree after several seconds of silence. She shivered, building up the strength to speak.

Vetch felt a pang of sympathy. His head was sore, but her kind were not good drinkers. Enthree's hangover would punish her for days.

"We face a difficult journey with an uncertain ending," said the alien. "That's perfect, because for humans, stasis is psychologically damaging. You need change, or rather you need action with the credible belief that it could lead to change."

"You're right," said Lily. "We're going crazy here. We all need to move on, though each in our different ways. Take Vetch, for a start. He needs a purpose, to convince himself he hasn't sold our souls in return for saving a Zhoogene girl we didn't know and will never see again. He needs a haircut too."

"What about me?" asked Darant. "Why should I head out to join these revolutionaries?"

"Because you need an outlet for your violent tendencies."

Darant shrugged, satisfied with his answer.

Lily stroked a hand down Enthree's hairy shoulder. "And as for you, my Muryani friend, your greatest desire is to be embedded in the adventures of humanoids."

"I concur," said Enthree. "What about you, Lily? What is it you seek?"

"Decent beer, late nights, and later mornings. I deserve a supply of hot running men, the badder the better."

Enthree tilted her head in denial. "Lily Hjon, that is not correct. What you describe is only a *distraction* from what you truly seek."

"Can't pull the wool over your antennae, can I, sister? It might be a distraction, but it would sure as hell be fun." Her face soured, and she closed her eyes, the lids slotting into the tattoos of magic fire-bolts or whatever the hell was supposed to be exploding out of her sockets. Sometimes, Lily looked less human than Enthree.

"I can't tell you what I'm looking for," she said in a shaky little voice. "But I know I haven't found it yet."

Hell, Lil'! Vetch finally realized the spikey tattoo lines on her face were a subconscious defense. Cover.

Lily was not in a good place.

"That's enough!" Vetch raised his voice as far as his throbbing head would allow and was relieved to see that Lily picked herself up from her introspection. "I looked up the term confabulist. They're people who make up elaborate lies to explain why they're right and anyone who disagrees is wrong. But they aren't lying—they believe their own crap. And here's the kicker—the more intelligent and educated they are, the better equipped they are to lie to themselves. I still don't really get it. Enthree, did you understand what that buffoon was talking about?"

"Oh, yes. Shepherd was a fascinating man. I believe I understood him far better than he understood himself."

"Then you can explain tonight. Darant, you're on watch. The rest of you, get some sleep. You'll need it. We head out at sunset."

* * * * *

Chapter Twelve:
Revered Leader In'Nalla

The unmarked car pulled out from the dusty hedge-lined road, onto a rough farm track. Asher's words were jolted out of her as the vehicle bucked violently and the rear seat slapped the backsides of the Revered Leader of Eiylah-Bremah and her private secretary, butts accustomed to being cosseted in official limos, cruising along the priority lanes of proper roads.

In'Nalla resisted the urge to glare at the driver. Or put a bullet through her brain. Such things looked petty, and appearances were everything in politics, especially in a period of transition such as this.

Within a few seconds, the driver had mastered the difficult terrain, the gravitics howling as the motors pushed the heavily armored vehicle high above the dirt bumps.

"You'll have to speak louder, Blayde."

Blayde Asher winced at the irritation in her mistress' voice and started again. "It's Secretary Gordon, ma'am. He's quietly agitating for the latest gun control bill."

"Gordon's always whining about what he likes to call the uncontrolled proliferation of firearms."

"Indeed, ma'am, but he's winning support in the Senate. He'll find a stooge to table the bill for him."

"Who, Blayde? Who is supporting this…this defiance of my will? And at a time like this?"

"That's difficult to say. You understand that senators are unwilling to speak openly unless they feel they have safety in numbers. Nonetheless, it is possible to read the runes, ma'am. I believe the talk of a Gordon-sponsored gun control bill is highly believable."

The car sank into a grassy knoll above a rippling field of rye. Her bodyguard, Halm, got out of the car to greet the Militia and police officers coming to meet them, which gave her a few moments to mull over the threat from Gordon. And the woman who had discerned it.

Asher was a reedy woman with pebble-lens spectacles who always wore a shabby hat that seemed two sizes too big for her head. She was easily dismissed by those who didn't know her as an inconsequential lackey, yet she was an astute political observer, and In'Nalla's spies had reported that Asher had perfect vision.

Blayde Asher was an act. But she was *her* act.

"Let Gordon make his move if he dares," In'Nalla said, with a sigh. "He will argue that, in these times of insurrection, we must not allow our enemies to arm themselves freely. And I will argue that it is precisely because the times are dangerous that our citizens must be armed, so they may defend themselves and our society."

Halm was walking back across the grass to the car. He looked satisfied that the area was secure.

"Gordon's a fool," she spat. "He'll never understand that, in the current situation, weapon control laws are a sideshow. What really matters is how the citizens choose to use the weapons already out there. And for that, we need to control not just the way they speak, but the way they think."

And Plan 19 will deliver exactly that, she thought, though she kept the dangerous words to herself. Committing mass atrocities against your loyal citizens was a regrettable necessity, but one the Court of Public Opinion was not ready to support.

The door opened, and Halm stuck his massive and rather handsome head through. "Area's secure, ma'am. It's safe to leave the vehicle."

* * *

The hellhole the fugitives had used stank of human sweat, animal stink, and of all things, cheap whiskey. A pair of basten goats were in here with them. She shuddered—the disgusting creatures had probably used the space to copulate.

But for once, she was glad of her small stature because the others kept scraping their hats along the dirt roof held together by tree roots.

She glared at the local police commander, a Sub-Commander Rea Konestogga, and enjoyed watching the Zhoogene go rigid with fear.

Serves you right. If it weren't for you, Sub-Commander, I wouldn't be in this shithole.

When In'Nalla was led to the hideout, a Zhoogene farmgirl had been hanging around the police commander, trying to conceal the lust burning like golden fire in her eyes. It was obvious she was the informant, and it was equally obvious what—or rather who—had made her sell out her cause.

It wasn't illegal for Zhoogenes to refuse hormone suppressants—though only because the federal courts would declare any such law unconstitutional—but it was a disgustingly aberrant behavior. How could anyone let their own body rule them? The farmgirl deserved all that was coming her way.

In'Nalla licked her lips and was preparing to unleash her anger on Rea Konestogga when a soft bleating interrupted her.

She looked down in surprise and saw one of the goats nudge her with its furry forehead. The creature looked up at her hopefully, blinking enormous eyes.

"Oh, you poor dear. Do you expect a treat?"

In response, the wretched animal rubbed against her shin.

In'Nalla gave it a solid kick that rewarded her with a snap of bone and hurled the goat against the wall.

The other goat looked in horror at its stunned companion.

Then it snarled at this aggressive human, ears back and fangs extended.

But In'Nalla had already drawn her Z'lox Needler pistol and chambered a flesh round. She put two shells through the goat that had dared to snarl at her, and another blew the skull of its friend into red paste.

The confined space concentrated the clap of the gunshots and made her ears ring, but In'Nalla decided the effect on Sub-Commander Rea Konestogga was most pleasing. If the police commander went any more rigid, she'd snap.

"Why was this place not discovered earlier?" she demanded.

"Ma'am," began Major Lyssin, the Militia commander, "I'm gratified that you've taken an unexpected interest in our operations, but this is a routine—"

"Shut up, Lyssin. I'm asking *you*, Sub-Commander Rea Konestogga."

"Ma'am, intelligence sources are, by nature, unpredictable. It's regrettable the information was not forthcoming earlier."

"You should have exploited your source more ruthlessly, Rea Konestogga. What was the problem? Did you fall in love with the girl you seduced?"

"Of course not, ma'am."

"I'm very glad to hear it. But she's hot for you, isn't she? Go get your reward. Now."

"Revered Leader, forgive me. I'm not sure I understand."

"Don't waste my time with coyness. Grab that farmgirl. Go into that farmhouse. Lock the door behind you and do whatever it is your bodies tell you to do with each other. Don't come out until you're both fully satisfied. That's an order."

If the sub-commander weren't wearing a beret, In'Nalla didn't doubt that her headgrowth would be waving like that rye outside in a hurricane. "Yes, Revered Leader."

Rea Konestogga saluted and left the burrow.

"If her informant had spoken earlier, you, Major Lyssin, would have caught your deserters, and I wouldn't be wasting my valuable time on this trip to a stinking pit. Asher, arrange for Rea Konestogga's immediate reassignment to the Northern Fringe. Let's see if she has more success seducing the polar wolves. As for the girl, she's a dangerous rebel. Arrest her the moment the sub-commander is gone and throw her into A-10."

Finally, she turned her attention to the reason for her visit. Major Lyssin, the human commander of the city garrison with whom she had a special arrangement—one that clearly needed realignment—and Lieutenant Ren Kay, a Zhoogene subordinate who was clearly in the major's confidence.

"Leave us," she told Asher, without breaking her observation of the Militia officers. "Tell Halm to make sure no one enters the burrow and then wait for me in the car."

Major Lyssin got straight down to business. "Why are you here, Revered Leader?"

"Why are *you* here, Major? The esteemed capital zone commander getting his hands dirty chasing a handful of Militia deserters…No, sir, it does not fit. What's special about them?"

Lyssin gave her a thoughtful look. It was refreshing to engage with someone who didn't fear her.

"These are individuals of concern to Joint Sector High Command."

"Why?"

"Ma'am, I do not know, and I did not ask. Even if I did know, I would not feel obliged to inform you. That's not part of our deal."

"Our deal? Hah!" She brought a boot down hard on a basten carcass, crunching bones and tendons. "Our deal appears to be as broken as this animal. Instead of implementing my wishes, you chase deserters who are of no consequence to me. May I remind you that I allow the Militia to exploit the considerable wealth of the belt mines with the understanding that, in return, you supply the brute force I need to push my people into the bright future they deserve?"

She nodded at the junior officer. "Him? Is he dependable?"

"You may speak freely in front of Lieutenant Ren Kay, ma'am."

"Good. Perhaps he can explain why you're dragging your heels over Plan 19."

"Because there's a limit to what the Militia is prepared to do. Let the rebels have the jungles and mountains to the east. You're safe here, in Kaylingen. For your benefit, Ren Kay, the Revered Leader wishes to discredit the rebellion by committing war crimes in their name."

"Ma'am, if I may," ventured the lieutenant. "If it's dirty work you need doing, perhaps hiring mercs is in order."

"You Militia *are* my fucking mercs!" she yelled.

"That is not accurate, *ma'am*."

In'Nalla felt a chill down her spine. The Militia major's voice was filled with contempt. Disgust. Condescension. At her!

She got in his face and whispered, "If you fail me, I shall destroy you. I shall demand of the Sub-Sector Marshal that he break you to the ranks and order you to lick my boots clean every day—dawn, noon, and dusk."

Lyssin wasn't the slightest bit fazed. "I advise you not to. And if you think you have any—" he had the good grace to give an embarrassed cough, "—dirt on me, then know that the Sub-Sector Marshal already has that and a whole lot more. It's your prerogative, of course, but I would think carefully before you make yourself a liability."

In that moment, she knew the Militia were no longer the answer. She needed another means to complete the improvement of Eiylah-Bremah.

Lyssin seemed to sense the change too. He swallowed hard, showing nervousness for the first time. "I take it we're dismissed, ma'am."

The major practically fled her presence, drawing the Zhoogene lieutenant with him.

In the end, the asshole had rediscovered his fear of her, but what exactly was he afraid of? If she could no longer rely on the Militia, then she had limited means to project power. Less, perhaps, than even the rebels. Most people assumed she held an unassailable position of authority, but it was just a house of cards, held up not by rifles and fighter craft, but by the support of the people.

And that depended on controlling the lies circulating through EB-Link.

She needed to shore up that support. Deepen it with fear. If Lyssin wouldn't implement Plan 19, then she needed to find a way to do so herself, and soon.

A howl of pain—quickly suppressed—came from outside the entrance to the hollow.

She pressed herself against a muddy wall and covered the entrance with her Needler.

"Easy," said Lieutenant Ren Kay, his arms up and spread wide. He halted with his chest a yard from her muzzle. "I offer you no threat, and your security guard is unconscious, but will be fit for action by tomorrow with no permanent damage done."

"Who are you really?"

"Oh, I really am Deroh Ren Kay, but I am more than a Militia lieutenant. I work for a federal agency called the Blue Chamber. I'm here to help."

"Blue Chamber?" She waved her pistol at him. "I have no qualms about firing a weapon in anger."

Ren Kay raised an eyebrow the color of golden wheat. "As the cute, fluffy animals discovered to their detriment. Look, Revered Leader, I don't blame you for not knowing about us. We don't exactly advertise our existence."

"The Federation is awash with secret societies and black ops departments. I think they're compartmentalized sections of the same two agencies. Which are you? Militia? Or are you really Legion?"

"If what you say is true, then how would I know from within the confines of my compartment? If I may…a more useful question for you to ask is why my organization would want to help you. To which the answer is that our objectives align perfectly. We want to discredit the Panhandlers. Unlike the official position of the Militia and its Senate backers, as represented by my superior, Major Lyssin, the Blue Chamber is not afraid to get our hands dirty with fabricated atrocities. In fact, we specialize in false flag ops."

"It's very kind of you to answer my own damned questions, but that wasn't top of the list. I was thinking more, why the hell should I accept your help?"

The green bastard shrugged. "Because you need us too much not to."

* * *

In the grass outside the burrow entrance, Ren Kay smiled at the muscled security human groaning in his semi-conscious state.

He'd lied about the severity of the human's injuries. A police medic was making his initial assessment, and if the man knew his trade, he would recommend amputation of Halm's hand and replacement by a prosthetic.

Sergeant Edrifice Halm was no longer a problem, though.

In'Nalla was.

In his first few moments of direct conversation, she'd demonstrated that she was highly perceptive, and that made her dangerous. He had to consider the possibility that she suspected the department had been running her as their asset from the very beginning of her ascent to power.

With Operation Blue Chamber suddenly moving faster than planned, threatening to spiral out of the department's control, he had to escalate or abort.

He watched the little human with the pockmarked face storm across the knoll back to her car. She didn't look like a woman who knew she was a pawn but then she'd used her disheveled demeanor to cause people to underestimate her in the early years of her ascent. Was Ren Kay underestimating her now?

No, he didn't think so.

Admittedly, he was working on gut feel, but the department had taught him when to trust his instincts, and now was such a time.

He wouldn't abort the operation.

He would accelerate it.

"Lieutenant!" called Lyssin. "Stop dawdling."

The major was in a huddle with a police tech support team. Drone operators from the look of their equipment cart.

"Sorry, sir."

"Hurry up, man. I need you to acquire the police data on our targets."

Ren Kay blinked slowly, wiping away the Department 9 operation commander, and becoming once again the junior Militia officer eager to ingratiate himself with his superior.

He rushed to Lyssin's side. "My apologies. Did I miss anything?"

* * * * *

Chapter Thirteen:
Vetch Arunsen

After reaching the coordinates Shepherd had given them, they had slithered through the mud in a chunk of featureless jungle and carried straight through. Five klicks farther on, Vetch took a breather to scan the area. Far from seeing signs of civilization, they were deeper and darker in the jungle.

With a squelch of sucking mud, Vetch resumed his march, scanning the tall trees for a welcoming party and finding none. Sunlight streamed through gaps in the canopy high above, shining off the peculiar metallic growths like polished steel short swords that formed the center of the leaf spirals. Were these swords a kind of stamen?

The foliage was green on this world, as it was throughout most of the Perseus Arm. Back in the Orion Spur, leaves were mostly purple, though the old myths said Earth had been an exception.

Why the difference? Was it because the quality of light from the older stars found in this region of the galaxy different? It wouldn't make any difference soon, because as they pressed on, the gaps in the canopy were shrinking. Before long, they would be encased in steamy shadows in which all colors would merge into a uniform darkness.

He shook his head sharply, realizing the monotony was making his mind drift.

"Stay alert," Vetch warned the party.

"Have you seen targets?" asked Darant hopefully.

"No."

"I don't like it," Darant complained. "I've got a brace of plasma pistols begging for some action."

"And again, no," said Vetch. "Our best defense is to approach openly and allow ourselves to be seen. Same as that recruiter did with us."

"More to the point," said Lily, looking behind her to see if they were being followed. "We allow ourselves to be heard."

The route ahead was blocked by chunky tangles of vines that moved like twitching fingers. Enthree got to work with short swords redeployed to machete clearance duty.

"I told you weapons safe," Vetch roared at the other humans. "Don't bunch up. Keep your separation."

As they slid apart from each other, still watching the shadows between the trees, a plaintive bleat emanated from Darant's pack.

Bleah? Bleah?

"Did you hear that?" Vetch asked.

"Hear what?" Darant responded innocently.

The noise came again, Darant tried to cover it with an unconvincing cough.

"Sounded like a dropship making atmos entry," Lily suggested.

"Or…" Vetch gasped in horror. "The hunting shriek of an atrox air-drifter."

Darant scowled at him. "You need your lugholes degreased again, big guy."

Vetch looked at him, hands gripping the shaft of his war hammer hard as if in fear, but in truth, taking full advantage of his thick beard to hide his grin.

Even his prodigious beard wasn't enough in the end. A little boy's giggle escaped his whiskers.

"Goddamned bunch of asshole jokers," Darant muttered. He knelt in the mud and undid the main flap of his pack. Hubert leapt out.

The miniature goat blinked at the familiar faces and then used all six limbs to skim across the slimy jungle floor like a guided torpedo.

Man, the little guy was fast!

"How long have you known?"

"Since your pack started wriggling a hundred yards after we set off from the hideout," said Lily. "Who knew our grumpy old book-worm was such a sweetie?"

"Stow it," Darant growled. "I've grown to like fresh milk in my coffee, that's all. Only way I could figure how to do that was to bring a supply with me."

"You know, Yat," said Vetch, stroking his beard thoughtfully, "on some planets you could legally adopt Hubert. You should look into it."

"That goat will be in a pie long before we get off this mudhole planet," Darant retorted. "Sooner, if you don't stop ragging me. Now, quit your giggling, you goddamned clowns, and keep alert."

"Shepherd sent us," said Enthree.

"What?" Vetch frowned at the Muryani who'd stopped hacking at the foliage. "I know. What's your point?"

"I wasn't addressing you, Mr. Arunsen."

With a sinking feeling, Vetch realized everyone else was looking up. He followed suit and saw the leaves bristling with rifle barrels pointed their way.

The rebel fighters soon had them on their knees in the mud, hands on heads, while the leader inspected them.

Works both ways, my friends, thought Vetch, as he assessed their captors.

They were armed with a random selection of rifles, pistols, and even a crossbow, most of which were sports models. Half of them carried their weapons as if they were an extension of their body, while the rest held them awkwardly as if they were armed with screaming infants.

Their heads were wrapped in folds of light gauzy material that revealed only their eyes and noses. Dull reds and greens were the dominant colors in the tough material of their plain jackets and pants. None of them wore camo. In fact, they didn't look like an army as much as a mob of desperate farmers off to rob a grain store.

The leader, a male Gliesan, stared into Vetch's face before nodding in satisfaction and moving on to Lily.

He gave her a good look and a sniff. "Forgive me," he told her.

What the hell kind of desperado rebel says forgive me?

The Gliesan wiped one of his delicate-boned fingers across Lily's cheek and then traced the spikey black lines that curled out from the corners of her eyes.

Lily took it stoically until he removed his touch and inspected his fingertip.

"It doesn't rub off, you know," she sneered at him. "It's called a tattoo. What the hell were you expecting?"

For several seconds, he contemplated her.

"Roses," he said and gestured to his soldiers to bind their captives. "And you ain't got 'em."

* * * * *

Chapter Fourteen:
Lily Hjon

The interrogation room was a small grain store in a village clearing by a fast-flowing stream. Bags of food were neatly stacked on one side, but the other half of the climate-controlled building had been made over into an operations room with printed local maps on the wall above a bank of comms equipment.

A human rebel in camo and beret, who looked like a soldier, beckoned Lily forward and motioned for Vetch and Darant to stay back with the grain bags. The man remained expressionless behind one of the face flaps that had been commonplace at their last hideout.

Back in the jungle, the rebels had bound their wrists behind them, but they hadn't known what to do with a Muryani. Enthree was waiting outside, with a half dozen weapons pointed at her.

Lily took a few steps toward the man who stood in front of a battered plastic table strewn with paper, more maps, and unwashed coffee mugs.

On the far side of the table, another man regarded the prisoners from the depths of a leather chair shrouded in cigar smoke. Dressed in tattered red boiler coveralls, he was quite the contrast to the soldier. Instead of a hood, beret, or wrapped fabric, his head was covered by a trucker's cap, its peak pulled low over his eyes. A corporate logo was emblazoned on the front above the words *Bori-Alice Space Truckin'*.

The soldier squared himself up. "They're undamaged, sir. As ordered."

Lily was convinced the two men were about to exchange salutes, but it turned out these rebels weren't Legion wannabees. The leader blew a smoke ring at his subordinate and then tipped his chair back against the wall so he could put his feet up on the desk.

Something about that looked familiar…

"We'll help you win your revolution," she told the smoking man, "but if you're not interested in joining us, then feed us and let us go. We've people to find off-world. Stuff to do. You know how it is."

"*We* join *you*?" asked the soldier in the beret, incredulous.

"Lily's not joking," said his leader. He lifted his cap and leaned forward out of the smoke to regard her through twinkling lilac eyes.

"Oh!" she said.

"Hello," said Fitz, grinning. He held out his cigar. It was almost half the length of Lily's forearm. "Filthy habit I'm revisiting from my youth. Izza would kill me if she ever found out. Not that she ever will."

"Fitz. What are you doing here as a rebel leader?"

"Waiting for you." His grin dissipated. "I gather our Muryani friend is waiting outside, but…" He grimaced. "I don't see Mr. Sward."

"Didn't make it," grunted Vetch behind her.

"I'm sorry." Fitz waved at his people to undo the captives' bonds. "I mean no disrespect to your absent friend, but it gladdens my heart to see the rest of you here and safe. I've been leaving threads for ages, hoping you'd pick one up and follow it to me. I'd almost abandoned hope that you'd make it here in time."

Freed at last, Lily rubbed her chafed wrists and allowed Vetch to storm over to the table and lean his bulk over it.

"What the hell are you doing here, Fitzwilliam?"

"Mr. Arunsen, please call me Fitz. Or Captain Fitz if you require formality like a damned jack. Speaking of which, Sybutu and his two little jack friends are not far from here. They're safe, but all their talk of 'I swore an oath to the Legion' has yet to convince the fine people who brought you here that they're on the same side. As for me…" He puffed on his cigar. "A little misunderstanding led to me being marooned here by my own crew. And now…"

Fitz's eyes blazed with violet light.

"I find I don't like the way the people here run their world," he said. He kept his voice level, but it was filled with the power of a fusion generator about to blow its containment field. "I don't like it at all."

Lily had never seen him truly angry before. The other rebel soldier recoiled in disgust from the mutant eyes that glowed like nebulae in the warmth of newly born stars, but what did he know? Fitz's freakish eyes were *awesome*!

"I'm going to tear down the tyrant, In'Nalla. Rip out their sick system of inform-on-your-neighbor. Dismiss the Churn. And did you know that humiliation is a major export industry? People across the Federation are shipped here as a lesson to those at home. A lesson on what happens if you upset the powerful. All that has to go."

"And you're what?" Lily asked, a little breathless. "The big cheese in this rebel outfit?"

Fitz grinned, and the anger was gone. No, not gone. Concealed within, but passion still drove him.

Hold on! Rewind...What was it he'd said about his wife?

"I'm working on it," Fitz responded. "I'm a senior zone advisor for now, with big plans to get this revolution moving."

"You said we got here just in time," said Darant. "In time for what?"

Fitz came out from behind the desk and walked over to Darant, cigar clamped between his teeth.

He choked on its smoke halfway over, coughed a little, but quickly recovered and slapped Darant heartily on the back.

"We're going to free the political prisoners in In'Nalla's flagship house of tortures. The Ameliorate-10 Re-Education Camp. A-10. It's 80 klicks northwest of here. We're going to bust it open, and you, my friends, are going to help me do it."

Darant punched the air. "Screw the system! Let's tear it down and start again. When do we go?"

"You have a day to rest, learn, and train with these excellent local people. Then we head out. Then it *starts*."

* * * * *

Chapter Fifteen: Deroh Ren Kay

The comm chimed on his way to the parade ground.

Ren Kay clicked his teeth in irritation. The tension between Major Lyssin and the tyrant notwithstanding, the opening of the Global Economic Forum was tomorrow, and Ren Kay was leading the honor guard. His troopers would look as smart and well-disciplined as any legionary, damnit.

It was a text message from Singh: *Tried to raise you earlier. Nothing urgent. Call me tonight?*

His heart skipped a beat.

Ren Kay was always aware of his surroundings, and he knew no one was around. He unlocked the door to a nearby tertiary armory and quickly stepped inside before that changed.

The message was code. Singh had urgent news.

Ren Kay keyed his comm to a non-standard channel that used Department 9 encryption. "What do you have for me, Singh?"

"Remember Lyssin had you chasing through farmyard muck, looking for those Militia deserters?"

He rolled his eyes. Lyssin's determination to bring in the bounty on those troopers' heads had been an enormous distraction, and Ren Kay had far more important matters to organize. "Of course, I do."

"Data digging turned something up. The police double agent gave the deserters a flock of basten goats to tend as cover. I think the deserters got lonely and treated the animals as pets."

"Get to the point."

"Sorry, sir. The goats were chipped. All but one was destroyed, but that one…It just turned up 200 klicks to the east in the middle of the rebel force concentration near my position. The chip says it's alive and well."

"I think you're right. Our deserters have an unhealthy liking for Zhoogene goats." He laughed. "Lucky for us." He thought a moment. These individuals were Major Lyssin's most wanted, so offering them up could win his favor. On the other hand, the department had its own reasons for keeping tabs on these troopers, and an even greater reason to keep Lyssin well away from Zone-41. "Good work, Singh. These individuals are suspected Naval Intelligence assets, but so's half the Federation. Track them, but don't contact me again on a high priority call. I've more urgent matters."

"Wait, sir! Surveillance is still trying to ID the deserters, but in looking for them, someone of much greater interest showed up. Tavistock Fitzwilliam! He appears to be a part of the RevRec forces we suspect are concentrating for an attack on A-10."

"Fitzwilliam is part of the Revolutionary Forces of Reconciliation? But that's…perfect! Do you believe in fate, Singh?"

"Sometimes," the agent replied cautiously.

Ren Kay didn't blame his reticence. Strong religious affiliation was frowned upon by the department. It could lead to unfortunate conflicts of interests, and Department 9 demanded its operatives' absolute loyalty in all matters. The future of the Federation depended on it.

"Let me rephrase that a better way. The Human Marine Corps of the Orion Era had a saying: When you see an opening, seize it with all six limbs."

"Six, sir?"

"It was a Jotun saying, most likely. But it's one I follow. Don't let Fitzwilliam slip away. I'm coming over in person to lead the department's operations in Zone-41. When the histories of the Federation's restoration are written, the events over the next few days will be the start of a new volume. This is where it kicks off, Singh. The shit is about to get real."

"And if an opportunity presents itself to eliminate Fitzwilliam and the other targets?"

"Singh, you've done so well. Don't disappoint me now. You kill them, of course."

* * * * *

Chapter Sixteen:
Yat Darant

"**N**ow, we're talking!" Darant roared his encouragement as the rest of the crowd's applause descended into a slow clap.

Twenty paces from the flames, the first fire jumper flexed like a professional high jumper. Then he started his run.

"Five credits says he'll bottle it," Darant yelled at the green-haired girl perched on another rough log seat, ten feet away.

Sitting astride the log, she shifted 90 degrees to face him. "You're in."

Idrielle. Her name was something like Idrielle. To be honest, Darant had quaffed too much of the local beer to be sure. Or to care.

The fire runner accelerated along ground strewn with soaking wet straw, cheered on by the mix of villagers and rebel soldiers billeted there overnight. But Darant wasn't watching. He was engrossed in the flames reflected in Idrielle's eyes.

She wasn't watching the jumper either. Her gaze was drinking in Darant and blazing with heat that wasn't coming from the fire.

Or was that the beer talking?

No, Darant was sure it wasn't. These rebels were giddy with the terrifying thrill of attacking the A-10 concentration camp. At dawn, they would set off on a forced march through the forest to their deployment zones. But tonight, they had thrown off their mouth masks and coverings.

In solidarity, the villagers had not only done the same but…

Huzzah!

By Orion's balls, these mad bastards were jumping over fires. For fun! The first was safely over, and plenty more were lining up for their turn.

Idrielle sauntered over and sat next to him, real snug like.

"Pay up!" she demanded.

Chuckling, Darant reached in his pouch for five credit chips. He hadn't doubted the jumper would successfully make his leap. It must take balls like asteroids to jump over waist-high flames, but it wasn't a difficult leap. No, this was a bet he'd been happy to lose.

Local men, with their heads bared, threw a few more logs on the jumping fire, making it sizzle and the crowd roar. The next jumper's leap would be just a bit more perilous.

Darant held out the credits in his palm and felt an unexpected pang of regret.

Five federal credits. That was a lot in these parts. Maybe a month's income.

Was he being too flash with his money?

Idrielle placed her hand over his coins and raised an eyebrow. "The next jumper looks hesitant," she said.

Darant snatched a look. She was right. The jumper was grim faced. Doubting…

"Let's make this more interesting," she said. "Double or quits?"

"Err…" Darant sucked in a smoky breath. Ten credits was a lot. What if he won and cleaned the girl out?

In Darant's philosophy, money was like the weather. You enjoyed the sunny spells of plenty, and you hunkered down and survived the bleak periods of poverty. Trying to control your financial situation was as dumb as trying to control the weather, and it would make you miserable to even try.

At the moment, the gods of plenty were shining on Darant.

Back when he'd briefly been a prison guard in the capital, Darant had quickly latched onto Sergeant Detennigen as someone with a suspicious air about him. Following Detennigen one day had led Darant to a large stash of small denomination chips buried beneath a loose stone in a cell that never seemed to house a prisoner. Darant had been overcome by a sudden duty of care for his fellow troopers. In the case of Detennigen, it meant relieving the rogue of a good chunk of his booty, purely to salve the sergeant's conscience, of course. After all, the guard sergeant's treasure was surely ill gotten and its possession a burden of guilt on the poor fellow.

Darant laughed at the irony. He was now a fighter for the Revolutionary Forces of Reconciliation. Fitz had explained that RevRec's idea of reconciliation wasn't to sit down with a mug of coffee and talk things over with In'Nalla and the gang of tyrants who had screwed up this planet. To this bunch, reconciliation would come about through firing squads that would be quite busy when In'Nalla fell.

And here he was, somehow caught up in an old-fashioned people's revolution, and scattered about his clothes, his person, and his belongings, were enough credits to make him ever-so-slightly rich.

"Well?" Idrielle demanded.

"I was just thinking. Ten credits? Are you sure?"

Her face fell. "Oh, you don't think I can pay."

"No, no. It's not that—"

She threw him a devilish grin. "I don't have ten credits," she said. "If I lose, we'll just have to think of another way I can pay."

Darant swallowed awkwardly.

Sod Vetch and Lily, he decided. They can moan about Eiylah-Bremah all they want. I like it here.

"Double or quits it is," he said. "You're my kind of people, Idrielle."

She looked at him askance. "Istrielle," she corrected but smiled. "I guess it's close enough for an ignorant off-worlder."

The crowd's rising excitement pulled Darant's attention back to the jumper, who hesitated halfway along his approach run, but made his leap over the fire to the delight of the cheering crowd.

But by then, Darant and Istrielle had already moved on.

* * *

Her lips tasted of cider and the eagerness of wanting much more than she dared hope for.

In fact, the enthusiasm with which Istrielle mashed her lips against Darant's, and the way she kept grabbing his ass cheek like it was an emergency pull cord, made him pause a moment.

She wasn't used to this, he realized.

It hadn't felt that way to him back at the fire, but now that he thought about it, in a world where everyone crapped themselves at the thought of speaking honestly to other people, flirting was probably an extreme sport for danger junkies only.

She released her pinch grip on his ass and squeezed his shoulders instead, staring into his eyes as she pushed him gently back against the outer wall of the hut.

Never mind that the wall was constructed from tough composite building material that added a trickle of solar power, would absorb toxins such as carbon monoxide, and could be configured to resemble wood, stone, and plenty besides at the click of a button. The village of Krunacao was home to only 3,000 souls when it wasn't hosting a rebel army on the eve of battle. Darant had been raised in the gutters of a major city. On the three sides of the village not bounded by river, the forest was only a hundred yards from the village boundary. In this remote place, Darant could only think of the dwellings as huts.

What did that make Istrielle, he wondered?

She was looking into his eyes, gathering the nerve to ask him something.

He gave her a little time.

"Take me to the Trucker," she begged. "Please."

"The Trucker?" He hadn't seen that coming. "That's what you people call Captain Fitz."

"Yes. Please, Yat. It would mean a lot to me, and it would be worth—"

Darant closed her lips by shoving his palm over them. That was a sentence he didn't want to hear to the end.

The happy train of events he thought he was riding had suddenly derailed. His ego was bruised. The little minx was using him to get to Fitz.

The hurt lasted for several seconds before Darant decided he didn't care.

"I can introduce you, if that's what you want, Istrielle. Do you want me to tell you something about him first?"

She blushed. This may have been the first time she had revealed her face to strangers since she was a little girl. She wasn't practiced at keeping her expression guarded. "Tell me where he's from."

He shrugged. "Dunno. He's a mystery."

She looked disappointed. "But you *do* know him?"

"Oh, yeah. I signed up as a marine on his ship. We're all part of Chimera Company."

A frown spoiled her pretty features. "People tell a lot of stories about you off-worlders, but they don't all add up. Some say you're part of the Trucker's crew, and others that you're Militia deserters who sprang a girl from prison in the capital. You can't be both."

"Yes, we can. The Militia thing was just a cover. Glad that's all over. Our real lives are on the *Phantom*. Best ship in the galaxy. We're daring renegades, rogues who are not afraid to stick it to the aristos. Then a tragic series of events saw us marooned on your planet, cut off from the *Phantom*."

"I'm so sorry. What happened?"

"Fitz's wife kicked him off the ship."

Confused emotions boiled across Istrielle's face.

"I didn't mean to burst your idolization, Istrielle. I mean, Fitz is a chancer, a supreme space jock who's clever with his handgun when the bolts start flying, but he's just a guy."

"Good." She kissed him hard. "Take me to meet him."

He laughed. This was a mighty strange night, but he was old enough to know when it was time to yield to the flow of events. "Sure, I will. But first, I'm gonna ask *you* a question. Why is the Trucker, as you call him, such a hero? He's only been here for a few months, and now it looks like he's running the whole damned revolution."

"Because…" She took a deep breath. "Because he *is* a hero. I think. In the formal hierarchy, Trucker is only a lieutenant. That's remarkable in itself, but he's not a big-shot general. And yet, he has staff and guards, all volunteers. This man has electrified the movement. The off-worlders who came here first—the Panhandlers—they just want to use us to replace the existing tyranny with their own. But I hear you, Yat, and your talk of running free along the rimward stars. About being rogues. I would love to hear your stories another night, but I know that life is not for me. I'm sure the reality is different—dirty, unglamorous, dangerous—but in my mind, it's romantic because it speaks of hope."

"Hope?" Darant shrugged. He hardly knew Fitz, but the man did seem to spend most of his time running away from people trying to kill him. Was that a form of hope?

She nodded, as if hearing his doubts. "Yes, hope. People of my world cover their faces and thoughts. They police their words. I want to believe we could be free of all that."

Darant straightened his back. "That's what we're here for, miss. I may not have the words and the swagger of Captain Fitz, but we're here to turn your hope into a reality. Starting with the attack on A-10."

She pushed her hot palms against his chest. "I think you do just fine with your words, Yat Darant."

"But…you still want to meet the Trucker?"

"You don't mind?"

"*Trucker*…Damned stupid name, but sure…I just need to do something first."

"No, Yat." She got to her feet. "Later. We have the whole night to enjoy each other."

"Oh." His face grew hot. "No, I didn't mean that."

She grinned at his red cheeks. "What, then?"

Darant blinked, not quite believing what he was about to say. "I need to see a man about a goat."

* * *

Darant found the others in the hastily erected beer hall. Vetch, Lily, Enthree, and…a small six-legged goat he had grown attached to.

"Vetch, look after the little guy, will you?"

The Viking gave Darant and Istrielle a dour look. "No. Dump the damned beast. It'll get you killed."

Darant sighed. What was wrong with Arunsen? "Enthree," he tried, "you're responsible for Hubert tonight. Okay?"

The Muryani was indulging in her peculiar beer drinking ritual—sticking a pair of front limbs in the cup and whisking them around before downing it. "Where will you be, Darant?" she asked, still whisking.

Lily looked up from the conversation she was having with Vetch and winked at Darant out of one space sorcerous eye. Man, her tattoo was getting freakier every day. Then she gave Istrielle a look of raw, needy hunger.

"Ask Lily where I'm headed," Darant told Enthree. "She understands. Now, will you look after the damned goat or not?"

"Your non-sentient friend will be safe with me, Darant."

"Thank you."

Lily gave him a cheery wave. "Have fun, Grandpa."

"Grandpa!" he muttered, allowing Istrielle to lead him away by the hand. "You must be nearly twice my age."

"Ignore Lily," said Enthree. "I know I'm twice *her* age. I think Lily just needs her ticket punched."

Darant howled with laughter. *Ticket punched!* Crazy alien. Where did she learn those expressions?

Once outside, he turned to Istrielle. "Now that you've met most of my embarrassing friends, there's just one more to go. Let's go find your goddamned Trucker."

* * * * *

Chapter Seventeen:
Yat Darant

They found the Trucker in a huddle of officers and planning staff who were moving away from the entertainment around the fire. Discussing the upcoming battle, Darant supposed. Fitz had a few of his supporters with him, but it was clear to Darant that the smuggler captain was not in charge.

He hadn't charmed everyone yet.

In fact, as he approached, Darant decided this wasn't a discussion so much as a full-blown argument.

Fitz noticed him and beamed with pleasure. "Good evening, Mr. Darant." He noticed Istrielle too and nodded politely at her as he strode Darant's way, scattering rebel bigwigs as he passed.

He hugged Darant.

Okaaay. That was a surprise.

And when he broke the embrace, he announced, "I sleep better knowing this man will be at my side when we make the assault on A-10."

Darant was too surprised to do more than watch dumbly as Fitz turned to Istrielle. "And you, madam. Are you a friend of Mr. Darant?"

"Looks that way."

"Then you and I are friends too, Ms. …?"

"Istrielle."

Fitz embraced her, planting a chaste kiss on each cheek.

The rebels opened their mouths wide in shock. Istrielle too. But when Fitz pulled back, her face flushed with giddy delight.

In Darant's experience, kissing as a greeting was common across most humanoid races and cultures, but these people hid behind masks. Man, this planet was a hot mess.

"Thank you," Istrielle whispered beneath fluttering eyes. "Sir, tell me straight. Will we triumph at A-10?"

"With the likes of you and Mr. Darant, our victory is as assured as it can be in matters of war."

"Thank you, Trucker, sir."

Darant was trying to remember why he'd brought this girl here as he watched her hyperventilating hero worship, when a sudden change came over her. She grabbed him by the wrist and pulled him away from her idol.

"Is that it?" he asked, though he was happy to be led away. "Have we ticked him off the list now?"

"Keep walking," she hissed. "Don't look back. I don't want to get caught up in this."

"In what?"

"Commander Slinh's just shown up. She's our greatest hero. Our leader. And I don't think she approves of Trucker."

Darant was only human. He planted his heels in the dirt and looked back.

At the head of a phalanx of subordinates, Slinh had pushed through the group and was standing up to Fitz with her hands on her hips and wings unfurled. White haired and bespectacled, the diminutive old Gliesan didn't lack for physical presence. There was an aura about her. An angry aura that was focused on Fitz like a ten-terawatt particle cannon.

"No!" she growled at him. "It's an antique, not a toy for childish adventurers. Don't ask again."

"Stop teasing," Fitz replied, with a cheeky grin. "You know you want to."

"You're right," Darant whispered to Istrielle. He squeezed her hand and walked away with her. "I've had enough of generals and attack plans. Let them debate and shape the future. I only care about tonight." He contemplated her face, still flushed with heat. "And about you."

Istrielle stopped. "My billet will be occupied." She ran her fingers over Darant's cheek, then brushed them along his neck and down over his chest. Her eyes began fluttering again, and this time her giddiness was all about him.

She took him by the hand once more and led him into the forest.

* * * * *

Chapter Eighteen:
Yat Darant

"Eiylah-Bremah is a strange frakker of a world," Darant opined as he caressed the firing control handles of the SG-7c assault support gun, or plasma squirter, as everyone who wasn't a total weapons tech nut called it. Like Deep Tone had been.

"*Bleeke*," cried a little voice when Darant's mutterings stalled on the memories of his friend.

"Deep used to rip me a new one every time I trained on one of these beasts," he told the basten goat chewing on a pile of leaves atop reserve plasma tank-3. "Said I had no feel for the gun."

He tightened his grip on the handles and looked through the holo-sights at the guard tower, 150 yards away across the killing ground behind Ameliorate-10 Re-education Camp.

All things considered, the rebels had worked wonders setting up this position so close to the target. Not only had the area been quietly cleared over several nights, but he was protected by a horseshoe of armor plating four-feet high and screened by shrubbery.

"Deep will be guiding my hands in a few minutes. He won't let me down, even though he'll be laughing his dead head off at my poor feed mix and telling me I aim my SG-7 like a drunk taking a piss."

Darant squealed when he felt a touch on his shoulder.

It wasn't Deep Tone stretching out his ghostly fingers; it was Vetch.

"Keep it down," the big man told him. "And that damned goat. Five Hells, man, I told you to leave the bloody animal behind. Its bleating will give us away."

Hubert narrowed his eyes, stood tall on his ammo tank, and hissed at Vetch.

"Animal noises are good, Sarge," Darant whispered. "It's the *lack* of animal noises that clues the enemy that something's up."

Hubert's hiss deepened into a growl.

"You know what?" Vetch asked. "Call it a hunch, but I'm guessing the enemy *already* knows something is up. I just don't want them looking in our direction."

From the outside, the A-10 camp was a fortress. The walls and guard towers were of similar design and construction to Fort Iceni, the Militia base where Darant had been stationed on Rho-Torkis. But this was bigger. *Much* bigger, with a lot of extras too. A-10 was several pages further on in the product catalog than Fort Iceni.

Under cover of the forest's edge, the main force of RevRec rebels was already assaulting the south gate with rockets and mortars. The wall was being raked by fire from 2,000 rifles in the hands of determined men and women with sharp eyes and a lifetime of regular trips to the range.

And shouting. There was a lot of shouting.

Roars of encouragement.

Screams of excitement and the moans of the wounded.

But mostly, the rebels taunted the Re-Education Enforcement Division defenders by openly yelling out speech crimes.

REEDs, the locals called the uniformed thugs behind the walls. And when those walls were breached, Darant wouldn't want to be caught wearing the all-black REED uniform with the distinctive red 'X' across the chest and knee guards.

For now, though, the action at the south gate was just a demonstration designed to suck in the REEDs. The breach would come from the northeast. From Fitz's team.

Darant looked around him through the trees. Enthree was nearby, standing rigid and silent, with det packs slung over her back. She'd be going into action soon.

He sighted the target once more. There was no sign that the north wall and the adjoining towers were manned. Had the REEDs all been redeployed to the battle at the south wall? Or had the sneaky bastards spotted the rebel force in the trees to the north and waited to flay them with fire as soon as they advanced into open ground?

"Anyway," he whispered to Hubert, who had returned to munching his leaves after the nasty human with a long beard slid back into the shadows. "As I was saying.…" The REEDs on the south wall began firing a noisy minigun, and Darant had to raise his voice. "As I was saying, you couldn't make this damned planet up. Taxes are low. Entrepreneurship is idolized. If you suggest roads or healthcare are better under public ownership, you get sent to a re-education camp like this until you're ready for your show trial, where you get to explain how wrong you were. They don't have many laws. Public opinion decides if you're a transgressor or not, and public opinion is tightly controlled by the government. They don't even bother with an army because the citizens are all armed. Not because that's a law or anything, but because if you don't carry a gun and regularly visit the shooting range, everyone's scared you might inform on them for thought crimes. Armed citizens—my kind of world. If we can just tip public opinion against In'Nalla…"

The goat gave Darant a warning rumble and flicked his ears in the direction of the trees to their right. The nervous tension in that section of the rebel line was so palpable it would probably show up on radar.

"Don't worry about it," Darant assured the goat. "I'm not sure what's going on there, but I'm guessing it's Captain Fitz giving a heroic speech. Now, Fitz is an interesting case. He's a damned mutant. If you make disparaging remarks about most personal characteristics, you've committed a speech crime. Even if you didn't intend an insult, you still need lengthy re-education. Not so for unprotected groups like mutants. The galaxy over you can insult devil-eyed mutant freaks as much as it likes."

He noticed Enthree checking that the straps of her det packs were secure against the bony parts of her back. It wouldn't be long now.

"See here, goat, I'm a rogue, living it up on the outer rim." He grinned, thinking of Istrielle hidden somewhere nearby in the trees, cradling a blaster rifle. "So, I spit on their speech crime nonsense. Let's see how many laws I can break in one sentence."

He mused in the cesspit of his vocabulary for the foulest way to describe the crater-faced dwarfish hag-witch, the Revered Asshole, In'Nalla.

Darant had just opened his mouth to begin his volley of abuse when his wrist slate pinged and started the twenty-second countdown.

He flipped the locks off the firing handle studs, re-sighted his target, and made some final adjustments to compensate for atmospheric conditions.

15...14...13...

"You might want to step back," he told Hubert as he pulled his goggles over his eyes. "Things are about to get exciting."

* * * * *

Chapter Nineteen:
Tavistock Fitzwilliam

Fitz crept forward, almost to the open ground before the north wall, heedless of the REEDs' ability to shoot him, so long as he got a good view of the entertainment. Darant was positioned in a clearing that had been quietly finished off the night before, and from there, he spat plasma from the barrel of his SG-7 like a dragon who'd learned the trick of indirect fire.

Strictly speaking, the gun was streaming pre-plasma that whipped itself into a high-energy state just before splashing against the firing ports of the defensive tower and quickly spreading through every gap it could find. Fitz's glasses flickered as they progressively darkened to shield his eyes from the beastly brightness. Anyone watching the plasma show directly would burn their retinas as surely as if they were staring at the sun.

Just as well, really. Fitz was relying on that.

He activated the second countdown. Twenty seconds, and he would be off in a light show of his own. Not so bright, but ten times as dangerous. For him.

Darant panned his plasma squirter right, dropping fire over the top of the wall butting up against the tower. But it was the tower's roof that Fitz examined now, tapping his glasses to select infrared view.

The former Militia gunner—and now a member of his marines, Fitz reminded himself—had kept the plasma away from the tower roof, but the glasses showed patches with temperatures up to 400° Kelvin. Fitz looked down at his boots. He'd have to jump like a desert lizard, but it wasn't his feet that were most vulnerable to the heat.

Much too soon, the arc of plasma fell away and died, leaving a scorched black gouge in the ground.

The countdown in his glasses said there were still 11 seconds to go.

He'd just have to be early for once in his life.

Fitz broke cover and ran for the wall. *Waddling* would have been a better description with the heavy contraption strapped to his back.

Without the covering fire from the plasma, he felt horribly exposed, but small arms fire lashed the wall from the trees, pitting the armored structure and, hopefully, encouraging the REEDs to keep their heads down.

He couldn't bear it. Earlier than planned, he thumbed the launch button on the right handle, and pushed forward the directional control on his left.

Three clusters of rocket nozzles deployed over the backs of his calves, and the jetpack sent him arcing into the air.

"You see, Commander Slinh?" he shouted. "There was no need to be so protective of your little toy. I *do* know how to use one of these."

He sailed over the top of the tower, tossing a handful of micro drones at the upper level, programmed with pre-instructions to sneak inside the firing ports.

He cut off the thrust and missed his intended landing completely and passed right over the tower roof, dropping instead into the interior of the camp. It was a dreary open area of cobblestones, with a speaker's dais and weather-hardened PA columns.

Crap!

He landed well and sprang into a bounding series of moon leaps by tapping the thrust button. Once he had enough distance for another try, he shuffled around to face the tower.

Bullets deflected off the ground at his feet in a spray of stone chips.

"About time you woke up," he declared, quick drawing his F-Cannon and firing the exotic handgun at the upper levels of the tower.

Ten meters along his firing trajectory, the 'blinder' round bloomed into a rounded rectangle about three meters high, two across, and one deep. The interior of this zone filled with smoke and particles with confusing motion, reflective properties, and EM-radiation.

It was as if someone had drawn a blind over the air.

Fitz took two side steps and then hit the thrust once more, boosting up and onto the tower. He remembered to grab the cigar from his jacket pocket and clamp it between his teeth so he would look good in front of the rebels.

This time he came down astride the center of the slightly domed roof, landing as gently as a kitten on a ton of extra-plump cushions.

He waved to the rebels still in the trees with one hand, and with the other, he keyed his glasses to show view panels feeding from the drones inside the tower.

They showed an upper floor, blackened and smoky, but devoid of flames or corpses. Far from the emptiness he was hoping for, three REEDs in breathing gear were beginning to assemble a crew-served gun that would shred any rebel attack force into bird food.

Unless, that was, he could persuade the REEDs to hand that gun over to him…

He guessed he had about a minute before the REEDs opened fire.

Fitz pushed an outstretched palm toward the rebels waiting in the trees. *Stay back!*

Then he carefully shrugged off the jetpack, still laden with fuel.

Bullets flew over his head.

Instinctively, he ducked, and started sliding off the roof. He pressed down with his hands and feet, praying for grip.

His prayers were answered. He arrested his slide, but the jet pack went over like a snow sled, tumbling fifty feet and landing with a hollow metallic thud on the inside of the re-education camp.

"No!"

He risked a look over the edge. The thrust nozzles were bent, and fuel was leaking onto the pavement.

Beneath the thunderous roar of battle, he thought he heard engines starting up. A lot of them, but they were hidden from view.

More rounds came his way, and he ducked again, but they were firing high. Probably couldn't get an angle on him from the ground, which left the broken jetpack as his main concern.

Slinh wasn't going to be happy about that. They didn't make Orion Era jetpacks anymore, and Fitz had argued with the old Glie-san for hours back in Krunacao before the commander agreed to part with her prized antique.

Can't be helped. Better give her a fantastic victory to take her mind off things.

Luckily, Fitz's cigar was unharmed, and taking care to keep as low a profile as he could, he activated it and took a puff before clambering onto the north side of the roof.

"Now, let's see about that gun."

* * * * *

Chapter Twenty:
Lily Hjon

Hooking up with Fitz again was proving damned entertaining.

In her position up a tree, Lily had her HC2 blaster's scope set to 'reaction mode,' giving her a field of view across the northeast tower and thirty feet of adjoining wall. Any movement the system couldn't discount as a natural phenomenon would be vividly highlighted and firing solutions would be prepared.

Only one unnatural phenomenon was registering: Captain Fitz, or in his new persona as a cigar-chomping revolutionary leader, the Trucker.

As she watched his exploits play out, she wondered if Vortex of Chaos might be a better name for the man.

First, he'd used a rocket pack to ascend the gently domed roof— a freaking rocket pack! He'd almost slid off the roof, but he'd still managed to wave at the RevRec rebels and flash them his trademark grin. In his stained red boiler overalls and trucker hat, he looked like a maintenance worker come to clear a blockage in the drains, but the RevRec fighters adored him.

All through his performance, Lily had been scanning for threats with her Hunndrin & Rax targeting system, but had found none. A few rounds from the interior of the camp had sought Fitz out, but he was now on the reverse side of the sloping roof, and the fire couldn't reach him. Maybe the REEDs really had abandoned the north wall and rushed to the sounds of battle to the south.

Amateurs!

Lily's heart pounded with excitement at what Fitz did next.

Leaning over the top of the tower, he fired two rounds through the armored wall. At least, that's how it appeared to Lily. She saw a bizarre green muzzle flash at the business end of Fitz's hand cannon and then...nothing came out.

He'd fired point-blank at the wall, but there was no sign of impact, nor of scorching of the target.

But Fitz clearly thought he'd done something impressive, because when he stuck his head up to face the rebels, his grin doubled, and he blew a triumphant smoke ring before giving a thumbs up.

Had he somehow shot someone inside the tower?

She sensed sudden and violent motion hurtling through the trees.

It was Enthree. She must have read the thumbs up as Go! Go! Go!

And, sister, she certainly *went.*

The Muryani charged out of the trees like a startled spider. A big one.

It was likely a sight no one in this world had seen before, and that probably saved Enthree's life, because it took three seconds before the astonished defenders—who had been hiding in the north wall all this time—came to their senses and began filling Lily's scope with movement alerts.

She fired first, unleashing a trio of bolts at one of the horizontal firing ports 178.2 yards away.

Hunndrin & Rax had named their HC2 blaster rifle the *Penetrator,* but the bolts seared against the firing port without finding a way through. Only Sward could have sent all three bolts through the slit, but she hoped her fire gave the REED on the other side of the port something to think about for a few seconds.

Already, she was unleashing bolts against other ports, settling for near misses in return for a higher firing rate.

Around her, the rebels in the trees opened up with a fusillade of bolts and bullets, but the REEDs were determined. Defensive fire flew out, and it was concentrated on the Muryani sprinting across the open ground.

* * * * *

Chapter Twenty-One:
Yat Darant

"I'm gonna need that ammo in a minute, bud," Darant warned the goat happily munching his leaves on top of tank-3. "Or do we run for it? Looks like you and me and the nice, tattooed lady have been designated the rearguard, because where the *fuck* did everyone go?"

The plasma feed was reporting fifteen percent remaining. When that went dry, it would take him around one hundred seconds to swap it out for tank-3. If anything came at them out of that camp, they would be totally defenseless until the swap was complete.

"Is this a goddamned joke?" he screamed at the empty trees. "Cause I ain't laughing."

Fitz was leaning out the tower, shouting at Darant, but his voice was inaudible over the plasma squirter's roar. So, Darant cupped an ear, and Fitz responded by pointing down behind the breach Enthree had blown.

"What does that madman want now?" he asked Hubert. "Does he want me to re-light his cigar with my plasma?"

A tingling sensation came over him when he realized what Fitz was trying to say. Something bad was about to emerge through the breach.

"Sorry, mate," he told the goat. "Looks like we're screwed."

But Hubert wasn't paying attention. The basten was looking over Darant's shoulder and bleating happily.

"Whoever you are," Darant growled at whatever had gotten Hubert's attention, "either put a bolt through me or leave me be, because I ain't turning around until tank-2 is spent."

He panned his plasma stream to the left and rained down hellfire inside the camp, just beyond the rubble of the breach. Any REEDs assembling there were getting a hot surprise.

"Do you need a hand swapping out plasma tanks?" asked Istrielle.

Despite the dire situation, his heart skipped a beat at her voice. "If you're not trained for it, then no."

"Holy skragg!" Something big and highly explosive cooked off beneath his plasma spray, sending up a fireball higher than the camp wall. "Get some! That'll keep you bastards quiet for a few seconds."

But without his plasma raining down on the wall, the REEDs at the firing posts began pouring bolt after bolt into the armor protecting his position. The fire set the screening foliage ablaze but didn't penetrate the armor shielding his gun.

Darant took a deep breath and confronted Istrielle. "We've been set up. Why?"

Istrielle remained tightlipped and grim faced. She wore navy blue coveralls burnt away on a shoulder to reveal severely burned skin. Her green hair was tucked inside a knitted black hat with loose flaps that covered her ears. She sure didn't look like a soldier, but she carried her blaster like she meant to use it, and boy was she pretty.

"Speak!" he demanded as he began detaching tank-2 from the SG-7.

"The villages are being massacred. Faeynsted, Bas-Hemel, and…Krunacao. The others went back to defend their homes."

"If the REEDs are massing for an attack, there won't *be* any homes by the time they get back." He sealed the spent tank and threw it behind the gun emplacement. "Here, they could have made a difference. So, what do we do now, RevRec girl? Your friends decided to leave the expendable off-worlders to sacrifice themselves as a rearguard. Is that it?"

"That's what many were saying." She cast her gaze to the ground in shame. "I didn't leave you, Yat."

She jerked, screaming, as something wafted in front of her face.

"What? You scared of a little splither of burning wood now?"

Then he saw the reason for the look of horror on Istrielle's face. The rebels had piled up bundles of shrubs to screen his gun's armor shield. And now, burning branches were falling inside that shield.

Onto the last two plasma tanks.

They each grabbed one of the tanks from under the burning wood and leaves and scraped away the flames, not daring to think what would happen if the plasma fuel cooked off.

Darant began furiously working on connecting tank-3.

"Here they come," warned Istrielle, who was peering through the gap in the armor.

"Be specific," snapped Darant as he screwed in the plasma feed.

"Hover vehicles. Six. More coming. Like armored bubbles. With four gun barrels out each nose."

"Holy skragg!" Darant looked through the gap to see for himself.

He saw a column of 'crab' light armored vehicles and, screaming above them, hover darts— narrow, two-man flitters that were nimble enough to get through the trees.

Explosions blossomed to their front and flanks, crumpling their armor shield and making Darant's head and chest ring.

Darant wasn't great with numbers, even when his head hadn't been beaten with a lump hammer, but the calculation he ran was not difficult. The crabs couldn't fly through the trees, but they'd be at the tree line pouring down cannon fire at him before he had any hope of readying the plasma gun to fire again.

"Run!" he screamed, scooping up Hubert and his pack as he fled into the depths of the trees.

He was pursued by bullets, bolts, and splinters of wood, shattering under the onslaught of fire pouring out of the crabs and hover darts.

The ground before him erupted into plumes of dust and fire as rounds struck.

Darant dodged right and ran around tree trunks and through bushes. His lungs burned with fatigue and the smoke from the trees, but the shouts of REEDs were close by, and he didn't dare stop.

An explosion ripped apart the air behind him, and he lost his footing. Thrown forward in a wave front of dirt and shattered wood, he thudded into a tree hard enough to bruise ribs. Maybe crack a few.

Stunned, he lay still on the forest floor. Every breath was a stab of agony cutting through his chest.

The throb of gravitic engines kneaded his ribs, and it was all he could do to keep from screaming out in pain. They sounded as if they were passing through the forest mere feet away. But he was half deafened, and his thoughts wouldn't come together properly in his head.

If they were that close, he was screwed, so he decided to lie still for the count of ten to clear some of the thunder rolling around the inside of his head. Then he'd make his move.

He got to four before blacking out.

With a gasp, he came to in the same litter of broken branches he'd passed out in.

Skragg it!

He rolled onto his side, which made him grunt with the pain in his ribs.

No one there.

He'd been left behind. No, not quite alone. A familiar sound of crunching leaves nearby told him he still had the damned goat for company.

And not just the goat. He heard shouts from deep in the forest. They grew urgent.

Then came the scream of heavy blaster fire.

Followed by silence.

He checked his wrist slate and found he'd only been out for a couple of minutes.

Memories flooded back and slotted themselves into an order that made some kind of sense.

"Sonofabitch!" he murmured, remembering that the rebels had left him to die.

Though not all of them.

"Istrielle!" he groaned and pushed himself up to sit against the tree. Pain flared from his chest like fireworks. They exploded across his vision. He needed to get back into the fight, but he needed to grab his med-kit first.

Back in the capital city of Kaylingen, he'd pilfered some of the good stuff they didn't issue to penal scum like him. Man, he was glad he'd taken that risk now. He stabbed himself in the chest with a rib trauma kit.

Fiery tentacles spread across his chest.

What was this? A pain enhancer? 'Rib trauma' had been written along the tube, but did it have the wrong contents?

He ground his teeth and held on to his consciousness because his mind was telling him his friends needed him.

Blue rained across his sight.

It was surreal, but cerulean clouds rained fat blue globules that pooled into an azure sea, which sloshed across the lower half of his sight. The waters quickly rose to completely fill his vision.

What the fuck?

Then he remembered hearing a long time ago about expensive medicines that confirmed with the patient they'd received the correct treatment and dosage. The cap he'd pulled off the tube was the same color blue as his vision. So was the writing on its side.

"Probably to distract you from the pain," he said, laughing, giddy with relief or, possibly, the drugs.

But it had worked. The pain in his ribs was gone. And it was more than a painkiller. Okay, so maybe this wasn't as classy as the medical nanites of the Orion Era, but his injuries should be repairing, the natural healing mechanisms of his body boosted to a massively accelerated rate. Which probably explained why his chest felt so hot, he expected to see steam curl up from it.

If only he could see through the blue.

"Over here!" called a voice not far away. "He's by that tree."

They'd come back for him. He wasn't alone.

"Istrielle?" he cried. "Is that you?"

He tried to peer through the blue filling his eyes but got nothing. It was his hearing that told him two people were standing over him.

Damn! He must seem pitiful, looking up at them blindly. Did his eyes look solid blue from the outside?

Hubert gave a warning hiss as the blue drained a little from his sight.

He could discern the vague outline of two people which was enough for him to orient his head in the right direction. "Who are you?" he asked the nearest.

The figure made no reply.

That wasn't good.

Darant gasped. Blinked. And finally *saw*.

They were humans, or close enough, and they were carrying blasters. Beneath glossy light combat armor, they were clad head to toe in loose black overalls like hazmat suits. The impression was emphasized by rubber boots and shiny gauntlets that ran as far as their elbows. Visored helmets with circular breathing filters over the mouth completely enclosed their heads and covered their necks.

Wide, red, cross belts fell across their chests in an 'X' pattern that was mirrored by red 'X's stitched into the knee armor. The only other color came from a circular sensor band in lurid pus-green that was mounted over the visor.

They looked like villains from a low-budget horror-holo. And he supposed that's exactly what the Re-Education Enforcement Division was.

"Easy, rebel," said the REED he'd mistaken for Istrielle. "We'll take good care of you. Docs will patch you up so you live long enough to understand the horror of your crimes and confess. You will pour out your sorry heart begging for atonement, and you will mean every single word."

"You'll get your chance to atone too," said the other REED, a human man. "They'll reconfigure your body so it's pressure sealed for vacuum and then sell you to the asteroid mining consortium. Soon, you'll forget what it was like to eat or breathe like worthwhile citizens who deserve those rights. Each day you deliver your work quota, they'll swap three cylinders out of your new body. One for air. One for nutrition. One for waste. Miss your target or fail to beg for atonement, and you don't get your swaps that day. Better hope you survive till the next one. Radiation'll kill you within a year anyway."

Out of the corner of his eye, he saw a fluffy six-legged goat stand tall—all of his twelve inches—and narrow his eyes at the two REEDs.

Darant waved Hubert away. "Get out of here! Scram!"

"Pathetic rebel scum," sneered the woman. "Do you really think we'll fall for the 'look behind you' trick?"

Hubert growled and jumped at the man, flicking out a wicked curved claw from each middle hoof. He landed on his target, behind the man's knee.

The goat's mid-limbs crossed in front of his little chest, and the REED went down.

Orion's balls! The little fella had sliced through the man's hamstrings.

"Heavens above, Ceritel," snapped the woman, looking at her comrade. "What's the matter with you?"

"Goat trouble," Darant explained as he drew his PHC-9 pistol and shot her five times, each time seeking weak points in her armor.

Turned out there weren't any because it was weak all over. The armor was just for show, and the slugs of his 9 had carved cavernous wound channels right through her.

"You want some too?" he challenged the other REED who was face down in the dirt. Hubert stood on top of his helmet like a hunter over a trophy kill.

The curly white fur around the goat's mouth was stained red and dripping with gore.

Pistol out and ready, Darant inspected the REED's wounds. Hubert had tunneled under the man's helmet and bitten out his throat.

The animal hopped off his vanquished foe and nuzzled against Darant's shins.

Crouching down, Darant fussed at the wool behind the goat's ears, marveling at its softness.

"Good boy, Hubert. So, you're cute *and* deadly, eh? Just how I like my women."

Istrielle...

Darant swapped a fresh mag into his pistol, grabbed his pack, and relieved the REEDs of a blaster and a couple of charge packs.

Hubert was eager to retrace their steps back to the camp. He looked over his shoulder, waiting for his human to follow, but Darant checked his purloined rifle first. The model looked like a local design, but its operation appeared generic.

He risked a test shot, sending a screaming bolt sizzling into the leaves between the dead REEDs.

Not bad. The rifle registered 23 standard power shots remaining.

The goat huffed at him.

"Somehow, coffee with your milk is never going to be quite the same again. OK, goat, let's move out."

He followed Hubert through the dense forest for twenty yards before he found Istrielle.

She was face down and unmoving, blown clear of a blackened crater that he guessed was from the same explosion that had thrown him against the tree.

He ran to her side. "Istrielle?"

She didn't reply.

Carefully he rolled her over.

Strands of green hair escaped her stupid knitted hat, framing unseeing eyes.

He forced himself to draw his gaze down her body and take in the destruction of her chest. A slimy mess of blood and intestines spilled out onto the forest floor.

"Not you too," he moaned.

He took off her hat because she'd told him she wanted to live free of the masks and coverings that had suffocated her.

After stroking her hair into the way she'd worn it that night at Krunacao, he closed her eyes.

He was about to move off, but hesitated. Instead, he safed the REED's blaster and threw it into the underbrush. He grabbed Istrielle's rifle and reached into the dead woman's thigh pouches to retrieve a couple of charge packs.

It was stupid sentimentality. But he wanted to have something of hers.

"Darant! Over here."

He followed the sound of Lily's voice and saw her waving him over from thirty yards away. Behind her, deeper into the trees, he saw the outline of a Viking in the shadows.

After a last, lingering look at Istrielle, he jogged over to his friends.

* * * * *

Chapter Twenty-Two:
Lily Hjon

"Never get attached," Lily murmured. "Never care."

"What's that?" asked Vetch.

She ignored him, unable to contemplate anything beyond Darant's haunted face. Her heart wept for his loss, but she had a part to play, and she wouldn't allow herself to weep openly.

She understood, though.

Everyone she'd loved had been separated from her. Usually by death.

"I'm sorry for your loss, Darant," Vetch told him. "You have two minutes to get your shit together, but then we're going back for Enthree and Fitz. We can't leave until we've at least looked for them."

Lily was surprised to feel Vetch stretch a comforting arm over her shoulders. Normally, any fool trying that would have gotten it snapped at the shoulder, but now? She didn't even flinch.

"You too, Lil'," said Vetch in a gruff voice that was the closest he got to soothing. "I won't lose faith in you just because you allow your eyes to leak a little."

They hunkered there in silence, but they never managed the two minutes.

Fate came a-calling.

* * * * *

Chapter Twenty-Three:
Vetch Arunsen

Vetch flicked the selector to high-power fire and watched the rifle's charge count above the butt stock drain from 21 to 4. There was a price to be paid for unleashing bolts of maximum destructive power, but he had no choice.

The whining gravitics of the two GAC-19 hover fliers grew louder. They were almost upon him.

Buried beneath a pile of half-rotten leaves, with just his barrel and sights poking out, he waited for the assault vehicles to come into view, trying to ignore the war hammer pressing painfully into his side. GAC-19s were ground assault craft and, as such, had thick belly armor. Ideally, he'd have shooters in the trees to fire down upon the upper vents of the rear engines where the armor was weakest.

But he'd have to settle for a few high-power shots into the side of the cockpit and pray for good luck.

Vetch steadied his breathing and tracked the red 'X' painted on the rounded nose of the lead flier as it came into view.

Hopefully, Lily and Darant had pulled themselves together sufficiently to be doing the same, but for the moment, Vetch's universe had shrunk to him, the scope, and the sleek black form of the flier. As he was panning up to the cockpit, he suddenly panicked. The pilot needed to die first, but did the pilot sit in front of the gunner, or was it the other way around?

He couldn't remember. But when he sighted the cockpit, his jaw was too busy dropping into his beard for him to care.

The sight picture slammed two surprises into him nearly simultaneously. First, there was only one occupant of the cockpit. Second, that pilot was Enthree.

The third surprise came a half-second later and barely registered. The cockpit was flooded with human blood.

"Hold your fire," he whispered, "but keep under cover until we know who's following."

Enthree piloted the GAC-19 to a gap in the trees a short distance away, then settled it down to land. Damn! She was out of sight, and a mechanical hiss indicated she'd retracted the cockpit canopy.

"Wait," warned Vetch as the second flier came into view. "Douse me in batter and fry me in oil. It's Fitz."

Lily ran out, waving a hand cheerfully. Vetch lay buried for a moment, frowning at Lily's reaction. Fitz presented himself as charming and resourceful, but Vetch still hadn't made up his mind about the man underneath.

* * *

Five people.

Four seats.

The dilemma was solved by Enthree balancing on the rear fuselage of one of the fliers as they headed southeast through the forest, retracing the route they'd taken from Krunacao. The Muryani's prodigious sense of balance was a well-established fact.

The next decision was a much tougher one. What should they do next?

"We can't go back to RevRec," said Lily. "But where can we go?"

"Don't be so hasty," Fitz retorted. "Slinh's people took a body blow they couldn't handle. They lost their belief in what they were doing. And while abandoning us was a cruel betrayal that I'll make sure Slinh comes to regret, it wasn't a premeditated one. We return to Krunacao."

"Those RevRec bastards don't deserve our help," said Vetch.

"I agree," said Fitz. "We're not going back for their sake, but for mine. I want to know who's really behind this. And besides, I've just been on the blower to Sergeant Sybutu. His team's going to meet us at Krunacao. Soon, we'll be one big happy Chimera Company family again."

* * * * *

Chapter Twenty-Four: Enthree

"**W**e could use a fresh pair of eyes and…" Fitz shrugged in a manner that Enthree had learned to describe as flippant. "And a fresh pair of antennae."

Enthree regarded the human twenty feet below her on the forest floor, though she took her role of lookout very seriously and kept her antennae sweeping the area for unexpected visitors.

The man wasn't even properly human. Those truly of that race often referred to him as a mutant, which was highly inaccurate. She decided to assign him the label of trans-human for now.

Vetch had ordered her to watch their six, by which he meant to use her superior senses of smell and vision to alert the remnant party to dangers approaching from the forest. And although she tried to perform her duty with diligence, she couldn't help but redirect her antennae away from the trees and toward the trans-human, agitating them laterally as she sought hidden meaning behind his words.

She trusted Vetch and Darant because they were transparent to her. Meatbolt had been like that too, and Lily to a degree, although her friend with the fascinating tattoos harbored a wellspring of sadness that corroded her from within.

Fitz, on the other hand, cloaked his true self under a chameleon disguise of personas. He swapped them out to suit whatever task was at hand, much as he did the cartridges of his Fitz-Cannon, as he liked to call his intriguing hand weapon.

Enthree had seen humans attempt to hold multiple personas before, and she concluded that the species was ill-advised and ill-equipped to do so, because each persona left a residue that gummed up the individual's psyche. Before long, so much psychological sediment built up that the underlying truth behind that person was obscured forever.

Such a person could not be trusted, and the 'trans' she placed in front of Fitz's species name did nothing to alleviate her fears.

Enthree did not trust Fitz's flippancy any more than the man behind it, but she couldn't see an immediate reason to refuse his request.

"Of course," Enthree answered, and she realized with a painful jolt along her spine that Lily had been standing behind Fitz all this time, and she hadn't noticed. Her concerns about the trans-human were inducing a troubling reduction in her observational effectiveness.

She helped Lily up to take her post in the branches and then clambered down to the others at the tree line surveying the village of Krunacao. She took binoculars from poor Darant who radiated grief and anger like a nuclear furnace.

The vision enhancing device was designed for tiny, forward-facing, humanoid eyes, and it took several moments of uncomfortable adjustment until she was able to see through the eye pieces. Doing so was not nearly as uncomfortable as the sights that awaited her in the burning village.

Krunacao.

The memories of the time she'd spent here two nights before remained happy and informative, but the very joy of that night now laid a poisonous foundation for the charnel house scene laid out before her.

She trained the binocs on the temporary canteen where she'd consumed alcoholic beverages. It was one of the few buildings that was no longer burning, its fabric outer layer having been consumed by flames to leave a blackened frame under which charred humanoid corpses slumped against metal tables. She surmised they were lunchtime diners caught unaware by the attack.

Why hadn't they fought back, she wondered? Almost all the adults in the village had been armed two nights ago.

"I want to know who did this," Fitz said. "Who are we facing? Any clues?"

"I am still assessing," Enthree replied, though she snagged for several seconds on Fitz's use of the word 'we.' She was no longer sure who 'we' *were*, and she was even less convinced they remained the allies of the rebel group that had abandoned her at the walls of Ameliorate-10.

So far, there had been no sign of Slinh's rebel army, which was presumably still headed here through the forest, traveling on foot. When they got here, they would find almost every building in flames or already burned out. Three thousand inhabitants had called Kruna-cao home, and their bodies were everywhere, many of the adults still gripping personal weapons. Something about their positioning was wrong, though. There were no signs of an organized defense. Nor were there signs of them fleeing headlong into the trees, which were just a hundred yards from the edge of the buildings.

Enthree tried selectively filtering out the crackle and roar of the flames, listening for a clue that would answer the questions forming in her mind.

Hisses and pops from vaporizing fluids were everywhere. Enthree pulled her jacket tight over the hearing hairs of her throat and chest because she didn't want to think about what was generating those sounds.

Instead, she relied on her eyesight to scan the tree line on the opposite side of the village. The humanoid binoculars used smart overlays to see through the smoke, but they were ineffective. Her vision was impaired by the tears dripping over her eyes, stimulated not by the smoke—which her outer nictitating membrane was perfectly capable of screening out with minimum loss of vision—but by thoughts of those joyful people so full of life that night and now…so very dead.

"Well?" Darant demanded from nearby. "What do we do now?"

"Give Enthree a few more moments," Vetch told him.

In those moments, Enthree saw enough to confirm her working theory. "There are no signs of weapons being fired into the trees, which I would expect if villagers fled there. The position of the corpses neither matches everyday peaceful activity, nor determined resistance or flight. I conclude that this massacre has been staged to make it look like something it is not."

"Thank you," said Fitz. "I concur."

Enthree handed Darant back his binoculars. "There is more. That smell invites further investigation." An 'S' shape reflected up and down her spine as she contemplated the sickening odor of devastation.

She got up to walk into the village but paused when she noted the looks of surprise on the humanoid faces. "I do not refer to the smell of death," she explained. "There is something else. Like over-ripe cheese smeared into old, well-oiled leather." She tasted the air with her antennae. "Definitely diglycerides and ammonia in the air."

"Knockout gas?" Vetch suggested.

"Very probable," Fitz agreed, grabbing Enthree by the rear leg to stop her from walking into the village. "Woah! Hold up, Ms. Enthree. We don't step out of cover without first concocting a plan."

"The two storehouses are not ablaze," she explained. "I want to know why. Maybe answers await us there."

"Have you considered," asked Fitz, "that it could be because whoever committed this atrocity is still here? They're the two most solidly built buildings in the village, and the gap between them is hidden from view. We will approach, but first, we ready the GAC-19s as a reserve and then we sneak up from either side in a coordinated reconnaissance."

"Wait!" Enthree angled her antennae at the road that fed in from the trees on the opposite side of the village. Then she screwed them into the dirt. "Wheeled vehicles are approaching. Three of them."

"Everybody, stay under cover," Fitz ordered. "Not everything is as it seems. Wait. Observe. Be ready."

"Remind me why this guy is giving the orders now," Darant demanded.

"Because I say he does," said Vetch. "For the moment. So, shut up and wait."

The rebels came screaming in on three trucks with fat tires and long travel suspension, but the narrow bodies were only about five feet wide. The armed passengers sat in a line behind the driver.

The vehicles screamed to a halt, though the occupants hesitated before disembarking. They stared wide eyed at the corpse-strewn ruins for a long while before finally jumping to the ground.

By then, a welcoming party had begun to assemble.

A Pryxian and a human had moved out from the gap between the storehouses, initially heading away from the rebels, but doubling back to flank the vehicles from behind concealment. Their clothing resembled Shepherd's, down to the neckerchief striped in the red and white of the Panhandlers, but unlike the old human man, these two stalked their prey with the stealth and certainty of jungle predators.

Something else about them spiked Enthree's interest—they didn't just move beside the burning buildings to use them as concealment, they walked *through* them too, seemingly unscathed.

Interesting.

She concentrated on her observation of the fireproof humanoids. If she ever met up with her Expansion handler, the memory she would extrude and store on the outside of her head would be well received.

"Are we going to sit back and watch this happen?" Darant asked, aghast.

"The massacre has already happened," Fitz answered. "I want to see how this plays out. Don't forget, those people in the trucks left us to die."

"Not everyone abandoned us," warned Darant.

Fitzwilliam's face paled. "You're right. Sorry. Lily told me about Istrielle." He straightened up. "And in her name, you and Vetch work around the rear of the vehicle convoy. Enthree, with me. We're going to take them from the side. Assume the rebels are our friends, and the welcome party are the perpetrators of this outrage. But the situation is fluid. Don't hold fast to your initial assumptions. Let's move it, gentle people, because we're doing it for Istrielle!"

* * * * *

Chapter Twenty-Five:
Vetch Arunsen

Hugging cover all the way, they crept up on the rebel convoy. The soldiers had unassed the trucks and were about to spread out and search the village when a lone figure strode out from the storehouses to meet them.

"Returned to the scene of your crime, have you?" It was a Zhoogene dressed in the same Panhandler neckerchief as the two they'd seen disappear into the burning village. He seemed familiar, but Vetch couldn't place him. "You've got nerve coming back here."

"This?" The RevRec leader gestured at the devastation. "You think we did this? Are you mad? Explain yourself, and you'd better make it fucking good." He made a show of charging his blaster. "I'm not in the mood for games."

"Keep moving," Vetch urged Darant.

They filtered along a row of blazing retail stores, keeping low beneath the walled-off loading yards at the back.

"You shot these defenseless civilians," thundered the Zhoogene, hidden from Vetch and Darants' view, but his voice ringing clear. "Massacred those who looked to you for protection. The people of this world will hold the Revolutionary Forces of Reconciliation responsible, and they will turn upon you and destroy you."

"Why are you saying that shit?"

Darant had pushed on ahead, making for the end of the shops from which they could drop behind the convoy.

"Because we have footage of you committing the massacre," the Zhoogene said.

Under the cover of the stunned silence, Vetch checked that Fitz and Enthree were in position a short distance behind them. Then he hurried to join up with Darant who suddenly shouldered his blaster and took aim.

Vetch moved alongside and saw one of the apparent Panhandlers walk out of the burning store on the end of the row and get ready to sneak behind the rear of the RevRec rebels. The Pryxian looked disoriented for a moment as he exited the blaze but otherwise unscathed. Why weren't his clothes even smoldering?

"Sorry, Lucerne," Vetch told his war hammer as he slung her over his back and cradled his light blaster in his hands. "You'll taste some skulls soon. I promise."

Once again, he checked Fitz and Enthree. They were holding position, and Fitz was waving at Vetch to hold fire. When he saw he'd gotten Vetch's attention, Fitz pointed back at the storehouse, trying to convey with gestures what was coming.

Vetch was no good at these party games. But he got the message that what was headed his way was big. And bad.

"Darant," he whispered. "We've got trouble inbound. Eight o'clock."

"Do I take the shot?"

Vetch sucked in a deep breath and almost choked on the smoke and stink of overcooked meat. What was he leading the remnants of Raven Company into? Fitz complicated everything. Vetch had wanted to thrash it out when they got downtime, but it couldn't wait. Soon as this action was over, Fitz would have some talking to do.

Meanwhile, Vetch didn't feel like taking orders. He felt much more like taking revenge.

"Wait for my signal," he whispered to Darant. "But yes. Waste the Pryxian."

* * * * *

Chapter Twenty-Six: Tavistock Fitzwilliam

"Hey, you! Skangat! Get your green ass back here!"

Fitz looked with interest through a gap in the burning buildings as the Zhoogene sauntered away from the RevRec rebels in the direction of the storehouses.

"Kill him!" ordered the rebel leader.

Suddenly struck with fear, the Zhoogene turned and spread out his long arms. "Please, no!" he pleaded. "We're on the same side."

The Revolutionary Forces of Reconciliation was not listening. The Zhoogene went down under a fusillade of blaster fire, his screams almost, but not quite, drowned out by the fury of the bolts ripping through the air.

Then he got up, dusted the soot off as best he could, and resumed his walk back to the storehouses, apparently without a care in the galaxy.

Desultory blaster fire pursued the Zhoogene who'd passed out of Fitz's narrow field of vision. He didn't need to see to know that it wouldn't penetrate the personal force shield.

It was a smoking hot variant. He'd never seen one so good. Damn!

Tire squeals announced the rebels were going to run down the fake Panhandler.

That wouldn't work either. The Zhoogene who'd dressed up like a Panhandler had staged his shooting. No doubt it would be edited to add fake blood later. If his team had taken out the entire village with ease, a handful of rebels wouldn't present much of a problem. Azhanti! He'd stumbled into an operation mounted by serious professionals. A false flag action designed to discredit the RevRec rebels.

And we all know who loves false flags. SpecMish…

"Captain Fitz!"

Enthree was pointing along the retail row at Darant and Arunsen who were exchanging fire with another apparent Panhandler, a Pryxian also wearing a shield. This one appeared to be a more conventional model, though, because it flashed ghostly colors, like an aurora, under the blaster assault.

"Enthree, tell those two buffoons to disengage and withdraw to the GAC-19s."

"You mean Darant and Sergeant Arunsen?"

"Yes, of course, those two buffoons."

"In the future, please be more specific in your instructions," Enthree corrected him and sprinted off to comply.

Fitz shook his head. "That Muryani's going to be even more trouble than Lynx," he murmured and then broke cover to head in the opposite direction, wanting a better look at what they were really facing.

The command and control issue his team faced needed resolving, fast, but it would have to wait. He'd been waiting until he'd gathered the legionary component of Chimera Company. Now that decision didn't seem so smart.

Boom! Boom!

Here it came…Enthree had stuck her feelers into the dirt and warned him about what was coming, but the sight of it still made Fitz's heart pound. And the sound of massive metal and ceramalloy feet slamming into the ground sent primal fear coursing through him.

He wanted to flee.

But he had to watch as the nine-foot high mech stomped out of the cover between the storehouses.

Its armor was painted a deep green, and it had unusually long and rounded arms that ended in miniguns. The cockpit was multifaceted, and its many armor reinforcing joints that jutted out of the hull gave the mech an insectoid look. In its own way, it was a chimera of sorts, but an ungainly one weighed down by oversized multiple rocket arrays mounted on its shoulders like shoulder pads of death.

Out of forty on each shoulder, only three tubes still contained rockets.

I'd bet the *Phantom* those rockets were loaded with knockout gas. It's the only way to explain how they staged the massacre.

The rocket pods also explained why the beast was stomping so much. Its driver had to be struggling to keep the mech's balance under such an ungainly load.

Rebel bolts, aimed mostly at the weak points at the joints, screamed into the mech.

The mech replied with both miniguns, unleashing a devastating hail of fire.

Return fire from the rebels swiftly dwindled.

The Zhoogene operative reappeared in Fitz's view, having armed himself with a blaster. Sheltered in the mech's shadow, he calmly observed the extermination of the rebels. Suddenly, he twisted around, looking straight at Fitz along a barrel he was holding in a C-clamp grip.

"Arrogant," muttered Fitz, then he jumped out of sight behind the blackened ruin of a wall and heard the bolts scream overhead.

"And he wants me alive. For now."

The professional false flag op.

The signature C-clamp grip they loved for some reason.

Neither was unique to the Special Missions Executive, but that's how Fitz was calling it. He'd lay money on that mech driver smoking a clay pipe inside the canopy.

He could even be facing the same team who'd taken out Nuysp. Department 9, Wei had called them. Whatever. He now knew to take them seriously.

Swingfire armor piercing or shield piercing? Which cartridge to select for his hand cannon?

The mech was still stomping destruction through the last of the rebels.

Cursing himself for not stumping that extra twenty thou for the dual magazine option, Fitz went for shield piercers.

His F-Cannon hummed as it reconfigured its loadout. While his pride and joy worked its alien-tech magic, he looked back to check on the status of his new marines.

He caught a glimpse of insectoid limbs moving into cover and surmised that Darant, Arunsen, and Enthree were falling back to Lily's position in the trees. They covered each other in their retreat, maintaining almost continuous blaster fire in the approximate direction of the mech. With the village in flames, he couldn't see what they were firing on, but their withdrawal was disciplined.

"I want nothing but the best in my marine squad," he declared to no one in particular, not caring that he didn't have a ship for them to operate out of.

Wiping the sweat from his eyes, he stepped out from cover expecting to snap a shot at the Zhoogene.

But there was no one there.

He swiveled his head back and forth, but all he could see was a burning village. All he could hear was a mech crashing through the debris of buildings…And it was heading his way.

"There is no escape, Fitzwilliam," boomed the monster through external speakers. "Or should I say, Lieutenant Commander Zi'Alfu?"

Azhanti! Where's Izza when I need her?

Fitz ran.

* * * * *

Chapter Twenty-Seven:
Lily Hjon

"Helluva time to learn how to fly!"

Lily pushed the gravitic control forward and simmered with satisfaction as the GAC-19 hover flier rose from its leafy concealment.

She was exhilarated by the power flowing through the yoke and vibrating her ass. This wasn't like the game sims. This was real!

She understood instantly why aviators and space jocks got addicted to this.

She eased back the gravitics slightly, then pushed on the thrust lever, and the flier accelerated forward.

Suddenly, tree trunks were flying at her. She turned the yoke, easily slaloming through the forest, before bursting out into the open area in front of the village.

"Oh, yeah!" she screamed. The yoke was just like her old hologame setup. This was going to be fun.

She kicked the pedal, yawed right, and swept around the open area, heading for the road into the village the RevRec rebels had driven along.

Stuck up a tree with no radio comms, she'd had to piece together what was going on. But when the miniguns started their furious rattle, she had decided it was time to shift from lookout to reserve force.

En route to the road, she saw a Pryxian dressed like a Panhandler step out of a burning building and send bolts her way from a weirdly stubby blaster.

Fireproof. That's a neat trick.

She pulled back the throttle and hit the stabilizer control. The flier was a hovering gun platform now, twisting to face its foe.

The Pryxian's blast fire mostly deflected off the GAC-19's heavily armored nose, but some bolts were skimming over the top and into the front of the canopy, which darkened under the impact.

"Don't know what you are—" she flicked the safety caps off the fire buttons on the yoke handles, "—but you ain't no Panhandler."

Quad heavy blasters spat fat bolts into the target.

The Pryxian held up his hand as if warding off a dazzling light. Around him, the outline of a force shield blazed in a baleful red.

But the shield held.

Bolts caught the Pryxian in his right flank—she guessed they were from her friends—and the shield's glow shifted from red to green.

Lily screamed when the flight canopy shattered around her. She ducked low but kept both thumbs down on the fire buttons, giving the Pryxian everything the war machine had.

"Lily!" someone screamed. "You got him."

She raised her head and saw Fitz yelling at her from within the confusing maze of flaming ruins. "Get out of here. Now!"

The Pryxian had been chewed into burned dogmeat beneath a cloud of dust.

The feet pounding through the rubble were the first indication of what was coming next. Then the dust began to clear, and she saw a hulking metal form cutting through a ruined building to get to her.

She was flying. For the first time. Not just flying but combat flying.

As it turned out, *getting out of here* wasn't going to be simple. The street was narrow, and the flames all around seemed to lick at her, eager to burn her up.

Hell, she'd had no experience running away from tight situations in the sims. That simply wasn't part of the game mechanics. But she did know the best way to beat boss-level opponents was to wear them down while ducking nimbly away from their big guns.

The mech lumbered her way, stopped, and began twisting its body to face her.

If that wasn't a boss, she didn't know what was. And if those guns got a lock on her, she was dead.

She throttled forward and flew at it, head on.

"Get some!" she yelled.

Moments before crashing into its torso, she remembered to fire. Bolts flew at the metal beast but didn't penetrate.

"It's not over yet," she assured her enemy and pushed the yoke forward to skim over its top and come around for another quick burst before it could bring its miniguns into play.

A distant memory surfaced of reversing the yoke control in her game setup.

Instead of flying over the top of the mech, she pitched down toward the ground. She pulled back, but it was too late. Her straps bit hard as she was thrown forward when her GAC-19 hit the ground and skimmed along, throwing up a plume of ash. The flier careened through the mech's legs and delivered a glancing blow to its ankle before coming to a stop in a gap between two houses.

Lily hit the quick release on her harness and scrambled out of the cockpit.

Behind her, the whine and hiss of the mech's servos sent a fresh adrenaline spike through her limbs, and she ran faster, trying to lose herself in the smoke and flames.

* * * * *

Chapter Twenty-Eight:
Hines "Bronze" Zy Pel

"What the hell are those brutes?" Sybutu pointed at the mech monsters parked fifty yards ahead in the gap between the two long buildings that were the only ones in the little town not on fire. Not even scorched.

"Hunters," Bronze replied. "Hansen-Hyperb Hunters with seriously large custom rocket pods on the shoulder mounts."

There were two of the forbidding machines. One appeared to be powered down, the other had its canopy open and looked about ready to go into action.

"The message from Fitzwilliam said to meet him here," said Sybutu. "He said nothing about mechs, nor this slaughter of civilians. Can't believe those machines are with Fitzwilliam, and they aren't painted with REED markings. So, who the hell are they?"

"SpecMish," Bronze growled in response, his voice rough with shame. "Bears all the hallmarks. Don't ask me how I know."

Sybutu gave him a piercing look. "Fine, I won't. Do you know how to pilot one of those beasts?"

"*Drive*, Sarge. Yes, I can drive one. They're designed to terrorize soft targets. Their mobility is limited. But stand in the way of their miniguns, and you'll be shredded."

"Let's not do that then. Zavage will head north and distract the one booting up. Bronze, you get in the other one and shoot it from the rear."

"No," said Bronze. "There's no need, and the situation is too chaotic for us to split up. Follow me."

He sprinted across the ground, making for the Hunter on standby.

A man popped his head out of the open mech and looked at him in astonishment.

Bronze fired at him, but missed, so he tossed a puffer grenade instead.

The man jerked his head back inside and closed the clamshell canopy.

The grenade bounced off the canopy's rim.

Bronze hit the ground and covered his head as the pressure wave blew over. The time wasn't wasted, though. Using his brain augments, he sent the secret SpecMish backdoor codes to shut down the mech.

Metal fingers the size of hams twitched beneath the miniguns.

"Bad luck, asshole," roared the mech's speakers. "That won't work with *us*. I'd like to know how you found those codes, but you won't live long enough to tell me."

The Hunter's body hummed with power as its fusion reactor went live. It lifted an enormous leg and stomped into the open.

"Just one chance," Bronze muttered and ran at the metal monster.

He must have presented an unlikely sight—a slender man wearing civilian garb, charging at a mech that weighed eleven hundred kilos. But he had no choice. He had to close with it before its targeting systems booted up and acquired him.

Twin miniguns cycled and then spat a hail of rounds through the air.

Bronze evaded the crossfire by mere inches and leapt for one of the armor plates over the knees.

The mech driver tried to flick its leg to shake him off, but mechs were no good at dancing, and despite the name, Hunters were more like mobile weapons platforms than those intended to engage in close combat. All it succeeded in doing was stumbling and flailing with one arm to avoid falling over.

His familiarity with the access recesses made Bronze's ascent easy. He climbed up the mech's torso, dodging the arms trying to brush him away, and clambered over the smooth dome that topped the canopy, before dropping down the other side.

He'd meant to climb down, but there were no climbing points, and the mech's gyrations finally won out. He lost his grip.

As he slid down the rear of the mech, fingertips of one hand still in contact with the Hunter's hull, he slammed the patch in his other hand over the point on the mech's back where the kidneys would be in a human. It was where Hansen-Hyperb mounted their fusion powerplants.

"And that," he shouted in triumph, "is why Hunters aren't combat rated."

He grunted as he landed and braced for the possibility of the mech transforming into a massive fusion bomb. Not that he would have time to know about it if the worst happened.

The device he'd slapped on it was a mag-spike. It played havoc with mag-clamps and quenched superconductors and screwed with linear accelerators and fusion containment fields.

He'd guessed the mag-spike wouldn't be powerful enough to collapse the containment field catastrophically, just enough to trip the failsafes that would shut it down hard.

Since he hadn't been blasted into a cloud of hot, ionized gases, he had to say he'd called that one right. The Hunter should be rebooting into safe mode, unwilling to activate until it had run a diagnostic over the fusion plant.

How long that would take, he had no idea.

"Hey, Bronze," called Zavage from the other mech. Its canopy was open, and the Kurlei was dangling from the harness inside as he booted the machine. "Are you gonna drive this thing or what?"

"Hell, yeah," he answered. "I'm in the mood to stomp a few heads."

Zavage jumped out, and Bronze clambered aboard.

"Neat trick!" called a voice before he could slot inside the haptic sleeve.

Bronze whirled around to face whoever had spoken. Before he'd even drawn his pistol, he knew it was Fitz. In a greasy trucker hat.

He drew his pistol anyway, not sure how much the smuggler with a past could be trusted.

"I had the same idea of stealing one of the mechs." Fitz pulled a cigar from a sleeve on his arm. "Gentlemen, thank you for making the rendezvous. The rest of the team are being pursued. They need help."

"The team?" Sybutu queried.

Bronze listened but concentrated on getting inside the sleeve and getting the mech battle ready.

"Yes, of course, the team," Fitz responded. "Chimera Company. That is why we're here, after all."

"Funny," said Sybutu. "I thought we'd been marooned here."

"We were." Fitz thought better of his cigar and stowed it away unsmoked. "We can discuss that another time. Come on! Focus, people! We've been scattered by these SpecMish murderers. There's one active mech and at least one operative on foot. Probably more."

Lights flared to either side of Bronze's head as the mech's systems came to life and reported green status.

"First things first," said Bronze, his voice through the external speakers making Sybutu jump. "The other mech could come to life at any moment."

As the clamshell shut with a hiss of pressure seals, Bronze lifted a leg inside the haptic sleeve, which, despite the name, consisted of a series of white bands that wrapped around his torso and limbs. Most of the haptic sensors were in the gloves and socks.

The mech lifted a leg in response and then followed its driver's lead in stomping it down, pounding an inches-deep print into the ground.

Yeah, the Hunter's controls were all too familiar. Driving this giant was like wading through thick mud on a heavy gravity planet while shackled to a ball of neutronium.

Bronze stomped off toward the other mech, crashing against it belly-to-belly like an overweight metal wrestler. He spread his fingers wide in the haptic glove, and his mech reached out with one hand and grabbed his opponent by the wrist.

He squeezed hard and his mech tried to obey by applying a crushing force with its metal fingers, but they were too fat to get behind the armor and sever an actuator cable or pressure feed.

No matter. Bronze raised his mech's free arm high and pointed it down at the other mech's elbow joint.

"Stand well clear," he yelled. He waited several seconds and then opened fire with his minigun. Sparks flew as the rounds ricocheted off the two metal giants. The thunderous noise had to be insanely loud outside the protection of his mech, but Bronze didn't care. He wielded his minigun's firepower like a blunt scalpel, slicing through the weak points at the elbow joint.

An amber warning flashed on the HUD schematic for his right minigun.

Ammo level 50%.

Damnit!

The minigun's demonic death rattle shut down with a coda of spinning barrels. Bronze gripped his opponent's shoulder with his right hand and pulled down on its wrist with his left.

The lower arm came away at the elbow, spraying coolant and hydraulic fluid. Bronze threw it to the ground.

"You're gonna be dis-armed, killer!" he roared at the SpecMish mech driver. "I'm gonna make you as helpless as those civilians you massacred. See how you like it!"

He grabbed for the other wrist, but his opponent's mech sprang to life as he moved across its front.

A burst of fire shredded the armor on Bronze's right flank. Before it could eat all the way through, he body-slammed his ton of mech into the other Hunter.

It staggered back...and used the space it had won to try grabbing the right hand of Bronze's mech. Bronze ripped his arm out of the enemy's grip and fired with his right minigun. It exploded, spraying shrapnel that bounced off their metal chests.

Damn! The skragg must have damaged it in his attack.

He tried angling his left minigun to do damage, but his enemy came in too close and began grappling.

Even with half an arm missing, this guy was good, and Bronze had to work hard to keep his balance.

A boarding alert flashed red. Rear quadrant.

Bronze glanced at the rear viewscreen to see what the hell was going on.

Had the rest of the SpecMish team arrived?

But the person climbing the rear of his Hunter wore a space trucking cap and had a cigar between his lips.

Fitz...what the hell...?

How the man got there without slipping off was mystery enough, but it got even weirder when Fitz took a hand off the mech and drew his weapon, aiming it through the mech's armor at the back of Bronze's head.

Bronze searched the controls frantically, looking for any anti-personnel defenses. The combat mech prototypes he'd trialed years ago could electrify the outer shell, pump out clouds of plasma, or even emit intense sonic pulses, but he could see none of that in this Hunter.

Sybutu and Zavage were out of sight.

His SpecMish opponent probably had no idea Bronze had been boarded, but he seemed to sense his opponent's distraction and made the most of it, pulling himself away from the grapple hold.

The other Hunter stumbled back a couple of steps, throwing out his half arm for balance, while the good arm brought its armament to bear on Bronze.

Bronze brought his left arm up too.

Fitz blew a smoke ring into the back of Bronze's mech and followed it with a round from his hand cannon.

Bronze flinched and fired at the same time.

But…he hadn't been injured.

And the other Hunter wasn't firing at him.

Other than his ruined gun, the status readouts on Bronze's mech were green across the board.

So, what the hell had happened?

"Hot holy shit!" Fitz was on the ground, hopping mad. "That was my last pop-up round." He took off his cap and glared up at the back of Bronze's mech. "The other driver's dead, Bronze. I shot him. Now disarm his mech and get moving. We need to save the rest of my marines."

My marines?

A round that could pass *through* Bronze, through multiple layers of thick armor, and kill the driver inside the other mech?

Colonel Malix had thought Tavistock Fitzwilliam was someone who could change the galaxy. Finally, Bronze was beginning to suspect he had a point.

"Do as Captain Fitz says." Sybutu was approaching from deeper inside the village. He and Zavage had acquired blaster rifles.

"On it, Sarge."

Bronze made short work of the other Hunter, kicking it from behind so it toppled over and then stamping on the remaining minigun until its barrels were as bent as a federal senator.

"Follow me," said Fitz.

They moved quickly through the burning village, Fitz leading them to where he said they'd hidden a hover flier. Zavage and Sybutu took the flanks while the Hunter marched behind as heavy fire support.

Everywhere…bodies! Bronze had to concentrate harder than he wanted to avoid squashing them. He would have preferred to focus on watching for threats, and if this had been a normal battlefield he would have. But these were civilians. There were things in his past for which he could never atone; their dignity was his priority.

As they approached the southeast edge of the village, they heard miniguns cycling short bursts of intense fire. It was coming from the trees.

"Hurry!" Fitz jogged toward the sound of the guns. "But stay alert. These are tricky bastards. That burst of fire might have been intended to lure us into the open."

Bronze threw caution to the wind and stormed ahead, each step of his lengthened stride a battle to avoid tripping. His human legs burned with lactic fire, but he gritted his teeth and pressed on anyway.

They met their opponents in the open ground between the village and the forest.

Arunsen and three of his troopers had their hands on their heads—four hands in the case of Enthree—as they were being marched out of the trees. Behind the prisoners were another Hunter mech and two men on foot, one human and one Zhoogene.

The two lines paused, just twenty yards apart.

"Fitzwilliam," called the Zhoogene. "I was hoping you would show. I need to know why so many people have an interest in you and then I want you dead. You won't leave this place alive, but I'll trade the rest of my prisoners for you. I'll let them scurry away into the woods to live their insignificant lives if you surrender yourself and your secrets."

Fitz stroked his chin for a moment and then screamed at the captive troopers. "Down!"

The troopers threw themselves to the ground, and Bronze opened up with his minigun, spitting a hail of 20mm rounds at the knee joints of the enemy mech.

He had to trust the wireframe sight picture in his radar targeting screen because the visual was blinded by the heavy enemy fire that rattled and screamed against his armor.

In place of conventional cameras, which were too vulnerable to use, the Hunter had an array of several hundred pinprick sensors that were stitched together into a field of view by the mech's computers.

All it could see was the searing light of blaster bolts and depleted-neutronium tipped mini-shells raking across its armor, destroying its outer layer in clouds of hot ceramalloy fragments.

Mechs were not built for maneuvering. It was a battle of attrition between two armored brutes, slugging it out until one side was overwhelmed. Miniguns against layers of composite-ceramalloy armor.

Who would succumb first?

Doubt edged Bronze's resolve. His enemy had two miniguns to his one.

The outer layer of Bronze's armor was shedding rapidly.

But not quickly enough for the enemy mech, it seemed.

After badly pitting Bronze's torso armor, the enemy drew their line of fire down and concentrated both streams on a single hip joint.

"Too late, sucker!"

The other Hunter swayed and shut off its guns. In the radar image in his targeting view, Bronze watched as both of its knees snapped, and it toppled forward into a mound of spent shell cases.

The firing had ceased—for the moment—but Bronze wasn't clear about the situation around him. Much of his torso armor had been shot away and nearly all his pinprick sensors along with it.

"Out of my way," he bellowed through his speakers and ran at the downed mech.

He had it in his radar. It was legless, but it was throwing its arms around to right itself, and those arms carried miniguns. He had to put it out of action.

The image of the flailing mech so consumed his attention that he'd taken three steps before he realized something was wrong.

His mech's right leg was trailing behind, dragging his meat leg back with it. He pushed with his thigh in its haptic sleeve, but he and the mech had become un-synced.

A grinding noise of protesting metal sounded from the mech's hip.

Bronze looked down and saw light streaming through jagged holes punched through the leg.

He screamed in panic and started unsnapping the haptic sleeve from around his leg.

Come on. Come on!

The metal thigh juddered, and he felt the mech overbalance through the haptic feedback.

His feet were still in the haptic socks. If the mech toppled over, it would rip his legs off.

"Bronze!" called Fitz from outside. "Quit fooling around and unwrap this bandit from his mech."

"Don't talk to me about unwrapping!"

Bronze slid both feet out of the haptic socks and drew them up into the main torso compartment. His knees were up against his chest, banging against his viewscreen.

Just in time. The Hunter's right leg snapped away from its torso, and the mech went over.

Bronze punched with his left arm and swiveled the Hunter through ninety degrees as he fell, catching himself with the mech's hands.

The overhead view showed the other mech immobilized.

"It's quite safe," Fitz explained. "I shot out the minigun motors."

"And the others?"

"All survived. The human and the Zhoogene, who apparently has been going by the name Lieutenant Deroh Ren Kay, ran off before we could chat with them. Our former Militia troopers are retrieving weapons and equipment from the woods. Now, would you oblige, Mr. Bronze? I want a chat with this mech driver."

Bronze was more than happy to oblige. He dragged his mech across the ground with its arms and pounded on the other mech's torso with its metal fists until he tore a hole in it. Then it was simply a matter of ripping the clamshell off to reveal the driver inside.

By the time Bronze had popped his own clamshell and jumped out of his ruined mech, Fitz was standing on the defeated war machine, one hand aiming his hand cannon at the driver, while the other activated a cigar. Meanwhile, Sybutu and Zavage kept watch.

"Who are you?" Fitz demanded.

"We're the Blue Chamber, rebel scum."

Fitz puffed smoke into the mech. "Oh, you can dispense with that 'rebel scum' bullshit. Same with Blue Chamber. Sounds to me like a cover name for Department 9."

"Department 9? I thought you were better than that, Fitzwilliam. Department 9 is one of those disinformation stories that gets pumped out to feed the conspiracy nutters. Ninety-nine percent of federal dirty tricks are really garbage pushed out by conspiracy theorists. It makes the one percent that's real as secure as can be."

Bronze whispered to Zavage to come over, and together they joined Fitz on the mech. Zavage used the position as a vantage point to peer through the flame and smoke of the village as best he could.

Other than the same red-and-white neck cloth, which he thought was a clumsy contrivance, the human driver looked plausibly like a Panhandler, if that was what you had been told to think.

A pretty beaten up one. One puffy eye was swollen closed, his face was raw and bloodied, and his left shoulder had been crushed.

Guess my Hunter punched harder than I thought.

Bronze had no sympathy for the man lying there smugly in his harness.

Fitz turned to Bronze and scratched under his cap. "Do you think it's too soon to start shooting limbs off to make him talk sense?"

"I've a better idea."

Locking gazes with the driver, Bronze unwrapped the loose folds of his head covering, pulling apart the flaps of false neck skin to expose the bronze plate beneath.

The man's eyebrows shot up at the sight.

Then he shrugged and reassumed his mantle of arrogance. "So, I'm in the presence of the Hero of Azoth Zol, the mysterious Hines

Zy Pel. You know, when they found you fighting alongside the real Panhandlers, I thought you were being expedient. Yet here you are again, fighting on the side of the rebels."

"I'm doing no such thing. You're massacring innocent civilians in a conflict you care nothing about. I just happened to get caught up in your atrocity."

"Atrocity?" He spat bloody spittle. "As if you haven't done far worse, Zy Pel."

"Once. Maybe. Haven't you heard, though? I'm retired."

"No one retires from SpecMish."

"So I keep hearing. I'm also hearing a lot about Department 9 these days. What is it you want with Fitzwilliam?"

"You'll learn nothing from me."

"Don't be so sure. I have talented friends."

Zavage and Fitz took the hint and peered down at the driver. Zavage flexed his empathetic dreadlock-like tendrils, and Fitz took off his glasses to reveal his mutant eyes.

The driver's good eye went wild, staring at his three interrogators. He twitched violently, jerking in his harness as if powerful electric shocks were running through him.

Then he lay still, white foam bubbling out of his nose.

"Damn!" Bronze roared in frustration.

"What happened?" asked Zavage.

"Suicide implant," explained Fitz from within a cloud of cigar smoke. "It's a simple AI. If it detects waking brain patterns consistent with its host about to divulge secrets…Pfft! The brain melts." He raised an eyebrow at Zavage. "Funny how a worldly-wise SpecMish operative seemed to believe a Kurlei could read his mind."

"You got that wrong," Zavage responded, untroubled. "It's the mutie eye he was scared of."

"Movement in the trees. Five o' clock," warned Sybutu. "It's…the Muryani. It's Enthree."

"Finally," said Fitz with feeling. "The team is reunite…ted…Oh, turds!"

As she cleared the trees, it became clear Enthree was on her own. And the way she waved one of her forelimbs at them looked frantic.

"Take cover behind the mechs," Sybutu shouted. "Prepare to give covering fire."

Rounded black fuselages nosed out of the trees, red crosses painted on the tips. Hover fliers. GAC-19s.

"Let's give them a hot welcome," said Sybutu.

"No," said Fitz. "At this range, you won't penetrate their armor. Hold your fire. Give their imagination a chance to ponder why there are two wrecked mechs here, and what was powerful enough to take them out."

"Do you recognize the markings?" Bronze asked.

"REEDs," said Fitz. "Re-Education Enforcement Division. Swept through the woods from A-10. They were waiting for us in force. Knew we were coming. But they didn't know about the mechs. Watch…"

The GAC-19s eased back into the forest, never having fully emerged. Bronze didn't blame them. The entire area was covered in a thick layer of ash, except for the ruined metal of the mech carcasses. That meant the enormous metal machines had only recently been destroyed, and whatever had done that could still be around, waiting for the fliers to leave the cover of the trees.

"They've captured the others," Enthree cried, as she drew close.

"Keep running!" Fitz shouted at the Muryani.

Enthree did exactly that, easily bounding over one of the Hunters in a single leap and continuing in the direction of the village.

"We run too," Fitz said. "Don't look back."

* * *

They escaped through the village and then deep into the trees, detecting no signs of pursuit. Enthree reported her party had been surprised by six of the GAC-19s, without infantry support, and offered the opinion that they had encountered the limit of the REED pursuit for the moment.

"If they can march some prisoners back to base," said Sybutu, "that's an easier mission conclusion than attacking the village against unknown forces."

"Was anyone hurt?" Fitz asked.

"No. We hadn't yet retrieved the weapons Ren Kay made us abandon. Vetch, Darant, and Lily are at their mercy. We must save my comrades."

Fitz put a hand to her face and stroked a mandible. "They're *our* comrades too, Ms. Enthree. The boss ordered us to get the team together, and that's precisely what we shall do."

"Thank you. And please, Captain Fitz, to clarify, the boss is Kanha Wei?"

Fitz grinned. "I'm glad someone has been paying attention. Now, Enthree, I had the pleasure of hitching a ride when you were climbing over the buildings of Bresca-Brevae like you were wearing a rocket pack. Am I right that dense forest is like a highway to you?"

"I travel faster through the branches than across open ground."

"Good. Follow our captured friends. Observe without being observed. Assess. Then return safely to us. We'll be at the rendezvous point at the caves near Shinala Parva. If my guess is correct, that's where I'll find Commander Slinh, and I think I speak for all of us when I say I'd like to have a few stern words with her."

Enthree nodded. She raced up the nearest tree and disappeared within seconds.

"As for the rest of us, we need allies to get our comrades back, and that means the Revolutionary Forces of Reconciliation. My father raised me never to strike old ladies with glasses, or Gliesans. Commander Slinh is both. But in the case of that hollow-boned treacherous ass, I intend to make an exception."

"Are you serious?" asked Sybutu. "You're going to punch out the leader of the revolution?"

"Damned right I am. This revolution is a shambles. The only solution is for me to lead it myself."

Sybutu growled. "I hate it when you make me sound like the damned voice of reason, but if you go up to the leader of the military forces in this zone and punch her out, won't the rebels shoot you?"

"We'll never learn the answer to that if we stand around yapping, will we, Sergeant? Come on, everybody. Time to get moving."

* * * * *

Chapter Twenty-Nine: Sasmita Aelikaur

The day had seemed a triumph on so many levels. Major Sasmita Aelikaur had led the Enforcement Division's elite unit, Strike Force Purity, in the counterattack against the rebels and driven them from the A-10 facility.

The damned Militia were forever mocking her enforcers. They called them prison guard brutes who hid behind faceless masks, not real soldiers. It was ironic, because that's pretty much how the Legion poured scorn on the Militia.

But she'd proved them wrong today. Strike Force Purity had fought a battle without Militia aid. And they'd won convincingly.

And yet…

Her forces were *still* winning, of course. She'd driven her enforcers on relentlessly in their pursuit, never allowing the enemy respite.

Now, as dusk closed in, she was about to converse with the Revered Leader herself on a direct line to the capital.

It should be the ultimate personal triumph.

And yet…

The rebel attack had collapsed moments *before* she launched her counterattack. Why?

Whatever the reason for the Revered Leader's call, it surely wasn't to praise the conduct of her enforcers.

No, Aelikaur and her strike force were too obscure for that.

In'Nalla was only interested in the sickening scenes around her in the ruins of Krunacao, scenes repeated in every settlement within twenty miles, though Krunacao was the largest.

Her wrist slate buzzed an alert. *Incoming call.*

Aelikaur checked the angle of her beret, took a deep breath, and tapped *Accept.*

The Revered Leader's face regarded her through the slate's surface. Her features were pinched as if pained by the burden of steering an entire world into becoming a more enlightened society, freed of its bigotry and willful blindness to its own corruptive elements. To her relief, In'Nalla didn't seem as angry as Aelikaur expected.

"I have seen online footage of so-called RevRec insurgents invading Krunacao and firing indiscriminately." The Revered Leader leaned into the camera. It felt like she was opening up Aelikaur's soul. "The implication is that this was an act of inter-factional fighting. However, I want you to forget what's being claimed online for the moment. You're my eyes and ears on the ground, Major. Tell me what happened there. What did your enforcers actually see?"

"Bodies everywhere, ma'am. The entire village slaughtered, its buildings burned. But it looks like the civilians fought back, because there are three war mechs here that were destroyed in the attack. They're enormous machines. We're trying to establish precisely what they are and how they got here. We have a suspect too. A patrol group spotted the counter-progress leader known as the Trucker. I think he's a populist responsible for further degrading the morals of the willfully cancerous dissenters until they're now capable of…"

Words temporarily failing her, Aelikaur tilted her wrist outward and panned the slate across the scene of slaughter.

"Major," barked the Revered Leader. "Complete your report."

"Forgive me, ma'am. Our forensic teams are en route and will supply further information. So will the prisoners we captured. They're Militia deserters from the capital. Our interrogators are readying to pry their secrets from them."

"Tell your interrogators to stand down. I want the public to see their trials and confessions, but they are not to learn of the prisoners' accounts. Anything they have to say now would be deemed highly significant and risks becoming unsanctioned news. They're not even WCDs. They're nothing more than gutter-scum deserters, so they will know nothing of importance. I repeat, they are not to be interrogated. Not even questioned."

"I…understand, ma'am. They are not to be questioned."

But Aelikaur *didn't* understand. Surely the captives knew *something* of value. Unproblematic people had a powerful instinct to immediately publicize anything related to a suspected misdeed, but there were special interrogators who could be trusted to break society's strongest taboos in defense of righteous authority. They knew how to keep a secret. How could she make In'Nalla see that without appearing to contradict the Revered Leader?

"The villagers, ma'am. They were known to harbor WCD insurrectionists, but this…this bloodbath was not the way to re-educate them. After being forced to confront the inappropriateness of their thoughts, some of them could have been rehabilitated as Class-3 citizens and led the remainder of their lives inoffensively. This was mass murder! A barbaric act."

"Calm down!"

"I'm sorry, ma'am, but you can't see what I do. You can't *smell* the scorched bodies. The rebels have to pay for this massacre."

196 | TIM C. TAYLOR

"I can assure you, they will, Major. To that end, you are to secure the site. Take footage but leave the scene undisturbed. I will have one of my professional teams there at first light to capture the brutality of this terrorist outrage and make sure the correct messages are clearly presented to the public. The people must know that acts such as the Krunacao Massacre are the only alternative to following my way. And when we have made them understand, they will rise in my name and wipe out the irredeemable WCDs who stand in the way of a liberated society. It will be a brutal bloodletting, but you must understand how necessary this is."

"After Krunacao...I do, ma'am. You can rely on me." The REED major looked around at the devastation. Tears began to stream down her cheeks. It was such a *wicked* waste of life. And wickedness must always be confronted with force.

"We have to purge this world for its own good, ma'am. It's the only way."

* * * * *

Chapter Thirty:
Gethren Wen

Gethren Wen flicked his gaze at the heavy door and prayed salvation would come that way. But how could rescuers find him? He didn't know where he was, himself.

"That's right," said the masked woman. "Take a good look."

His captor nonchalantly reached into the leather bag by her seat and brought out a metal canister.

What was that?

"I told you to look at the door!" she barked when she caught Wen staring wide eyed at the canister.

The woman's anger was so sudden, so brutally intense, that Wen flinched and almost toppled the chair he was tied to. Wen made himself stare at the door, but his attention was on the cap she was unscrewing from the cannister. *What was inside?*

"It's coffee, you piece of filth. Now, the door, damn you! The *door*! Tell me what you see. Where do you think we are?"

"Er…it's rusted. Metal. Looks heavy. It was originally painted blue, but it's mostly primer and bare metal now."

"More!"

Wen heard coffee being poured into a plastic cup and breathed in the rich aroma. It was expensive real-caff, not synth.

"I'm waiting…"

"Yes, the door. Sorry. The air's dank. Musty. There's mold on the walls. I...I think we're underground." He looked at the rows of metal filing cabinets, but any identifying information had long ago moldered away. The cardboard boxes on the shelves by the metal door were thoroughly rotted.

The woman pulled down her face mask to widen the gap over her lips.

Wen watched her drink her coffee. *Good* coffee. Suddenly, he squeaked in fear. If help didn't come through that damned door, he would never taste coffee again. It felt as if his life was falling away from him, shedding the little details of mundanity first.

"Not very imaginative, are we, Gethren?"

He frowned at the coffee drinker, suddenly struck by the way she'd spoken his name.

It was familiar. He couldn't place her, but if she knew *him*...this was personal.

What could he possibly have done to deserve being kidnapped?

The masked woman nodded as if to say she was aware of every thought passing through Wen's head. And that she approved.

In fact, she seemed to be drinking up Wen's fears as much as the coffee, savoring the exquisite taste.

"Regrettably, I have an appointment later," she told him, "so I'll have to chivvy you along. Perhaps you're nervous? Are you? Are you nervous, Mr. Wen?"

"Yes. I'm scared. It's a mistake. I can't think what I could have done to deserve this. Let me go now, and I won't tell anyone. I promise."

"Very well, Mr. Wen."

"Really? You'll let me go?"

"No, of course not. What would be the point of bringing you here, then letting you leave before we've properly started? I merely mean that I accept that anxiety is clouding your analytical mind." She laughed as she poured herself more coffee. "And I have to accept some responsibility for your mental state. So, let me help you along."

She walked over to the door and rapped on it with her knuckles, which produced a dull thud. "This place is rotted and forgotten, but the door and its surround remain thick and strong. We're underneath the oldest government complex in Kaylingen. Like most of the earliest buildings in what was then a fledgling colony, it had to do double duty as a shelter. These rooms once had their own independent air supply. The corridor out there leads to another door like this. Technically, it isn't actually a corridor. It's an airlock." She rapped on the door again. "And this faithful old hatch was probably repurposed after a career on a colony starship. So, please, I invite you to scream, Gethren. No one will hear."

She walked over to him and squatted down so her face was inches from Wen's. "I want you to fully appreciate the hopelessness of your plight. After all, I have gone to considerable effort to bring you here. And at no small risk, I can tell you."

"What do you want from me?"

"For now? I want to tell you a story, Gethren."

She took a sip of her drink. "It starts with a man. His name was Cornflower."

Cornflower...Gethren racked his brains. He didn't know anyone of that name. He'd worked at the Ministry for Offworld Mining most of his life. It had never been a big department; In'Nalla believed in keeping government small. He would have known if there was a Cornflower. This *had* to be a stupid, damned mistake.

"We met at work. Five years ago, it was. We were far from teen-agers in years, but the intensity of the way I felt for him…it was as if I was in love for the very first time. I contrived reasons to walk past his work pod. To arrange meetings, projects, and, in time, significant government expenditure…all for the chance to be near him.

"But he was a subordinate. A relationship was strictly forbidden. Which is why we almost never called each other by our real names.

"Maybe if Cornflower hadn't felt the same way, I'd have taken a long fishing trip to the polar region with a case of brandy and forgot-ten him. But his beautiful corn blue eyes lit up with delight whenever I passed, and he was even less guarded than me. People began to notice. All those furtive glances…We needed to end that. I told him so."

The masked woman fell silent, awash in her memories.

"What did he say?" Wen asked.

The woman frowned. She checked that the cap on her coffee flask was screwed in tightly and then struck it hard across Wen's temple.

Pain lanced through his head, blurring his vision.

"I'm telling the story, Mr. Wen. It is rude to interrupt."

"Sorry," Wen whispered, wincing with pain.

"Cornflower, of course, had been waiting for this moment. Pre-paring for it. He'd already established a false identity and used it to rent an apartment near Tattenhoe. I went there whenever I could." She sighed. "Eiylah-Bremah is not a world in which it is easy to be happy. But we were. For a time. For a little over a year, we were free, and it was beautiful."

She fixed Wen with a fierce glare. "And now, we go further back in time. A year before I met Cornflower, he was at a bar, simply enjoying an evening with friends. The drink must have flowed a little too freely because the topic of conversation strayed into politics."

Wen took a sharp breath. He began to see where this might be heading, but Cornflower…? Who *was* this man?

"Yes, you see, Gethren. I did tell you he wasn't as guarded as me. He expressed the opinion that we should engage in dialog with political dissenters rather than dehumanize and criminalize them. WCDs we called them. Willfully Cancerous Dissenters. He even dared to suggest that using the term for anyone who harbors inappropriate thoughts was unhelpful.

"I must point out that Cornflower despised the WCDs. He was no rebel idealist. In fact, he hated dissent in all its forms, but he felt our intolerance for them only drove the WCDs to breed like a plague of vermin."

She reached into her bag. "That hardly made him a WCD, did it, Gethren?"

Wen shook his head but didn't dare speak.

"Cornflower never told me what he said that night. Perhaps he was so drunk he forgot. But he'd been recorded, and his sentiment logged.

"I never learned how or who. Perhaps his friends had secretly recorded everything in case a speech crime was committed. Or it could have been the bar's surveillance, or a hidden camera planted by the REDDs."

"I'm not…" Wen mouthed.

"What's that? Speak up, man!"

"I've nothing to do with the Re-Education Discovery Division," he whispered. "Please don't hit me again."

"You don't work for the REDDs, Gethren. But you *are* connected. Oh, yes. Fast forward two years to In'Nalla's proudest achievement—the Night of Cleansing. All those new speech and thought crimes announced at midnight and applied retrospectively. All those cases readied in secret by the REDDs to pass over to the enforcement division. Did you know in advance about the Night of Cleansing, Gethren?"

Mouth trembling, Wen nodded.

"I'm sure you did. And so—" The woman choked on her memories. "And so did I. Far more than you."

Wen realized he was sniveling. He steadied his resolve and tried to think. He was a cabinet minister. How could his captor possibly have known more about the Night of Cleansing? Was she a REDD herself?

"The Night of Cleansing murdered my happiness," said the woman, as bitterly as if the events had occurred yesterday. "It became a level 2 speech crime to express anything less than total condemnation of RevRec, of WCDs in general, and of all of their cancerous ideas. But holding the idea that dialog or compromise was worth exploring became a level 1 thought crime. Retrospective indefinitely."

"I'm…I'm…"

"What's that, Gethren? You're *sorry*? No, that can't be it. To express sympathy for a WCD is a speech crime. You must have meant to say *I'm afraid.*"

"Yes, I am. I'm scared."

"Good. Be afraid. *He* was."

"Did…did they execute him?"

The woman choked and swallowed hard several times. "Cornflower begged for execution. He was marched to the scaffold on Execution Square, but as he stood trembling in his final moments, they played their little mind game. His sentence was switched to indenture."

"That's better. Isn't it?"

"Better?" she roared. "To live as a slave? A plaything for the well connected?"

The universe froze, clamping Gethren Wen in a moment of chilling realization.

When it released him and he could speak, he felt a strange calm wrap itself around him. There was nothing he could do now. He knew who Cornflower was. "Chl…Chlorel-Lee?"

"Yes. He'll always be Cornflower to me. He lasted three weeks before he came at you with a knife."

"Chlorel-Lee was never a slave. He was an indentured, and I was his contract holder—never his owner. If he'd served his atonement to my satisfaction—"

Pain erupted through his head when Conflower's lover struck him once more with the base of her flask.

He moaned, fighting for consciousness.

After a minute or so, the muzziness faded a little. Enough for him to see that his captor had drawn a knife. Long and sharp.

"Please. Chlorel-Lee was upset. If he'd settled down—"

"He would never have served his atonement to your satisfaction. To you, he was nothing but a filthy WCD. Less than human. Worse than an animal. But to me, he was everything."

"Who are you?" Wen demanded. "If you're going to kill me, at least have the courage to show your face."

The woman played the tip of her knife around Wen's throat. Instantly, the Minister for Offworld Mining's courage dissipated, and he soiled himself in fear.

"Cornflower killed two of your bodyguards but couldn't get to you through the third. I hope that, as you saw him die, you were terrified by how close he came to slicing your throat."

The woman pulled off her mask.

"You!"

"Yes, me, Gethren. Ironic, don't you think?"

The knife slashed through Wen's throat, cutting off his protests in a pulsing fan of blood.

His killer poured herself the last of her coffee and sat back to watch Gethren Wen die.

* * * * *

Chapter Thirty-One:
Vetch Arunsen

It finally happened on the eighth day after being brought to A-10. Vetch was heading along corridor 221E on his way to morning confession, when the prisoner in front slowed down and rippled the thick slabs of muscle down his back, which were clearly visible under the stale white vest.

Vetch turned and...surprise, surprise! Two other prisoners were upon him. He was caught in an ambush. Which had happened at every other prison he'd enjoyed.

"Hey! New meat!" called the leader of this ambush. "The Colonel wants to talk to you. Now."

Vetch took the measure of this man. He was an Ellondyte, a member of a hirsute, pointy-chinned race who were normally peaceful communal beings. Split them from their tribes and townships, though, and they quickly went sour.

The third member of this ugly greeting committee was a human man with whiskers designed to ape the Ellondyte.

Behind Vetch, the Colonel's enforcer cracked his knuckles. Vetch refused to show his fear. He'd heard of this Colonel, a fellow inmate who seemed to run the inside of A-10 from the political wing. Vetch needed to tread a dangerous line between being disrespectful and showing weakness.

"Are you coming, or do you need persuading?" asked the Ellondyte.

"Tell the Colonel that if he wants to talk, we'll talk. He knows where I am."

The Ellondyte's hair stood up, and he bared his teeth.

This wasn't Vetch's first prison. He knew he mustn't look like a victim, so he glared back.

"Your ears must have gotten clogged by that hairy mane of yours," the Ellondyte said snarling.

"Rich coming from an Ellondyte."

"First!" The alien spat. "The Colonel doesn't come to you. Second, the Colonel is a she. And third, I find you insulting. Apologize."

"Of course." Vetch brought his hands up in surrender. "I'm sorry. It's just that…Well…"

"Come on, beardy. Spit it out."

Vetch shrugged. "I am truly sorry. But…" He punched the Ellondyte, ramming his knuckles into the base of the alien's nose.

"But my fists…" Vetch grinned. "They're not sorry at all."

The Ellondyte staggered back, hands clasping a nose fountaining blood, and Vetch grinned at the shocked human watching the Ellondyte stumbling beside him.

The man glanced behind Vetch, and it was clear the team's enforcer was moving to attack.

Vetch was a big man. People assumed that meant he was slow and inflexible.

He was neither.

Dropping low to the ground, he spun around like a street dancer and hooked a leg under the back of the enforcer's knees.

The brute went down like a sack of rocks. As the man lay propped up on his elbows, Vetch put him out of action by shoving the back of his head hard against the floor.

Vetch turned to face the other two, but the Ellondyte was sitting on his butt, moaning with pain, and the other one had his hands out to ward Vetch off.

"Tell your Colonel I will be happy to meet in a neutral location if that's convenient for her. Now, if you will all excuse me, I'm late for confession."

Vetch continued his way, stomping on the enforcer's chest on his way out.

* * * * *

Chapter Thirty-Two: Vetch Arunsen

In Vetch's early stage of atonement, confession in A-10 consisted of reading speeches the re-educators had prepared for him. He wasn't yet expected to believe the words he was reading—that would come later—but he was told to read them *as if* he believed them. It was all part of the process of breaking you down until you truly thought you had committed heinous crimes against society, and you begged the public for forgiveness and punishment.

The re-educators boasted that they would make him believe that two plus two equaled five. The truth was whatever they said it was. He just didn't realize it yet.

And if you didn't cooperate, there would always be consequences.

He'd already had shock sticks rolled over every nook and cranny of his body by a pair of REEDs in their sinister uniforms with fully enclosed helmets and masks. The torture wasn't a consequence of Vetch's behavior, it was because Darant had read his prepared confession in a comedic voice, and the REEDs wanted to know whether hurting Vetch would get through to Darant.

Darant had watched the proceedings and laughed as if he thought Vetch's shrieks were funny. But the REEDs told him the next time, he would be watching Lily being electro lashed.

Vetch cooperated, figuring he would be dead or freed long before they could break his spirit.

"In my arrogance, I thought my status as an off-worlder gave me the privilege to abuse the moral and legal rights of the people of Eiylah-Bremah to dignity and fair treatment."

Bollocks to that. Here's what I actually think—this is complete bullshit.

"My actions caused lasting harm to innocent individuals."

No, they didn't. But I'd dearly love to do harm to whoever wrote this crap. Tap some manners into them with my hammer. I hope Enthree's treating Lucerne well.

"Although I acknowledge the great depth of my guilt, my flawed worldview, my bigotry, and my crimes are so great, no amount of atonement can ever be enough."

Damn right. At least we can agree on that. Saying sorry will only encourage the bastards.

Vetch suppressed a sigh and blanked his mind while he read the rest of the printed sheet. It wasn't exactly difficult. It was all generic. Other than his being an off-worlder, they didn't seem to know anything about him and—inexplicably—didn't want to.

In any case, he was much more interested in the handwritten note at the bottom of the sheet which read, "The Colonel will see you at the public confession at 14:30 hours."

Vetch looked around the room, wondering who had written the note. There were ten other prisoners busy reciting statements for their personalized brainwashings. A re-educator technician was listening in, and a REED stood impassive in their blacked-out hazmat helmet, silently dominating the space.

It could have been anybody. The point was, the Colonel had demonstrated her power inside this camp.

And that could prove useful.

Vetch couldn't wait to meet her.

* * * * *

Chapter Thirty-Three: Azheelah

Senior Truth Definer Azheelah fidgeted her wings and rapped her knuckles on the polished wooden table. *What was the damned wait?*

The foam café was quiet this morning. There were a few humanoid office workers in half-brimmed hats and students in berets that sported unproblematic political slogans. How the youths could afford to drink here was beyond her, but the point was that the place was almost empty.

So why was she sitting here hungry and thirsty? She had new WCDs to process by lunchtime. This was not good enough.

The Deception Foam Café on Progress and 34th Street was not a particularly remarkable establishment, but that was why Azheelah had settled on it as her early morning haunt for the past few years. On the lapel of her business suit, the red ribbon framed in white and green marked her as a member of the Re-Education Discovery Division.

REDDs were not used to waiting.

All she demanded from a place like this was the deference she deserved and to be chronically undercharged.

She heard a bustle from the preparation room, and a waiter liveried in iridescent blue robes pushed through the door. The human female hurried her way.

214 | TIM C. TAYLOR

"Tell your wretched manager the service today has been unacceptable," she informed the waiter while the dolt placed a mug of steaming liquid on her table. "Who are you, anyway? Where are all the normal servers?"

"My deepest apologies, Re-educator. The *former* manager and several members of the staff were arrested for expressing *inappropriate* sentiments."

Understanding leeched away a little of Azheelah's anger. The unvirtuous had to be rooted out of decent society, but it was an unfortunate fact of life that their removal could be disruptive. She smiled and shook her wings within the pouches sewn into the back of her jacket. Wouldn't it be amusingly ironic if the Deception's manager was one of her WCDs on this morning's list? She would make the cancerous creature regret disturbing her most important client's morning drink.

A plate filled with a cream pastry rodent joined the drink on her table. "The acting manager sends his apologies," groveled the waiter. "He asks that you accept this complimentary beverage and pastry."

"Is it caramel and wheat foam coffee?"

The waiter bowed. "Yes, Re-educator. Your regular. My name is Chlorel-Lee, and I will be your server this morning. It would be the Deception Foam Café's pleasure to meet your every desire today and every day. Just ask, and I shall serve."

Azheelah grunted a vague acknowledgment. Not an acceptance of the apology, of course, but, at least, the café seemed to understand its failure.

She brought the cup to her lips, breathed in the richly bitter aroma, and drank. *Ah, she needed this.*

The liquid bubbled and roiled in her mouth, cooling as it did so. Then it swelled, delicate clouds of flavored foam brushing the roof of her mouth. Bubbles burst with a delightful tingling fizz, which was unusually fierce in this morning's cup, but she decided she liked it.

Widening her mouth, she enjoyed the playful foam spreading to her cheeks and caressing the back of her throat.

For some inexplicable reason, the waiter drew out a photograph and placed it before her.

Azheelah half choked in delight as the foam pushed down into her throat, but she managed to compose herself and regard the photo.

It was an un-posed picture of a young human male. His curly black hair was scandalously uncovered, and his unbuttoned shirt revealed a meaty man-chest.

I would love to interrogate you, she thought, giddy from the tickling foam. The bubbles were bursting like miniature exploding shells far down her throat. She'd never tasted anything like it.

It felt edgy…

She pulled her beret over her eyes, embarrassed to be enjoying herself so freely in such a public place. Godsabove! She had been on the edge of moaning. What was in this drink?

The waiter—Chlorel-Lee, she thought she was called…an unusual name for a human woman—tapped the photo with her finger. "Don't worry if you've forgotten him, ma'am, because I assure you I haven't."

The impertinent human glared at her. It was a clear threat display. How dare she? And at a senior re-educator too.

Before she finished work that day, Azheelah vowed to have this worm beaten, stripped naked, and begging for her forgiveness. And after she'd officially clocked out…she would stay late at the office. It was a common sight to see a desperate citizen at the REDD complex who was not officially there. Some were being given an unofficial yet terrifying ordeal by a benevolent re-educator, scaring those who had strayed into unvirtuous thoughts before they became irredeemably problematic. Others considered it a perk of the job to enjoy defense-less citizens, who would willingly submit to any humiliation to avoid being formally charged.

It made their pleading for forgiveness so *enthusiastic*.

But Azheelah couldn't bring the words to her lips that would transform the waiter's insolence into terror.

Her words wouldn't come at all.

Something was wrong. Her throat felt like it was filled with rocks.

She couldn't breathe!

And when she tried to bang on the table with her fists, she lacked the strength to move her arms. Frozen muscles locked her into place.

The waiter gave her a fulsome smile. "For maximum pleasure, I prepared your drink so the foam was firm. Almost *solid*."

She leaned over the table and whispered in Azheelah's ear. "For *my* pleasure."

As the waiter took back the photograph, Azheelah suddenly recognized who had done this to her.

"I'll leave you to enjoy your drink, Re-educator. If you need any assistance, all you need to do is ask."

Senior Truth Definer Azheelah felt her final heartbeat.

Her chest was still now.

She had moments left. She used them to watch the woman walk to the preparation room. She never saw her reach the door.

* * * * *

Chapter Thirty-Four:
Revered Leader In'Nalla

I n'Nalla internalized her seething anger until they had walked calmly into a private breakout room and Asher had locked the door behind them.

Only then did she scream.

"Why must they be so stubborn?" she growled, waving her flexi-viewscreens and paper notes. "Why can't they cooperate? It's a time of global crisis, but the transport corporations show no signs of noticing. They would rather exploit a small advantage over their rivals than cooperate and provide a vastly superior service for their passengers. In the war of ideas with the WCDs, I need to demonstrate provision of decent basic services. Instead, I'm betrayed by trans-cos who are greedy, petty, and led by utterly short-sighted assholes. It would be better if we had fewer companies, and they were steered by a central authority."

Asher was as impassive as ever, but In'Nalla thought she detected the merest twitch of an eyebrow.

Grimacing, In'Nalla reluctantly accepted she'd gone too far. What was wrong with her? Was the relentless advance of the rebels finally getting to her nerves?

She'd just endured a breakout debate on regional transport networks for the lower zones. It had been soul-sapping, dysfunctional, and bloody. But this was the Global Economic Forum; it had always been that way.

She cleared her throat and composed herself for the benefit of her aide. "Obviously, I would never condone government ownership of corporations. Jacobin socialism and leveler ideology are dangers that seduce the simpleminded into treacherous thoughts. Nonetheless, this crisis demands we open up to new ways of thinking to support the people of our world. They expect nothing less of me."

"Of course, ma'am. The people would struggle to follow even their Revered Leader into such ideologies. Not without a significant preparatory campaign. Now, two rather more prosaic matters, if you please. The police have announced another murder. A REDD truth definer poisoned in a downtown foam café. They're ruling nothing out, but it seems unlikely that it is a terrorist act because there have been no claims of responsibility or demands. Most likely, it's a demented serial killer. Old school criminality is not to be underestimated, ma'am, despite all the additional forms of criminality we have defined in the modern age."

"If this is, as you say, a drooling old-school psychopath, I don't see why this would be of interest to me."

Asher adjusted her pebble spectacles, her way of politely disagreeing with her Revered Leader. "Nonetheless, ma'am, it would be prudent to select a permanent replacement for your personal bodyguard since Halm met with that unfortunate accident."

"I don't pay you to beat around the bush, Blayde. You've already selected someone, haven't you?"

"Guilty, ma'am." Blayde Asher grinned and gestured to the door. "If you have a few moments to see him now…"

In'Nalla waved at her to get on with it.

Asher opened the door and in came a heavily built man with an air of danger. He wore black military-style battledress devoid of insignia.

"He's an off-worlder," said Asher. "No allegiance to any Eiylah-Bremah political group or ideology."

In'Nalla addressed him. "So, your allegiance is to money. That right?"

"No, ma'am. I am completely loyal to whomever I'm contracted to protect. I would defend you with my life until such time as my contract expires."

She gave a curt nod. "I can work with that. Strip to your underwear. And hurry. I must reconvene a meeting in five minutes."

The man didn't hesitate to comply.

He was a handsome creature. If she'd had more time, she would have enjoyed her power over him, caressing her gaze over his muscled body.

"Do you know why I wanted you stripped?" she asked, deciding not to put a teasing edge on her words.

"On Eiylah-Bremah, political allegiance is frequently displayed in tattoos. You wish to see mine."

She smiled. In his case, checking for ink was a pleasure she did little to hide.

Her gaze rested on the left side of his chest. A woman was tattooed there, a young girl with lilac hair spread out in zero-g.

In'Nalla had enjoyed a lover in the Legion for a year—a woman called Leyla. Both had been of Jeanneppien descent, their skin color a pale blue, like shallow polar waters. Leyla had worn the exact same tattoo on her breast—the image of the Immortal Empress.

In'Nalla had never liked it on Leyla. She considered the design to be crudely stuck on such a handsome woman, but this man was different. His skin was far darker than Leyla's had been. The tattoo felt organic, as if it had been exuded naturally by his body, an expression of his inner Legion spirit.

"What is your name?" she asked him.

"Marc Sanderson."

"Why did you leave the Legion?"

"Excessive use of force against civilians."

"Are you a murderer, Sanderson?"

He regarded her through cold, dark eyes. "I get the job done, ma'am."

She closed her eyes and soaked in his danger. "I believe you will. Asher, arrange the details of Sanderson's employment. I want him at my side before I leave the conference this evening."

As she gathered her papers to leave, In'Nalla paused and looked back at the big man. "Sanderson, in which unit did you serve?"

"Chimera Company."

"I don't recognize that name. Should I?"

"Not yet, ma'am." He gave a wolfish grin. "One day you will."

* * * * *

Chapter Thirty-Five:
Vetch Arunsen

"I unleashed verbal violence against innocent Colonists. I caused real hurt in doing so, but my bigotry blinded me to the damage I was inflicting upon members of an entrenched group. Worse…"

The Zhoogene girl sitting alone at the confession desk sniffed.

In the confession audience, Vetch rubbed dampness from his tattooed eyes. He couldn't see the girl's face clearly at this distance, but he was convinced this was the person they had rescued from prison in Kaylingen. It was Carnolin Indoh.

"My greatest crime," the girl continued, her voice trembling, "was to continue my arrogance after my imprisonment. Instead of accepting society's just and lawful program of atonement, I helped a group of Militia troopers desert in return for taking me with them."

The breeze blowing through the gap Enthree had blown in the camp's outer wall suddenly felt very cold on Vetch's bare legs. He thought of his friend and comrade, Sward, buried beneath an Eiylah-Bremah hillside. Killed in this girl's rescue.

It had all been for nothing.

Carnolin couldn't finish the speech prepared for her. It was too much. REEDs advanced on the girl in their sinister black hazmat suits with the gas mask helmets.

Two hundred prisoners were lined up to watch this afternoon's confession practice. Standing with Vetch were Zhoogenes, Pryxians,

221

Gliesans, Ellondytes, and several more races, but mostly humans. Lily was there, too, in the second rank of the lineup. Her tattoo had changed in the days since their capture, taking on bright shards of color until her flesh looked like it had been painted with dazzle camo. More cover. It had never changed so fast, and he worried that it reflected a frail mental state.

They lined up with the young and the old, with members of every gender. Many were off-worlders sent by the authorities of their own planets to the world that had made atonement services a major export industry. And every one of them was dressed in plain white shorts and vests, hair uncovered and feet unshod.

Facing them, with their backs to the scaffolding of the breach repair building site, was a line of armed REEDs. Their faces were hidden behind the black visors of the helmets that stretched down to their necks. Bullies were the same the galaxy over. They had absolute power over their prisoners, and they were itching for any sign of disobedience so they could exert that power with shock sticks, knuckle dusters, and metal-toed boots.

The REEDs dragged Carnolin, who was screaming in terror, off her chair. There was a cry of pain. Then nothing.

Vetch searched the faces of his fellow prisoners, looking for darting eyes and angry visages—signs that an outraged group of wronged prisoners would launch themselves at the REEDs and punish them for their abuse of this innocent girl.

But their grim faces were as impassive as the REEDs'.

He searched inward, but he didn't find the spark that would launch him at the guards with his fists and bare feet, knowing the fight would be hopeless, but making him fight anyway because it was the right thing to do.

I've been here less than two weeks. Has this place beaten me already?

It seemed the answer was clear because Vetch did nothing as Carnolin was dragged away.

Another prisoner righted Carnolin's chair, which had fallen over onto the stone ground. She took Carnolin's place at the desk, facing her fellow prisoners through the screen of REEDs.

She was a silver-haired human with an unmistakably military bearing. The upper reaches of her arms and thighs were smeared with livid bruises. She read her prepared speech with dignity and passion, as if she meant every word of her confession.

Vetch tuned out the words—this atonement garbage was always the same rehashed phrases—and concentrated instead on the reactions of the other prisoners.

They had endured Carnolin's performance with outward indifference, but now they stood proudly as if the woman reading her confession was giving a rousing speech to her assembled troops.

Vetch suddenly guessed who she must be.

"Is that the Colonel?" he whispered to the elderly Zhoogene next to him.

"It is," he hissed. "Shut up."

Vetch blinked in surprise. Not because of anything his neighbor had said, but because his ears picked up a word in the Colonel's speech that fired memories in his brain.

Irisur.

The wicked crimes the Colonel was admitting to had occurred on Irisur. The same place Sybutu's lieutenant had been killed.

"Is that Colonel Lantosh?" he whispered.

A REED tilted its head to regard Vetch directly. The Zhoogene said nothing after that, and Vetch kept his mouth shut too, his eyes rigidly focused on the Colonel like a good little prisoner.

Since he'd arrived, everyone had told him—prisoners and re-educators alike—that A-10 broke everyone in the end. Even, it seemed, the Colonel.

To his mind, she'd given a perfect confession, humble, with profound regret for her misdeeds.

And when she'd finished, she stood up and neatly tucked her chair back under the table. She took a few steps back before spreading her legs a little and stretching out her arms as if halfway through a star jump.

REEDs smacked heavy shock sticks against her bare upper arms and legs, adding to the collection of bruises.

The Colonel seemed to welcome the pain. The REEDs looked bored by their own brutality and soon escorted the Colonel out of sight. They returned with a trembling Gliesan who they led to the confession chair.

Before the new prisoner could begin, the REED who had looked Vetch's way earlier beckoned him over with a finger in a rubberized black gauntlet.

Heart pounding, Vetch jogged over, expecting the blows to begin without warning.

But this wasn't a public beating; the shock stick remained on the REEDs belt. Instead, the sinister figure pointed through the breach in the wall to the outside.

Vetch guessed that his interrogation was finally about to begin. Despite being made to read confessions, he'd not yet been questioned. Darant and Lily reported the same. He wasn't sure whether the re-educators realized they were the same Militia deserters Carnolin had just spoken of in her confession.

"You want me to go outside the walls?" he checked.

"That's right, you piece of filth," said the REED, a Zhoogene woman from the sound of her voice. "Move your fat human arse."

"And do what? Escape?"

"Idiot. If you attempt to get to the trees, sharpshooters on the walls will gun you down. Quit talking and beat those feet before I do so, literally."

Vetch hurried to the breach and ran up the wooden boards on one side of the mound of earth piled up before it. He cut through to the inner breach an instant before a hulking Pryxian prisoner crested the other side of the mound, pushing a wheelbarrow of rubble.

He passed through a scene straight out of pre-history—barefoot prisoners reworking the wall's interior by hand before the professionals finished off the outer layers.

Ouch! He cursed the alloy scaffolding as he banged his head against it.

Bet the ancients didn't have to put up with low-slung metal scaffolding, he thought, though he quickly decided they'd probably had far worse. At least this scaffolding wouldn't collapse.

On the far side of the breach, he saw a group of four prisoners waiting for him.

"Hey, Viking!" one called out to him. "Get over here!"

He really needed to get his eyes checked, because it was only when he drew close that he realized the smaller of the prisoners was the woman he suspected was Lantosh.

"You damaged some of my people," she told him. "There must be consequences."

"There are far bigger matters at play here than camp politics," Vetch answered. "And worlds beyond Eiylah-Bremah."

"No doubt," replied the Colonel. "Nonetheless, I find myself on extended furlough in this lovely woodland facility. The galaxy outside is dead to me."

She nodded. Vetch allowed his arms to be pinned behind him by two of the prisoners. A powerfully built Zhoogene drew up in front of him and regarded Vetch's vulnerable stomach hungrily, waiting for the Colonel's signal.

But it was Vetch who spoke first. "It's a long way home," he said hastily, repeating the code phrase he'd overheard Sybutu giving to Fitz when they'd first met, "but I'm setting off tomorrow."

The Colonel's only reaction was to give him a filthy look. "What is your name?"

"Arunsen, Colonel Lantosh."

"Well, Arunsen, you're not going anywhere without the say so of the REEDs, and they are strict about granting leave from this place. It's clear the tide has gone out in your mind, and your sanity has slipped its moorings."

Wait…wasn't something like that part of the recognition phrases too?

"I feel sorry for you, Arunsen. Go easy on him, boys, but make it look good. After curfew tonight, bring him to my quarters."

She pushed in front of the Zhoogene who was revving up to apply pain and looked up into Vetch's face. "You know, Arunsen, it would have been so much easier on all of us if you had obeyed my summons in the first place."

A flash of color just above her vest caught his eye. It was lilac, the outer reaches of an inked woman that was mostly hidden under her clothing.

She caught his attention and raised an eyebrow. "I'm proud of what the Empress' image says about me. Let's see if there's anything you're proud of."

She lifted his vest and revealed the black raven emblazoned across his chest. The bird was perched on a branch over his right nipple, leaning over to pluck an eyeball covering his left.

He'd spent everything he owned getting the quality artwork inked, but Lantosh looked disappointed, the first time she seemed thrown by anything.

"This shows your gang allegiance?" she asked.

"Raven Company, Colonel. Currently of no fixed abode, but originally of the 532nd Regiment of Militia."

"The Militia *is* a gang, Arunsen. One I intend to eradicate." She stood back and waved on the Zhoogene.

If this was taking it easy, Vetch would hate to make the Colonel angry. The blows kept coming until he was a ball of pain, groaning on the ground.

* * * * *

Chapter Thirty-Six:
Revered Leader In'Nalla

The orange light above the door lit.

It was a hatch, really, sealed hermetically in a privacy room set inside a Faraday cage, which was surrounded by rotating hoops. Inside the hollow hoops was a mixture of plasma jets, randomly pulsing superconductors, and rattling carbon cubes that produced a highly effective field of low-tech audio interference.

The ten-by-four-foot box beneath her residence in the capital was as private as you could get, and the orange lamp meant the person she was about to see was being thoroughly scanned for any possible surveillance technology under the watchful gaze of her new bodyguard, Sanderson.

The lamp turned green, and the hatch opened.

Ren Kay sauntered in, his sleek green cheekbones and slender form making her feel suddenly old and bone weary.

Dammit! She hated this reminder of her lost youth but took strength from it all the same. She wouldn't live forever, which was why Eiylah-Bremah's progress toward a permanently virtuous society had to be accelerated, so her legacy to this world wouldn't die with her.

He grabbed her hand and gave it an unwelcome two-handed shake.

She slipped her hand from his grip. "We don't shake hands on Eiylah-Bremah."

"True, but you aren't native to this world, are you, Revered Leader? I believe you were born on Jeanneppi."

"This room is private, Lieutenant. That doesn't give you license to speak unvirtuous words. If that was a crude and insulting attempt to ask whether my loyalty is to Eiylah-Bremah, the answer is yes. I'm a loyal citizen of the Federation. I respect the Senate, my home world, and the federal institutions…when they do their jobs properly. But my primary loyalty is to the people of Eiylah-Bremah."

"I see." Ren Kay sat. "Why have you requested my presence?"

"Your initial action was disappointing."

The Zhoogene's golden eyebrows shot up. "Really? The feeds are full of the atrocities carried out in Zones 40 and 41. They very clearly show RevRec rebels in trucks gunning down civilians who refused to yield to their demands."

"That's not all the public is saying," In'Nalla replied icily. "They also caught wind of the mechs you left behind to be discovered. They're asking whether the armored brutes are real or fake. They're wondering whose mechs they are. Because they sure as hell didn't belong to the villagers. At all times, the public needs to be given simple and robust messages. Otherwise, the messages can escape my control. Your sloppy work has undermined the killings with the elements of doubt and mystery."

"My thoughts exactly. We made a mistake at Krunacao. The rebels were much better armed than we expected. If you want a stronger message to unite your people against the rebels, we need something new. Something big."

"We, Ren Kay? Remind me why this outcome would be as desirable to you as it is to me."

He shrugged. "Personally, Revered Leader, I don't care who runs this shithole planet, but the Blue Chamber does. We need strong planetary governments with obedient populations. We need leaders who understand that you cannot make an omelet without breaking eggs. Sometimes, a lot of eggs."

"I understand that peace, prosperity, and the security of the overwhelming majority will always be reliant on the broken lives of those who would get in society's way. But who is the Blue Chamber? And why would you want this outcome for Eiylah-Bremah?"

"We're not just trying to shape this world, but the entire Federation, ma'am. It's the same story everywhere. Governments bribe their supporters and pay off the Militia to turn a blind eye while they suppress opposition. The Outer Torellian Commerce Guild and other powerful organizations spread their influence and milk it for money. The Federation is divided, corrupt, and weak. It would collapse in the face of an external threat."

"External threat?" In'Nalla took a sharp breath. "Is there one coming?"

Until then, Ren Kay had affected a boyish charm. Now, his face pinched as he said one word, "Muryani."

Dread tore at her guts. The prospect of a Muryani attack horrified her, always had. Yet, there were examples from early human and Zhoogene history of tiny nations resisting the clutches of their powerful imperial neighbors. In every case, the plucky defenders who beat off the great empires of their time had only done so because they were united and strongly led.

Despite the initial horror, Ren Kay's revelation took a weight off her mind. If the Federation were ever going to be strong enough to fight off an attack by the Muryani, more than a few eggs would have to be broken. The deaths of thousands on her world was a horrible crime that would haunt her until her dying day. Yet balanced against the prospect of entire species being eradicated at the hands of the Muryani, those deaths would barely move the scales.

Her mind was made up.

"I want a dirty bomb," she said. "Radiation. Fallout. Fear!"

She regarded the spy, or whatever the Zhoogene really was. Would he shoot to his feet and condemn her for even conceiving such an evil act?

Ren Kay answered with a lazy grin. "Not a problem. I can do that."

"The willfully cancerous dissenters are edging closer to the capital, but they draw their strongest support from Zones 81 through 84 in the plains to the east of the Ashclombe Mountains."

"Won't pinning the blame on the rebels look odd if they nuke their own supporters?"

"Of course, it will," she snapped. "It is to the east of those zones, on the shores of the Amber Sea, that they are pushing hardest to spread their lies and extend their control. They hope to make that region their heartland of the future. I trust my assistant, Blayde Asher, with the details of our strategy. She will contact you within two days with the coordinates of one of the towns or small cities that is resisting the lure of the rebels. Petty, brutal, with evil seething through every cell of their bodies, the so-called and self-appointed Revolutionary Forces of Reconciliation will explode a bomb to terrorize the town into submission."

Ren Kay considered the proposal seriously. "Wouldn't it be better to blame the bomb on the Panhandlers? You want to unite the public behind you, right? Wouldn't that be easier if you blame offworlders?"

"You're right, damn you. Nuke that city into radioactive glass and make it look like a Panhandler atrocity. Blame them both if you can."

"Whoa, there. Back off, Revered Leader! It's gonna look unconvincing if you glass an entire city. Even a small one. The Panhandlers want to deliver a message, and their ideology allows them to justify any action whatsoever as long as it supports their objectives, but you're suggesting a level of unnecessary cruelty the people might not buy into. No, we need a small yield. No more than a hundred kilotons. Just enough for EB-Link to trend with images of radioactive clouds that will terrify people over thousands of square miles, not to mention poison the sea."

Doubts crept in again. Was she doing the right thing?

Ren Kay seemed to register her misgivings. "Remember the Muryani. If we're not strong enough to stand up to them, they will annex Eiylah-Bremah and ship its people across their empire to be slaves until the end of time. Are you strong enough to do this, Revered Leader In'Nalla? Or do we need to find somebody else?"

"Such a decision should never come easily, Ren Kay. Only a megalomaniac could order such a thing without doubts, and such an individual is not fit to lead. I am the lawfully elected leader of this world, and that gives me the moral authority. I worry about your casual attitude toward the destruction of my citizens."

He looked serious for a moment. "It is good that you think carefully before such a course of action, In'Nalla. I shall await a communication from this Blayde Asher. I will not contact you again until after the action has concluded. It is best you do not know the details in advance."

* * *

After she'd dismissed him, In'Nalla spent several valuable minutes staring at the hatch Ren Kay had left through, trying to corral her doubts. She subdued her moral struggles, but she couldn't tame her distrust of this man and the Blue Chamber who controlled him.

In the ten years since she'd sworn off alcohol, she'd never needed a drink more than now. Her gut told her to trust these dangerous allies just long enough to win her final victory, but it also told her to prepare for contingencies. That was okay, though. Asher was excellent at that kind of thing.

Soon...soon she could relax. That, or she'd be dead.

"When it's all over," she said to the empty space. "When the people rise up and reject the WCDs forever, then...then I'll drink a whole damned case of Scalian whiskey."

It was a promise to herself she intended to keep. In'Nalla stood, straight backed, and walked out of the room.

She was Revered Leader In'Nalla.

And she had a job to do.

* * * * *

Chapter Thirty-Seven:
Vetch Arunsen

Halfway through the morning's confession practice, Lantosh walked into the claustrophobic room and leaned over Vetch's table. "Follow me," she whispered into his ear.

He glanced up at the re-educator technician and the REED guard who completely ignored Lantosh's presence.

In these confession sessions, you read your prepared speech and didn't let another word slip past your lips. Beatings for any exceptions were savage.

Obedience to the rigid regime had become so ingrained in the short time they'd been here, Vetch found the idea of walking out the door inconceivable. It just wasn't...*what he was supposed to do.*

"That's an order," snapped Lantosh.

Yeah, she sounded like an officer all right.

After another nervous glance at the re-educators, who were still pretending they couldn't hear, he glared up at Lantosh. "I don't work for you."

"Yes, you do. The moment you told me that phrase you overheard, you were mine."

Was he?

He decided he was. He'd repeated Sybutu's words on the cusp of the moment, but he didn't regret it. He'd gotten Lily and Darant incarcerated here, and he would damned well get them out. But for that, he needed allies.

He complied, following her out of the confession complex and across the exercise grounds to a row of storage sheds the guards sometimes used for beatings.

They never hit you in your face or on your hands, but the REEDs were determined you would always hurt and would never feel safe from a beating.

He'd been beaten in public. Sometimes, indoors in tiny cupboards. He'd been dragged from his sleep one night and brought to one of these storage sheds where they'd strung him up by his beard. He'd had to stand on tiptoe for hours to avoid ripping his beard out of his chin.

Damned REEDs thought that was funny.

These were just the random beatings. Actual punishments were far harsher.

No one had asked Vetch who he really was. Nor had they shown any signs of connecting him to the events in Kaylingen or those at Krunacao.

He followed Lantosh into a shed that was cool and musty. Under a single, flickering strip light, random stacks of boxes topped with discarded machinery dominated the gloomy edges of the shed. At its center, two REEDs faced each other across the room.

Knowing A-10, the darkness and the sense this place had been abandoned and then forgotten, had been carefully constructed. This was the kind of place where prisoners might disappear.

Uh, oh! What have you led me into, Lantosh?

The former Legion colonel walked into the space between the two REEDs and faced the one standing with their back to the north wall. Vetch joined her. The REED ordered them to stand at attention and keep their mouths shut if they didn't want a shock stick rammed down their throats.

Somewhere behind that black gas mask helmet and the shiny hazmat uniform with the blood red cross was a human woman, or what had once been, judging by her voice. Vetch found it hard to consider the person inside to be human.

He didn't recognize her voice, and that was unusual. He'd soon realized every prisoner was assigned a limited number of re-educators, so the bastards could learn the best ways to torture and manipulate that individual.

The REED standing behind them bothered Vetch the most. The backs of his legs tingled as he expected a stick to thwack against his tendons without warning.

But the strike didn't come. Instead, the REED to Vetch's rear walked out the door without a word, leaving Vetch standing with Lantosh and the REED woman in gloomy silence.

Your psychodrama games won't work with me.

Vetch withdrew inside himself. He thought of the friends he'd lost since riding out of Fort Iceni saddled up on an exuberant Saruswine—Deep Tone, Rynter, Sward, and that poor kid, Meatbolt. As for Green Fish, if she were still alive, he would likely never see her again. As he went through the list, he drew strength from the knowledge that his friends had never given up. Never stopped believing in him. No matter what Lantosh and the REEDs were about to throw his way, he would stay strong for the sake of his fallen friends, because he would never let them down.

The door opened.

Vetch turned and looked to see who had joined them.

"Good to see you," he said to Lily and Darant, who walked in with the REED. Darant had a swollen left eye.

"I told you to keep quiet," said the REED who'd stayed with them.

"Fuck you," Vetch told her. All his rage boiled over. He couldn't hold it in anymore.

Vetch bunched his fists, knowing he was about to do something *really* stupid and that he no longer cared.

"I admire your spirit, Mr. Arunsen," said the REED. "Just as well. I expect my marines to possess a certain get up and go."

"*Your* marines?" asked all the prisoners in unison, Lantosh more stridently than the others.

The REED removed her helmet and revealed the human inside.

It was Captain Fitzwilliam.

"Nice voice changer," said Lily. "Had me fooled."

Fitz grinned. "One picks up a trick or two in my line of work."

"Fitzwilliam..." Lantosh whispered, astonished almost beyond words.

"I assumed you knew who this was," Vetch told her.

"Not that it was him. Well, well, well. My dear old friend. I never expected to see your face again."

Fitz's expression soured. "Less of the old friend, Lantosh. The last person to call me that was Obinquin Nuysp. He was murdered hours later. Does the name Department 9 mean anything to you?"

"It does, unfortunately."

"Well, they're here. They murdered Nuysp and tried to kill me. And as for Cisco..." Fitz swallowed hard. "Cisco was always my friend. Now, he's frozen radioactive dust on Rho-Torkis. Galaxy's gone to the dogs, Lantosh. I tell you, I don't like it. As for you, don't try to tell me I was under deep cover all this time. I'm not coming in from the void. I'm not your dear old friend. And I do not work for the Firm."

"Of course, I don't expect you to return to the fold, Fitzwilliam. Hell, it feels so strange to call you that name to your face. Operation Redeal is underway. The name is not an accident, Fitzwilliam. The old petty allegiances are gone now. Redeal changes everything. *Everything*."

"I agree," said the man in the REED's uniform standing behind them. His voice was Bronze's. "Everything's changing. But there is one thing we need to concentrate on changing first—how to get you out of here."

"Right on," said Vetch. "But first, Enthree…Is she okay?"

"She's desperately worried about you," Fitz replied. "I'm seeing her tomorrow. Do any of you have words of encouragement I can pass on to let her know your spirits are high?"

"Yeah," said Darant. "Tell her, when this is over, I'll teach her to dance. Human style."

"You?" Fitz laughed. "You're a dancer?"

"Yeah. You got a problem with that?"

"Not at all. Just confirming the capabilities of my new personnel. Now, to business. Lily, I have a job for you. I have a particularly odious skragg-bucket I want you to beat the shit out of. Are you up to the task?"

Lily sighed luxuriously like a waking cat…

* * * * *

Chapter Thirty-Eight:
Vol Zavage

Fitz cleared his throat. "You haven't lost her, you know?"

Zavage gripped the steering wheel tightly but made no reply.

The human didn't get the hint. Zavage was beginning to think the smuggler captain feared silence. "I may not possess your marvelous kesah-kihisia," said Fitz from the passenger seat, "but I *can* read people. The connection between you and Green Fish is not something easily broken."

Zavage ground his jaw.

Their six-wheeled truck was still five klicks out from Kaylingen's official capital-zone boundary, but they had already passed three checkpoints of hard-faced citizen armed action groups, a spontaneous militia of civilians organized through EB-Link messaging pads. They were the result of the panic spreading across the planet in the wake of the atrocities in the village of Krunacao.

Most on EB-Link agreed they would not stand by and allow their hard-won progress toward a virtuous society be derailed, but not everyone agreed on who to blame.

An increasing number of human civilians seemed to think the mysterious mechs were evidence of a Muryani invasion. As a Kurlei, Zavage had been born into a minority race that was possibly dwindling toward extinction in this region of the galaxy. He'd had no choice but to live and work among humans, and the race still managed to amaze him. Only humans could see mechs in the form of giant humanoids and convince themselves they were driven by six-limbed Muryani. Humans constructed such elaborate stories sometimes.

Captain Fitz was a case in point. No doubt, in the human's mind, he was trying to cheer up his Kurlei companion by persuading him that Green Fish was waiting just beyond the next adventure, when, really, it was all about Izza. If Fitz could convince himself that Green Fish wasn't lost, then maybe his wife wasn't either.

A ferocious snore from the cargo bed cut through the modest road noise. Enthree was in the back, asleep in a transportation box designed for dangerous animals. If they'd known how many checkpoints had sprung up since the day before, Zavage would never have agreed to bring Enthree in via this route.

"The next few days could be rather dangerous," said Fitz.

"Just say what you need to say and then keep your mind on mission," Zavage replied.

"I am. A person needs hope when the situation seems hopeless. And I tell you, I'm quite certain Green Fish will come back for you. You can spread your fish lumps over me if you like. Then you'd *know* I meant what I say."

That was it. The human had gone too far.

Zavage perked up. He gave Fitz a hard, contemplative look, despite the man's head being wrapped in a hood that revealed only his dark shades and a slit for his mouth. "Your marriage looks pretty shattered from where I'm standing. I don't know whether to punch you or console you, but no amount of self-delusion will bring them back. We are on our own now, Fitzwilliam."

Fitz leaned over the center console that divided them and tapped his shades to render them transparent. His eyes glowed as he looked into Zavage's soul.

Their minds linked.

For the first time, Zavage felt the true shape of Fitz's mind. It was human…yes…but it was also something else. He radiated confidence that he would be reunited with his Izza. It was not the brittleness of self-delusion Zavage was expecting—a crust of wishful thinking that reality would eventually sink through. Instead, Zavage felt robust confidence laid over deep foundations of experience and trust.

Fitz winked a violet eye and then the moment was gone, though it left Zavage stunned.

And hopeful.

A light flicked across the road a hundred yards ahead.

It was a checkpoint Zavage had been too distracted to notice. Two columns had been sunk into the edge of the road. Lasers fired from one to the other, the beams reflecting off the polished surfaces to form a barrier grid of coherent light. They didn't look that powerful, but the truck was an unarmored civilian model. Driving through the laser gate would be a desperate gamble the truck—and possibly its occupants—would probably not survive.

A half dozen humanoid citizens wearing armbands and black hats manned the checkpoint. Four of them had rifles; the two who didn't walked over to the truck.

"Who are you?" demanded one of them. He wore a blue armband and gray flat cap, and he acted like a leader. The armbands of the others, Zavage noted, were black. "What is your purpose?"

"We've been contracted by the Kaylingen Municipal Menagerie," Zavage explained. "We're transporting an adult *Artraxa ensata*, a spearheaded atraxian, caught in the jungles of Zone-75."

They looked more disgusted by Zavage than worried by a dangerous animal.

"Your head is uncovered," one told Zavage, himself wearing a half-brimmed green felt hat. "That's disgusting, especially at a time like this when decent folk need to show solidarity. Cover up."

"I shall not," Zavage retorted. "My kesah-kihisia that disgust you so much are a part of my natural sensory organs. It would be both unnatural and unhealthy for me to cover them. I'm offended by your suggestion."

"Don't say another word," the man in the blue armband warned his fellow. He released a heavy sigh. "Zykan, place yourself under arrest and surrender yourself to the nearest police registration kiosk."

Zykan went wide eyed with rage and glared at his comrade. "Are you shitting me, DeRenzi?"

"Your words sounded to me like a potential speech crime," DeRenzi answered resolutely. "During this crisis, we must be super vigilant. We must demonstrate faith in the system."

Zykan looked at Zavage with sheer hatred before storming away, presumably to turn himself in to the authorities.

DeRenzi leaned through the open window of the cab and glowered at Zavage. "I *will* destroy you. This crisis has left Zykan overwrought. Normally, he would never commit speech crimes. I blame you."

"If you hate my Kurlei friend so much," said Fitz, "why did you ask poor Mr. Zykan to turn himself in?"

DeRenzi slid the full fury of his gaze to Fitz and held him in his glare. "I did it because the incident was seen, recorded, and uploaded on EB-Link. If I hadn't spoken up, I would have been guilty of a speech crime myself, and right now, I'm needed here at the barricades and checkpoints."

Fitz shook his head, confused. "But isn't that…and I mean no disrespect to your local customs…completely batshit crazy?"

Although DeRenzi's facial expression cooled into an impassive stony face, Zavage sensed surprise. Suspicion quickly followed, and it wasn't difficult to figure out why. Off-worlders were assumed to be behind the fearsome Krunacao mechs.

"We're off-world contractors," Zavage explained. "Dangerous wild animals like our spearheaded atraxian in the back don't catch themselves, you know."

DeRenzi's suspicion intensified. He looked back anxiously at the other men and women at the checkpoint. One made a show of charging their blaster rifle.

"We don't understand," said Fitz. "Could you explain?"

"If you see a crime committed, you must report it," DeRenzi said coldly. "If you do not, you are guilty of the same crime you left unreported and face the same penalty."

"So," said Fitz eagerly, like a boy with a new toy. He made a pretend gun with his fingers and put them to Zavage's head. "If I blow my friend's head off, you have to report the murder. If you don't, you're guilty of murder yourself?"

"Correct. For which the penalty would be public execution."

"But what if, after murdering my friend, I turn my pistol on you and tell you that if you report me, I will kill you and your family.

Would you still be guilty of murder if you don't report me immediately?"

"No, of course not. We're not savages. But I would use all means to report your crime the moment it was safe to do so."

"Fascinating," said Fitz. "Why doesn't anyone do anything about this insanity?"

"How dare you?" thundered DeRenzi. "Who the hell do you think you are?"

Fitz grinned and reached for a cigar that wasn't there. "We're Chimera Company. Spread the word."

"You're what?"

"Ignore him," Zavage begged. "He has a disorder. Anxiety makes him withdraw into an alternate personality, which makes him talk complete crap."

DeRenzi narrowed his eyes and gave Zavage a predatory smile. "Everything you say is being recorded," he said, tapping a circular patch on the lapel of his jacket. "I will report you to the authorities for potential speech offenses, but—" he screwed up his face in fake dismay, "—regrettably, the authorities are currently overburdened by multiple crises. Which is why I'll also send it to the city menagerie. We'll see whether your employer still wants to be associated with you once your comments have gone viral on EB-Link."

"Do what you have to, pal," said Fitz. "Now, this is a checkpoint, right? Are you going to do some checking or what?"

"Open up the back of the truck," DeRenzi demanded. "I hope, for Zykan's sake, I find something incriminating."

Zavage got out of the cab. He walked around the back and opened it up.

"Easy, boy," he told Hubert, who bunched his legs and bleated aggressively at DeRenzi from the cargo bay.

Enthree had been taking care of Darant's pet, but in the little goat's mind, it was he who had been protecting Enthree. Was Hubert going to wake his Muryani friend?

Enthree continued snoring inside her box. She'd been so excited last night that she couldn't sleep. She kept saying something about dancing for some reason that made no sense to Zavage.

"It certainly sounds like a fierce beast," DeRenzi admitted.

"You have no idea. Would you like me to open the box? It's sealed to keep it dark inside. I warn you, though, sunlight will wake up the beast, and it will feel threatened."

"No. No. There's no need for that," DeRenzi said hurriedly. "I hope I judged you wrong, off-worlder. Stay pure. Stay vigilant. These days carry great danger." He nodded at Enthree's box. "They are even more dangerous than your wild animal."

The laser gate was switched off, and Zavage drove on. Fitz roared with laughter the moment they passed through the gate.

"Oh, that was beautiful," he said when his laughter subsided. "To cover your smelly fish dreads would be *an outrage*! Bet that never stopped you wearing your battle helm when you armored up."

As a matter of fact, Zavage's kesah-kihisia did itch within the tight confines of his armor helm, but he didn't feel like sharing that detail.

"You humans are crazy," he said instead.

Zavage meant it as a throwaway comment, but it sobered Fitz.

"I can't argue with that," he said. "Humans are weird."

"So, what are we doing here, Fitz? Really. The main objective of this trip is to smuggle Enthree in and get the intel on A-10 security out. But long term? If we depose In'Nalla, then what? Would the Panhandlers be any better? Would RevRec? Perhaps we'll have a nice little civil war in which the ideologies get ever more extreme until we end up with the Cora's World death camps."

"We're here to put the team together and get back to my real job. Find that mystery ship they dug up in Rho-Torkis and figure out our little mystery man, Lord Khallini."

"What about the regular people on this planet? Are we going to abandon them?"

"You can't save every soul in the galaxy, Vol. You can choose to be paralyzed with guilt over that, or you can do the best you can, knowing there will always be more left undone. I have discussed the topic of what happens next at length with Commander Slinh. I believe in her."

"You punched her in the face and told her she was a disgrace."

"True, but I called her out for her military leadership. And because she left me to die. As a political leader, she's the best hope for this planet. But we get ahead of ourselves. In'Nalla, for the moment, is still very much in charge. First, we must destroy her."

* * * * *

Chapter Thirty-Nine: General Gzeiter

"It's a goddamned lie!"

General Gzeiter frowned at the strategic map display in the middle of his operations room.

Eiylah-Bremah's central continent was on display, color coded according to strength of support for the rebellion. The black, white, and red PHPA symbol represented force concentrations. Not that there were many. The Rebellion had few combat troops on Eiylah-Bremah. They weren't here to win a war on this planet.

The strategy he'd been tasked with implementing was to wage a war of attrition. The Rebellion was to recruit local allies that would wear down the Militia troopers through guerilla warfare.

This was not a war of massed hover tanks and orbital drops. It was a stab in the back in some dark alleyway. Tired troopers ambushed by guerillas who would melt back into the local villages, indistinguishable from the local civilians because, in many cases, they *were* the local civilians.

Gzeiter got some satisfaction from knowing that Eiylah-Bremah already had a reputation in the Militia as a posting no one wanted.

And the cycle of attrition had become almost self-sustaining. The Militia controlled the rich asteroid mines, which meant they couldn't afford to lose the system. So replacement troopers were constantly fed into the war. As their retaliation against the civilians grew more

249

brutal—particularly in the jungles of the Zone 40s—fresh recruits swelled the ranks of the guerillas.

The orders from rebel high command were to keep the war going. Bringing down In'Nalla wasn't the objective here. The purpose of Eiylah-Bremah and a dozen worlds like it, was to grind down the Militia until their situation was so dire, they would be forced to bring in the Legion.

For the Legion to suppress Federation citizens would be an unconstitutional outrage. Better still, it would expose the fragile Legion logistics for the pathetic lie they really were.

And when the Legion supply chain was stretched to the breaking point, the carefully hoarded Rebel Navy would strike at their logistics. The legionaries would be stranded behind enemy lines with top of the range military hardware that had no ammo, no fuel, no power, and no spares. The famous PA-71 railguns would be nothing more than high-tech clubs.

Until that skragg-bastard Trucker had come along and pissed all over Gzeiter's neat war.

Now his map was meaningless.

The strategy was broken.

He deactivated the screen. "Might as well be staring at used toilet paper for inspiration," he growled.

"Sir?"

Gzeiter rolled his eyes—he'd thought he was alone with his frustrations—turned around, and saw Corporal Woods looking embarrassed.

"It's been a long day, Corporal. Go ahead."

"Human male wants to see you. He checks out as Candor Shepherd, recruitment and subversion specialist."

"Good. I wasn't expecting him till morning, but this is better. Show him in and make sure no one disturbs us."

"Yes, sir."

Woods disappeared, and a friend from many campaigns took his place.

"I would have come even if you hadn't summoned me," said Shepherd.

Gzeiter embraced the old political warrior. "Thank you, Carnor. I could do with your input. My lieutenants all tell me the same thing: our campaign here is a success. Nothing has changed following that business with those goddamned mechs in Zone-40."

"They're wrong, of course," stated Shepherd. "Everything has changed."

Reluctantly, Gzeiter nodded in agreement, but then he brightened. From an equipment cupboard, he drew out his bottle of Swift Endeavor whiskey and two glasses. Silently, they savored the amber liquid and each other's companionship as they sat beside the planning table.

Gzeiter switched on the map. "Tell me what you're hearing, Shepherd."

Shepherd drew himself up as was his way when he had a detailed explanation to deliver.

"*Concisely*, my old friend," prompted Gzeiter with a grin. "There will be time to catch up properly when this business is done. Perhaps you and I can go fishing for sword trout along the banks of the River Kezell."

"I'd like that." The recruiter frowned. "The Krunacao Massacre the public is calling it. I assume it is a false flag operation?"

"Almost certainly."

"Almost?"

"The obvious explanation is that In'Nalla is murdering her own civilians to shore up support among the public and to choke off the flow of recruits to our cause. And yet there are doubts. Where in the Five Hells did those damned mechs come from? And the outsiders? I'm informed that you encountered some of them near Kaylingen. Militia deserters. A Viking, a tattooed woman, and, of all things, a Muryani."

"They match the group I saw. There was one more. A male human."

"Was his name Trucker? A cigar-smoking pop-up folk hero with a cap that reads *Bori-Alice Space Truckin*?"

"I'm sorry, General. The other man I met was called Darant. He was an introvert who reads novels and keeps a pet alien goat. No, I don't think it can be the same man."

"My intelligence says the group you interviewed knew Trucker. Did they speak of additional members of their group? Maybe someone they left behind?"

"No. They were closed to the idea of discussing anyone outside the group. It's not uncommon. Deserting is psychologically traumatic. You're literally removing yourself from your old life."

Gzeiter felt Shepherd's appraising look as he took a long drink of his whiskey and poured himself a refill. Damn that Trucker.

"As I said, General, Eiylah-Bremah is horrified by the atrocity and appalled by its mystery. The people of this world have lived regimented lives for generations. They crave certainty and boundaries. Tens of thousands die in the war every year, but they feel they understand why. The war's body count is far greater than the number who died in this one horrible incident in a remote village. They don't know why this happened. They don't know who carried this out. And it is that very uncertainty that is driving them back to In'Nalla. For even those who hate her, at least, In'Nalla is the devil they know. One thing I will say with confidence. Whoever is behind this is likely to strike again. And again. Each outrage more shocking than before. Even our own natural sympathizers will eventually turn to In'Nalla if she promises security from this unknown threat."

"My thinking exactly," said Gzeiter soberly. "Our campaign here will fail."

"It will. Which is why you are preparing a new strategy to turn guerilla warfare into conventional combat operations."

"Who told you that, Carnor?"

"My own eyes as I walked through this camp. Our combat forces on this world are few, and it is obvious that what little we have are concentrating at this encampment. There is an unmistakable air of expectation about troops preparing for an assault, and it is rich in this camp. What is your target, General?"

"The capital."

Shepherd's eyebrows shot up.

Gzeiter's heart sank. Shock wasn't the reaction he was hoping for. "Do you think that's too risky a move?"

Shepherd rubbed his chin for a few moments. "I'm not informed enough to answer that question. No, my surprise, my *pleasant* surprise, is that you have chosen such a bold step."

"It doesn't sit naturally, I can tell you, Carnor. I know my reputation for caution, but Eiylah-Bremah balances on a knife's edge. If we don't seize the opportunities that present, someone else will."

"Well said, General. If I may offer bold counsel, your previous campaigns have yielded victories that came too easily. Now, you

254 | TIM C. TAYLOR

must embrace the risk of failure like most generals throughout history. This Trucker you speak of, why does he bother you so much?"

"It is not only we who have limited conventional forces. Our RevRec allies are primarily a guerrilla force. We were secretly training an assault battalion as a reserve. The process was far from complete, but they launched an unauthorized attack on A-10. And now, under the new leadership of this Trucker—an individual I know nothing at all about beyond his physical description—they've called for an attack on the capital and demanded our support. It's as if they've woken up and decided it's *their* war now. After all we've done for them…"

"So, he's a populist leader who also knows the off-world deserters. Yes, that is a conundrum. One of the deserters I interviewed was a former Militia officer. My guess is that the Trucker is also an ex-Militia officer. Do you fear the Trucker will seek to replace In'Nalla himself?"

Gzeiter drained his glass. "Damned right. And that's what's bugging me. Is the Trucker playing me for a fool? And what third parties are involved that I have no knowledge of, other than these damned mechs they left behind? My biggest fear is the Infection. I ordered everyone checked this morning. No sign of feathers or other strange growths. But the Infection could be rampant in the areas we control, hiding itself. We've seen this play out on other worlds."

"I can't speak about the Infection, but I don't think this Trucker is the threat you fear him to be. He may have temporarily won the support of the civilian populace, but if he tries to take In'Nalla's place, they will turn on him instantly. You have plenty of matters to worry about, General, but the Trucker's loyalty is not one of them."

* * * * *

Chapter Forty: Lily Hjon

"Why does it always fall to me?" Lily muttered. She pushed through the gate, noting the unusual absence of guards, and made her way into the exercise compound.

Because, Lily, you get things done.

"Oh, yeah. Let's get Dangerous Lil' to do the dirty work. Crazy Lil'. Just look at the tattoos on her face. Lily will do anything. Why can't it be someone else for once? How about that damned Zhoogene girl?"

Carnolin can't do anything like this. She's just a frightened little civilian.

"I'm frightened too," she snapped at herself.

The prisoners didn't cease pushing weights or their callisthenic drills, but her appearance did generate a ripple of unease. They sensed something was up.

And the Zhoogene prisoners could hear her one-sided argument with herself. Not that she cared much.

You're the right one for the job, Lily. Suck it up and get it done.

"I know," she murmured, seeking out her target. "I'm getting real tired of that."

Bullshit. You're about to kick things off. People on this planet will be talking about you for centuries. Admit it. You love it.

"Never said I didn't," she whispered.

Lily found what she was looking for by a corner of the high fence. A group of four men were doing press-ups, jumping jacks, and all that kind of crap.

"Hey!" she called, jogging over. She tapped a man with dark curly hair, who was about to transition up from a set of press-ups, on the shoulder. "Are you Stefan Gamal?"

The man slapped her away. Around him, his lieutenants halted their exercises and began looming aggressively instead.

"Who the hell are you?" snapped the man Lily knew damn well was Gamal.

She tutted. "Really! Such rudeness. I only asked—*politely*—because my friends told me you're a piece of filth who gets his rocks off by torturing children."

It wasn't true, and she laughed when she saw Gamal's eyes widen in shock. He had no shame about all the horrific things he'd actually done, but accuse him of something he hadn't, and the poor dear was mortally offended.

His dismay allowed her enough time to land one really satisfying punch before his men bundled her to the ground and began pummeling the hell out of her.

"Are we going to stand for this?" yelled one of Lantosh's plants.

Initially, the call was echoed only by those in on Lantosh and Fitz's plan, but soon, it spread throughout the exercise area and beyond.

Gamal and his thugs were pulled off Lily before she suffered too bad a beating.

Already, REEDs were thundering in to break up this unprecedented display of disorder.

They soon found the prisoners turning their fists and makeshift clubs on them, which only drew in more REEDs from other areas of the camp.

Lily sat up and wiped the blood off her face with her arm. She shuffled back a few feet so she could get a view of the top of the main gate.

According to Fitz, Zavage and Enthree had unexpectedly become best buddies, combining their skills in signal tech and hacking to great effect.

The main gate slid open under Zavage and Enthree's remote control.

She couldn't hear Lantosh and her best fighters move in to secure the gate, but she could hear the struggle—screams and punches and the occasional blaster bolt screeching through the air.

And in the distance, she could hear the rebel army approaching.

The REEDs froze, looking at themselves. Behind their gas masks, Lily hoped there was terror on their faces.

They'd been caught with their rubberized hazmat pants down, and they knew it.

She heard disciplined volleys of blaster fire from the area of the main gate.

Lily couldn't see the battle, but she knew what the result was going to be.

So did the REEDs. Some hurried to join the battle for A-10, but most abandoned the hopeless fight and ran deeper into the camp.

"Run as much as you like," Lily told them. "But you can't hide. Today is Payback Day."

And tomorrow, said her inner voice, *you get to rest, Lil'. But there's gonna be at least one more big battle before this planet'll let you get away. And you know you're going to be right in the thick of it...*

* * * * *

Chapter Forty-One:
Blayde Asher

Asher pushed open the door to Shelter 66. Immediately, she froze.

It was the worst thing she could possibly do in a place like this. Like all speak-free coffee houses, it was rumored to be crawling with police spies.

She frowned and rubbed her chest, trying to pass off her hesitation as a momentary pang of heartburn, then she panicked when she feared she might drop the precious object concealed in her right hand.

She supposed her trouble really was a pain in her heart. Cornflower had brought her here a few times in those heady early days of reckless love before she forbade it.

Well, now I'm back, darling. And I'm here for you.

Her sense of purpose restored, she walked over to the east wall, surreptitiously looking for her contact among the late-morning drinkers lined up against the shelf carved out of the stone.

Tens of meters of solid rock and a lead-lined roof above her head made these former emergency shelters popular locations for speak-frees. They had been built in the early years of the Eiylah-Bremah colony and abandoned a thousand years later. In the modern world, people had to shield from dangers more subtle than radiation storms, terraforming disasters, and alien invasion fleets.

The shelters were called speak-frees, but it was difficult to tell how accurate that description was. Even for her.

Although the breakout from the A-10 camp had shaken their totalitarian reputation, the authorities still promoted the narrative that Eiylah-Bremah's citizens were protected by an all-encompassing police state. Widespread, hidden recording equipment and informers were impossible to evade.

Asher knew the reality was different. Police recruitment numbers were far below target, and even if they weren't, they would fall far short of the numbers required for the police state people imagined. But that was the sick genius of the system. If you didn't report a crime you observed, you were awarded the same punishment as the perpetrator if you were found out.

There was an all-seeing police state, but its eyes and ears and recording devices were those of the public, coerced into oppressing themselves.

It had been that way for generations. In'Nalla had just refined the system for her own ends.

But very soon, it was going to end for good if Blayde Asher had anything to do with it.

She walked almost the length of the wall before she saw a man wearing clothes that matched the description she was looking for. He wore a loose hood over smartly pressed coveralls. Dark blue with gold stitching and lining, except where the left sleeve joined the rest of the garment. That stitching was silver.

She took a stool next to the man.

After apparently trying the service request console in front of her and finding it didn't work, she leaned across the man, who was nursing a tall, cream-colored drink, and used his.

"Excuse me," she said.

"No problem," he replied in an accent that sounded vaguely Zone 40-ish but had a hint of somewhere far more exotic.

Asher swiped through the beverage options. Normally, she would have chosen a foam coffee, but having used one as a murder weapon, she'd lost her taste for them.

That's an unintended consequence of becoming a serial killer they don't tell you about, Cornflower.

She selected a plain synth-caff instead and drew two sachets of sugar from the dispenser and dropped an identical sachet she'd been concealing in her hand since she came in.

The man shifted his arm on the shelf. It was the barest motion, but the sachet in which she'd concealed the recording of incriminating evidence disappeared.

Asher took heart. Whoever the hell this was, claiming to represent the Trucker, was good.

"We can speak freely," he said, "as long as you face the wall to defeat any lip readers. There are no active recording devices nearby. And if spies in Shelter 66 take an undue interest in us, I have friends here who will warn me."

He glanced casually at his wrist slate, as if checking whether he had time for another drink before his lunchtime appointments.

She glanced over, and his slate was indeed showing appointments. At least, from the angle she was observing, it appeared to do so. She guessed he was viewing something quite different—the recording of In'Nalla she'd passed him inside the sachet.

"I've not been on your world long," he told her. "And most of that was as a prisoner of RevRec, but even I can guess who you are,

Blayde Asher. When we release this, it will incriminate you too. Why do this?"

"My world is hopelessly screwed up. The Trucker is the only one who can change that. And he needs this."

Her contact sucked his drink through a straw, ice cubes clanging against the glass. He gave a satisfied sigh. "I don't believe you. What's the real reason?"

"Revenge."

She spoke quietly, but with such intensity, he didn't question her motives again. Instead, he asked the question that terrified her the most.

"Will this be enough, though? I'm guessing this is not the first time someone has shared a recording that compromises In'Nalla."

"You're right. It's not enough, and it's not the first time. Every few years, someone throws her words back at her and tries to destroy her. Most people think she would be the perfect victim of such an attack. After all, the Churn is all about those who abuse their power and authority being ruthlessly cut down by an outraged, baying public. But In'Nalla controls the information flows to the public and the way in which the public communicates with itself. The Churn belongs to her. Each time someone tries, In'Nalla turns the matter over to a binding Court of Public Opinion. And because she controls the message and the medium, she always wins. For my recording to be enough, you must take away her control of EB-Link, the data sphere, and the media conglomerates."

"And I suppose In'Nalla knows all this and guards her sources of power jealously."

"Of course. I can't help you defeat her defenses. That kind of thing's not my specialty."

With a slurp, the man finished his drink. "Luckily, it is mine. Thank you, Asher. We won't waste what you have delivered to us."

He pulled a clay pipe from his coveralls and was about to light it when her synth-caff appeared in his dispensing receptacle.

He handed it over. "Yours, I believe."

Those were the last words he spoke to her. Soon, he was wreathed in a cloud of smoke.

When she got up to leave a short while later, he showed no sign of acknowledging her.

I hope it's enough, Cornflower, she said inside her head as she left Shelter 66, but she was petrified it would not be.

Nonetheless, as she headed back along the underground street, making her way to the city above, she felt a lightness in her step she hadn't felt since the day they took her lover away.

* * * * *

Chapter Forty-Two: General Gzeiter

The viewscreens arranged across the wooden kitchen table showed the same image. The capital city of Kaylingen was tense—barricades were even more numerous and more heavily manned than after the surprise A-10 breakout—but there were no signs of violence. Not, at any rate, visible to the drones feeding the images.

"You should get rest, sir," insisted his aide for the hundredth time.

"I can never sleep before battle," Gzeiter replied tersely. Then more gently—because Captain Bryn meant well—he added, "I'll just chill in front of the screens. I find it relaxing to see the battlefield. But you, Bryn, could sleep under the barking guns of a field artillery battery. I swear you're gene-spliced with a kill droid. Go. Rest. Be back at 05:00."

Bryn saluted and left Gzeiter alone in the farmhouse kitchen.

Although he couldn't sleep, this was a restful place. Homey.

The Zhoogene farmer who had lived here was one of their field agents, and Gzeiter had expected his command section to be warmly greeted and updated with the latest intelligence. But it seemed she'd left in a hurry weeks ago. His staff had given the place a quick wipe over to remove mold, dust, and rotten food, but he could still smell putrid meat from somewhere and a faint whiff of despair.

265

He hoped she was safe but strongly doubted that was the case.

His eye was drawn to the shelf on which silver plates and sports trophies were displayed and then to the shelf below where cut glass tumblers were interleaved with bottles of exotic liquor, most of which he didn't recognize.

He shook away the temptation to drink and studied the lowlight-enhanced images from the drones. A few pedestrians were walking along peaceful nighttime streets, oblivious to his attention. In the morning, those streets would transform into assault vectors.

Appearances could be deceptive, he reminded himself. The people were oppressed by a sickening totalitarian regime. As he saw the city and its people—if not with his own eyes, then at least in real-time—he began to wonder if this campaign was really such a disaster.

True, he'd abandoned the idea of waging the long, drawn-out war of attrition he'd been sent here to fight. But he hadn't joined the Rebellion to conduct industrial scale slaughter. He'd been propelled by ideals; he still was. Taking out In'Nalla, and the sickness that supported her, would be a victory worth celebrating.

Hers was a strange ideology. One of convenience, he suspected, freely mixing her own innovations into what had gone before, caring little about the philosophy so long as it won her power. She was in favor of small government, ironically enough, understanding that it wasn't the same as weak government. She stood for both the preeminence of unrestricted free markets and the progressive march of social engineering. High economic productivity was almost a religion to her, as was the delivery of universal and free lifetime education. Anybody who was not in favor of those things either kept quiet or disappeared into one of the jails and amelioration camps until they were ready for their show trial.

His informers told him In'Nalla was on a passionate crusade to improve the world she lived in. He didn't believe that for a moment, but it made no difference either way. Tomorrow, her era would be over. And, too, if his plan came to fruition, it would be the end of the Trucker and RevRec's miniature field army.

The Pan-Human Progressive Alliance would rule Eiylah-Bremah unchallenged.

His wrist slate chimed.

"Go for Gzeiter."

"Signal ops, sir. North Strike Actual reports attacks in Zones 10 through 13 proceeding according to plan. Orbital Eyes confirm Militia troop transports and other air assets redeploying from Greater Kaylingen region, headed to reinforce defenses against the North Strike feint attacks."

Gzeiter dismissed the signal operator and walked over to the row of liquor bottles. He halfheartedly inspected the exotic labels again, but he couldn't concentrate. Everything was going according to plan. Everything depended on what happened the next day.

Tempting as they were, he resisted the lure of the bottles.

There would be plenty of time to toast victory on the morrow.

* * * * *

Chapter Forty-Three: Izza Zan Fey

She sighed.

It was no use. No matter how hard she tried to distract herself, *he* was always in her mind, beaming at her with that ridiculous human grin.

Carefully, she lifted the sleeping woman's arm off her and rolled over the man snoring on the other side of the bed.

The woman moaned, her hand tapping the sheet as it sought the warm body it had been resting against.

Izza pulled the man's hand until it rested over the woman's and grasped it slightly.

The woman purred happily and settled back to sleep.

Izza admired her two human lovers for a few moments. They did look sweet together, but they were nothing more than protective concealment to shield her heart. They would never replace *him*.

She padded along the cool deck plating of the main walkway, enjoying the comforting hum of the *Phantom* during ship's night. It was almost as if the ship were gently snoring along with its humanoid crewmembers. On the flight deck, she locked the door and settled back into the pilot's seat, resting her heels on the console on the spot Fitz had worn a little smooth.

When *Phantom* and her crew were awake, the pilot station was hers. She *owned* it, and neither she nor anyone else questioned that for a moment.

But in the quiet, with the lights set to sim-night dimness, touched gently by the distant stars watching her from the other side of the cockpit window, she could feel him out there somewhere in the galaxy.

She could smell his scent, feel his essence in the leather of the seat.

All her imagination, of course. He'd just had the seats re-upholstered, and she'd ordered them thoroughly cleaned after he came back from that damned space station covered in grease and dirt.

Imaginary or not, she rubbed her naked skin against the leather and felt a connection to him.

Within buried system menus, she activated a quantum-entangled comm link no one else on the ship knew about.

She looked out of the cockpit and stared a long while at the stars. One of them held him. She could summon an overlay to highlight the location of Eiylah-Bremah, if that were still his location, but she preferred not to know.

"I miss you." Her words were the lightest whisper on the edge of the comm's pickup threshold.

There was no reply, of course. She hadn't expected one. Even if he had heard, contact was too dangerous. Just the thought that he *might* be listening was enough for her. No doubt he had already re-cruited new allies, charmed new followers, and wrung the best out of his Chimera Company.

Laughing, she captured a static image of herself, blowing him a kiss as she lounged provocatively in his seat. It was an ill-disciplined waste of the limited q-bit capacity link, but that was the point—he liked his extravagant statements.

She rolled her eyes. *Human men!*

Besides, it would be good to remind him what he was missing.

"I miss you," she said once more. Louder.

She sat in silence waiting for a reply, as patient as the stars watching her through the cockpit.

When none came, she dozed off and dreamed of adventure.

* * * * *

Chapter Forty-Four: Vaylen-Zis

He blamed the humans.

Brilliantly creative, brave, stubborn, ignorant— there was something different about the way that infuriating species saw the universe. Vaylen-Zis sometimes wondered over a pipe and a ch'alla-soaked biscuit whether the humans who'd arrived long ago had come from another universe altogether. Something about them just didn't fit in the Perseus Arm.

He was proud to call himself an Ellondyte, but he admitted the best of the Federation was human. They were also the worst. Such as the WCD army waiting in ominous silence outside the city, just half a klick away from the barricade across Progress Avenue.

Kaylingen was a redoubt of decency in a seething swamp of WCDs.

Willfully cancerous dissenters.

The view through his blaster scope showed the rebel army was comprised of grim-faced civilians, bearing sporting rifles and low-powered blasters. There were heavier weapons too, perhaps looted during the breakout from A-10 a few days earlier. Some of the rebel soldiers might even be A-10 criminals, but all of them looked proud and determined. In fact, other than their crude Zone 40s sense of fashion and the Easterner burr to their accents that he couldn't hear at this distance but had no doubt was there, they weren't all that dif-

273

ferent from the brave citizens of Kaylingen standing with him at the barricade.

This army of dissenters didn't consider themselves cancerous at all.

And for that, Vaylen-Zis blamed the humans.

Most of these WCDs were human. He didn't think it was a coincidence.

Crazy humans.

"What are they waiting for?"

There was panic in the voice of the man beside him on the upper firing step. Vaylen-Zis dropped his scope and turned just in time to slap down a barrel being aimed at the army.

"Don't be a fool, Ignet!"

"I can't take it anymore." Ignet Jens was pleading. What did the idiot think Vaylen-Zis could do?

"You'll have to embrace the suck. That's what the Militia likes to say, except the Militia are nowhere to be seen, which is why we have to stand firm in their place. We includes *you*, Ignet. And that means no firing at the enemy until they close. There's over two thousand out there. There's sixty-six of us. If we're to die, we must make every shot count."

"I'm not a soldier," Ignet wailed. "I see someone threatening me, I don't wait to discuss tactics. I shoot them dead. And to see that army of WCDs out there. It's…" Vaylen-Zis sighed with relief when Ignet allowed one of the women from the lower firing step to safely take his rifle, but Ignet wasn't finished. He shuddered with horror. "To see those WCDs…to merely look at them is a sight crime."

"So, what are you saying, Harvey?" Vaylen-Zis asked angrily. "If I could give you a button to press that would agonizingly kill every single one of them and their families, would you press it?"

"In a heartbeat. Sure, I'd feel sorry for the families, but only because I'm a soft-hearted person. We have to harden ourselves toward those who don't deserve our tolerance." Ignet gave him a suspicious look. "Why? Wouldn't you kill them all if you could?"

"If it came to a fight, I suppose so."

"Waiting for a fight makes no sense," said Ignet. The steel was back in his soul, and he was looking around for his rifle. "We need to kill those WCDs first. They're not people. They're something less. *Sub*-people."

"Funny thing," muttered Vaylen-Zis. "I reckon they think the exact same of us."

"What's that?"

"Nothing."

Damned Militia. Where the hell are they? Situation's going to flash into disaster any moment.

Ignoring the human glaring at him, Vaylen-Zis raised his hands high and stood on tiptoe so he was clearly visible to the WCD fighters.

"I'm not surrendering," he announced in a loud voice. "I'm going to ask them what they're doing."

"I told you," shouted Ignet, "they're sub-people. You can't reason with them."

That won grunts of approval, so Vaylen-Zis replied, "The longer I stall them, the more time we buy for reinforcements to arrive."

"Reinforcements?"

"Is the Militia coming?"

276 | TIM C. TAYLOR

"I heard the Legion was setting up kill zones to wipe the WCD stain from the galaxy."

Vaylen-Zis left the rumors flying and clambered over the barricade and down the far side.

Conscious that he had the starring role in two thousand sight pictures, he lifted his hands and strode toward the WCD army. The blue band around his right arm felt more like a target with every step.

He closed about half the distance before stopping and yelling at the invaders. "I ain't surrendering. I just want to know what you're doing there. I ask as the elected leader of this citizen armed response team. The people's militia."

"We're the Revolutionary Forces of Reconciliation," came a shouted reply. "It's we who are the true people's army."

"People's army? That's the Militia." Vaylen-Zis couldn't help shrugging, and he added in a quieter voice, "Wherever the hell they are."

"The Militia and the Amilxi people forever," sneered the WCD spokesperson. Vaylen-Zis couldn't see who he was communicating with. "The corrupt Militia has bargained with In'Nalla to suppress disorder in return for the riches of the asteroid mine—wealth that rightfully belongs to us all. The Militia is not the people's army. They're mercenaries. Oppressors. We are the true people's army."

"Then why don't you attack?" asked Vaylen-Zis, immediately cursing himself for saying something so stupid a human could have said it. "We *will* fight. You will kill us, but there are barricades across all the main approaches, and you will have to go over our dead bodies to take this city, because we *will* stand up to you."

"What's your name?"

He hesitated. The WCDs could twist the most innocent of words into their perverted narratives, but he couldn't see the harm in telling them his name. "I ain't ashamed of my own name. I'm Vaylen-Zis."

"Well met, Vaylen-Zis. Tell us, what is it you do for a living?"

"I'm a butcher. Got a shop just off Restitution Plaza."

"Then I say to you, Vaylen-Zis, the butcher, this city needs people like you. I hope you survive this day. And to answer your question, we hope we won't need to fight, but if the city does not yield to us willingly, we will seize it by force."

"That saddens my old heart, because we will not yield, and many must die today."

"Have hope, butcher. This day will be long, and it has barely begun. Now, return to your friends."

Vaylen-Zis took a last look at the enemy and then turned back to the barricade.

Where the hell was the Militia?

* * * * *

Chapter Forty-Five: Major Lyssin

"Where the fuck are your people?" demanded In'Nalla. "There's an army outside my city. Where are your air assets? Why don't you bomb them into atoms?"

Major Lyssin silently cursed the woman fuming on his wrist slate.

This, he knew, was the end of a good posting. He'd be lucky to survive the day.

"Why don't you answer, damn you? Is this mutiny, Lyssin? Where is the Militia?"

Lyssin ground his jaw, searching for the right words.

The real answer was that the system marshal, safe in her asteroid belt command post, had redeployed assets to the north to defend against what even the most incompetent of trainees would realize was a feint attack. It was a half-baked military deception that wouldn't fool a semi-trained baboon. Had it fooled the marshal, though? Lyssin thought it just as likely that she'd been bribed or had decided it was time for a regime change.

Lyssin guessed the latter. This smelled of politics and bribery. Somebody had already decided what the fate of the city and its regime would be.

"Revered Leader, I regret that the sector marshal called away our air assets and rapid deployment battalions in error. I have recalled them."

It was a lie, of course. He'd done no such thing.

"Idiots! How long?"

"About an hour," he told her. "In the interim, I'm organizing a zonal defense with the assets I have. We just have to hold on until reinforcements arrive."

"Make sure you do. But your contemptible handful of troopers won't decide the city's fate. I will go ahead with my planned speech from Execution Square, but now it will be a rallying cry to call the people to the barricades. Make sure I am protected, Lyssin."

"Of course, ma'am."

Her face vanished as she cut the connection.

"Shit!"

What to do…what to do…what the hell could he do?

To start with, he took deep breaths and calmed down. It was a fearsome ordeal to be the target of In'Nalla's temper, but the old bitch wasn't his mistress. That was the sector marshal, and her last words to him this morning had been, "Protect the city."

He had five understrength companies, and they were *not* contemptible. It was time to remind the galaxy that the Militia could be more than ceremonial prison guards and do more than carry out reprisals for rebel atrocities. When pressed into service, they could be proper soldiers too.

* * * * *

Chapter Forty-Six: General Gzeiter

For once, Gzeiter agreed with the Trucker. Their combined assault force would first attempt to scare away the civilians manning the barricade across the Western Approach before blasting through to seize the objectives in the city center. After all, their aim was to win over the citizens of Kaylingen to the PHPA cause, not to slaughter them.

All the approaches into the city were blocked in some way, but none with any strength Gzeiter could see. Most of the armed citizen bands were facing Commander Slinh's Reserve Brigade on the far side of the city. Gzeiter's plan had been to bypass the main barricades and infiltrate the city across a wide zone, but the Trucker had argued they needed to move fast, hard and...*dramatically*.

The man had emphasized his last point with a curling smoke ring. Now that Gzeiter had seen the mysterious RevRec leader up close, he wondered whether, for him, this was all about the drama. The fate of the world could change today, but to the Trucker, it was just a performance.

"Ready on your order, sir," reported his artillery commander, Ipstein, through his earpiece.

"Fire at will, Lieutenant."

"Shots away," Ipstein reported a few seconds later. The artillery battery only boasted three light pieces designed to be carried on dropboats plus a couple of missile launchers, but Gzeiter's ears rang with the battery's roar.

Here, to the west of the city, the terrain was dominated by the broad Pa-Hukshen River, which curved along the valley floor and flowed through the center of Kaylingen.

The area was littered with boatsheds, jetties, cafés, and other facilities for enjoying the gently flowing Pa-Hukshen. After scaring off the civilians with an advance force, the combined RevRec strike company and Gzeiter's direct command had quietly deployed behind this concealment.

A series of *crumps* assailed the barricade.

The first salvo fired were crowd dispersion rounds. Thick clouds comprised of choking gas and skin irritants roiled out when the flash bangs inside burst. To drive home the point, one of Gzeiter's two missile launchers fired from the upper veranda of the café from which he was watching events. A standard explosive warhead hit a spot painted twenty feet in front of the barricade, sending up a plume of dust and road surface fragments through the gas clouds and leaving a deep crater in the road.

"Loading HELBeR," reported the artillery commander.

High Explosive Limited Blast Radius. If any brave fools still held the barricade, they would be churned to mincemeat when those HELBeRs hit.

"They're fleeing," said Trucker.

Gzeiter looked. The enhanced view through his binocs showed the armbanded rabble jumping off the heap of doors, vehicles, planters, and other crap that happened to have been within reach. Its defenders were now desperate to get away.

"Take that barricade down, Ipstein."

"Consider it done, General."

As the next salvo arced through the air, the mountainsides echoing with its firing, the RevRec leader began removing his clothing.

Behind him, Corporal Woods edged his hand toward his sidearm, but Trucker pretended not to notice as he stepped out of his stained coveralls like an insect bursting free of its cocoon.

Under the coveralls, Trucker wore a chic brown smuggler jacket and an elaborate thigh holster that held an exotic hand blaster.

"The game is on," said the Trucker, extending his hand to Gzeiter.

Gzeiter looked at the man's dirty hand dubiously, then at his face. Trucker seemed to have shed a couple of decades along with his coveralls. He was surprisingly young.

Trucker took off his shades and stashed them in a jacket pocket.

Gzeiter recoiled at the sight. Those eyes! Trucker was a damned mutant!

"You're…"

"The hero who's gonna save your ass, General? Or were you going to say something else? Tell me, does the PHPA have a policy of discriminating against my kind?"

"No, of course not." Gzeiter shook hands.

"To victory," said Trucker.

"Indeed."

"By nightfall, the city and Eiylah-Bremah will be ours."

"To our victory," Gzeiter repeated, but he wasn't anticipating a *joint* victory. Power would fall to the Pan-Human Progressive Alliance alone. RevRec would be decimated, and Trucker's lilac eyes would be staring lifelessly out of his corpse.

Trucker's two captured GAC-19s came out from cover, and Gzeiter narrowed his focus to the here and now.

The attack was on.

* * * * *

Chapter Forty-Seven:
Major Lyssin

"Ren Kay, update!"

"No change," the lieutenant reported. "The main rebel army remains in position to the east of the city, awaiting orders. I'm not detecting the tension I would expect if they were planning to attack imminently."

"The longer they wait, the happier I'll be," said Lyssin. "Wait long enough, and they'll be chewed up when the flying dollies come back here and do their job. There's nothing more you can do there. Return to the city and rejoin my command squad."

"Roger that."

"And fast. The fighting's already started. Out."

Lyssin wished he hadn't sent Ren Kay to scout the rebel forces. He would have been more useful here, helping put backbone in the defense force he'd scraped together. But regrets were for after the battle.

For now, he had to do the best he could with the hand he'd been dealt.

As much as it pained him to risk Militia personnel and equipment for In'Nalla's defense, the key to the city was Execution Square, and the pallid old hag was playing demagogue there this afternoon.

Lyssin keyed the commander of his armor column, which consisted of two tanks and a squad of dependable infantry. It wasn't much, but he hadn't been able to form up his troops before the enemy made their move, and that was all he could get to Execution Square in time. Just five more minutes, and his mobile strike force would have been ready to counterattack any advance from the enemy.

"Lieutenant Atiff."

"Sir."

"Advance on Execution Square. Defend it to the last trooper."

"Roger that." Outside the window of the school building he'd commandeered as a command post, Lyssin heard the sounds of tank engines revving up. "Any rebels get in my way, they'll be in for a big surprise."

* * * * *

Chapter Forty-Eight:
Yat Darant

The flying machine juddered as its quad blasters spat heavy bolts from its nose. It was loud, but what made Darant's ears bleed were the pilot's whoops of delight.

"I'd tell you to calm down," he told Lily, "but I'll need my breath to scream when you crash."

They were in a GAC-19a, the red crosses of the REEDs still visible under its coat of forest green paint. Unlike the hover fliers they'd seen at Krunacao, this variant had a rear-facing gun, which meant Darant was watching Fitz's RevReccers and the Panhandlers move up to assault and not whatever Lily was flying them into.

It was no use. He couldn't resist. Darant twisted around for a look.

The GAC was traveling slowly. Although flying parallel to the ground, its nose was pitched down, unleashing red bolts of energy that screamed into a barricade already mostly wrecked by the artillery.

Flames and debris erupted under the devastating pounding.

A little higher and to their right, Bronze was shooting the shit out of the obstacle from the other GAC. From the rear seat, Vetch grinned at Darant and gave him a thumbs up.

Darant stared at Vetch dumbly. He would have given anything to swap seats with the hairy bastard. He didn't trust that Bronze character, but he seemed to know how to do pretty much anything. Flying a GAC-19 was no exception.

Suddenly, his stomach backflipped, and their craft dove through the gap they'd blasted into the mound of smoldering debris. They were so low, their armored belly scraped sparks off the road.

"Holy shit, Lil'! That was totally unnecessary."

"I know!" she screamed excitedly.

"For fuck's sake! Please, Lil'. The last time you flew one of these, you crashed."

"Bite my ass."

The flier gained ten feet of altitude. "Not a chance. There isn't enough beer in the galaxy to wash away the foul taste. I'll get Hubert to bite you for me, assuming he's survived Enthree's tender care."

Darant's screen showed nominal damage on the belly armor as a few bullets pinged their underside. He remembered he had an auto-cannon and was supposed to be shooting at people.

By the time he'd reset his screen to targeting mode, the GAC had left the remains of the barricade behind and was following a curve in the road surrounded by four-story stone buildings.

"Do you think this crazy scheme will work?" he asked. "I mean, Fitz sounded convincing, but I don't like the trust we're placing in that jack you tortured."

"Who cares?" Lily replied. "I got to fly again."

"Asshole."

"You're just jealous. When this is done, you can sit up front on my lap, and I'll teach you."

"I'd rather sit on Bronze's lap," Darant replied, but his retort died before he could think of a good punchline because the walls looking down on them as they flew into the heart of the city were making him itch. Kaylingen didn't have proper military fortifications at the best of times, and the rapid response unit based just outside had been led away by a false trail.

Even so, it wouldn't take much to swat them out of the air.

Despite the improved upper armor of the GAC-19a variant, autocannons on rooftops or SAM pods deployed at major crossroads could shred them.

It really wouldn't take much.

Could they really make it to their target so easily?

"Armor ahead!" said Bronze in Darant's earpiece. "With squad level infantry support."

"Ahh shit!" Lily shouted.

Darant wanted to turn and look, but he kept quiet and focused on his gun's targeting display.

"Two light hover tanks," Bronze said calmly. "Aim at the weak rear armor over the powerplant vents. You'll see it easier in infrared. Follow me."

Their GAC wiggled its butt as Lily adjusted position. Then the horizontal thrusters growled as the craft picked up speed.

He could hear Bronze fire and then their GAC shuddered as Lily joined in.

There was a sudden screaming pulse from the gravitics, and their craft jumped up.

A tank round shot through the air just below them.

The flier passed the tanks. Darant noted they were light reconnaissance models pressed into duty they weren't suited for. One tank was on fire, and its crew was bailing out. The other looked badly scratched and scorched, but it was still very much in the fight. It was traversing its turret and elevating its main gun, expecting Lily to fly overhead.

She didn't.

Lily brought the GAC's nose up.

And *kept* lifting it. They were ascending vertically, engines screaming to the accompaniment of blaster fire lashing them from the troopers on the ground.

"Five Hells, Lily!" he said under his breath.

Darant wasn't built for this. It felt like his internal organs were shifting into unnatural positions, but he understood what Lil' was doing.

"Make it quick!" she yelled.

The blocky rectangle of the tank took center stage on Darant's targeting screen, surrounded by a score of shadowy humanoids with bright heat signatures on their chests.

Brightest, by far, was a strip behind the tank's turret—the exhaust vent.

"Quick! I can't hold it much longer," screamed Lily.

Darant tapped his screen to lock the targeting on the vent. Then he closed both firing grips and unleased a long burst at the tank at a full 3,000 rounds per minute cyclic rate.

It was just as well he'd locked the targeting system, because the GAC bucked and writhed, hovering with its nose up in the air and twerking its ass at the tanks and support troopers on the ground. Whether it was the recoil, the gravitic craft reaching its limit, the small arms fire hitting their rear, or the sheer weight of the heavy rounds Darant was throwing off, it was too much for the hover flier.

The engines cut out, and the GAC tipped over backward.

For a long moment, it seemed to hang there, Darant looking down out of the top of his cockpit at the troopers who were looking up in astonishment.

Lily screamed.

So did the uniformed Militia troopers.

Darant didn't. He was too terrified.

They fell, but the lateral engines and gravitics cut back in, pulsing in a carefully calculated sequence that caused them to loop the loop. They were accelerating away in level flight through a fan of flame when the tank Darant had shot up finally decided to blow up.

"You beauty," Darant said in wonder. "Neat flying, Lil'."

"It wasn't me," Lily replied in an unusually quiet voice. "Some kind of automatic anti-stall. I had no idea we had one."

Darant fired over the receding troopers to persuade them to keep their heads down. Firing at Militia troopers still didn't feel right. He kept his bursts short because he'd expended half his ammo taking out the tank.

He'd need every round soon; this was just a sideshow.

The real business was waiting for them up ahead in Execution Square.

* * * * *

Chapter Forty-Nine:
Revered Leader In'Nalla

"We can't let the willfully cancerous dissenters destroy what we have built here."

The crowd filling Execution Square booed the WCDs.

In'Nalla cocked an ear toward the crowd through the bullet-proof, transparent blast shield protecting the stage. "I can't hear you," she mouthed.

The crowd went wild, screaming their hatred of WCDs.

In'Nalla gestured at them to calm.

"To the east of our great city awaits an army. Army? Hah! More like the discharge from a blocked sewer. In their ranks are communists, perverts, fascists—the filth of our world united in their intolerance of everyone who does not yield to their perverted ideologies."

She gave the throng a moment to cheer and howl their anger before pressing on. "These *people*—though I don't believe they deserve to be called people, don't you agree?—are united in their hatred. Hatred of us." She picked out a screaming human woman in the front row and pointed her out. "Of *you*."

After letting the camera team fill the big screen with the woman's face for a few seconds, In'Nalla pointed out other individuals, rapid fire. "They hate you. And you. And you." She shrugged. "I don't know. Maybe they're right? Do you think we should invite the WCDs in?"

Execution Square went absolutely wild.

Relayed through speakers on her side of the blast shield, the sound was an incoherent white noise, but it was music to In'Nalla's ears, because it was filled with the passion she demanded of these people. *Her* people.

The clamor soon took the form of a chant that echoed off the high walls surrounding the square.

"Kill the WCDs."

"Kill the WCDs."

She raised her arms high in the air, her face wild with excitement. The chant grew in intensity.

From stage left, Sanderson marched over to her. The new bodyguard had been waving at her with increasing urgency for over a minute.

She put one hand out to ward him off, but he would not be deterred.

So, she cut the mic. "Not now," she yelled at the stupid man. "I need this moment. Can't you hear their passion?"

"Kill the WCDs!"

"Kill the WCDs!"

"An attack is imminent," he said. "They're coming for you."

"An attack? Sanderson, look at them. Four thousand people literally screaming to kill the enemy. Half of them are armed, maybe more. They're not like the scraps Major Lyssin allocated me. They're an army. *My* army."

"Ma'am, with all due respect, I've served in a real army. What you see here is an armed rabble. Highly motivated. Dangerous and unpredictable. And no match for an army with proper training, discipline, and real machinery of war."

"Machinery of war." She guffawed. "Such as what? More of those fantasy mechs?"

He pointed at one of the approach roads. "Such as that, ma'am." Two green-painted needle craft flew in from the approach road and circled the square.

Several brave souls from the crowd below shot at them, flashes blooming on the underside of the fliers as bolts hit home and bullets ricocheted away.

The fliers ignored the attacks and calmly blew away the rooftop positions where Lyssin sometimes deployed sharpshooters.

"Come with me, ma'am," urged Sanderson.

He lunged at her and tried to grab her around the waist, but she ordered him to stop with such a force of command that he hesitated. She glanced backstage where six worried Militia troopers looked on. They were all Lyssin had managed to provide her.

"No, Sanderson," she said. "Major Lyssin promised me tanks. Instead, I have six nervous wrecks and you. If these aircraft want to kill us, there's nothing we can do."

The fliers descended and blasted away one side of the stage, then hovered like oversized dragonflies with nose-mounted heavy blasters.

Their fire, she noted, was meticulous. No one was injured, and the blast screen remained intact. In fact, the only injuries had come from ricochets and rounds fired by the crowd that fell back into the square.

"Ma'am!" Sanderson was about to try to grab her again despite her Militia guards pointing their blasters at him.

"Oh, for pity's sake, stand down, Sanderson. The rebels aren't shooting at people, which means they're here to play politics. Let them. Politics is a game I play to win."

The green fliers descended below the blast screen, hovering a few feet above the stage.

"Surrender!" ordered a woman through an external speaker.

In'Nalla could see her through the cockpit of the nearest flier. She shuddered at the sight of the woman's hideously disfigured face.

Lyssin's troopers ran, the rebels content to let them go.

Out beyond the blast shield, some of her bravest citizens were trying to clamber over the barrier to protect her.

She let them come while she assessed her opponents' next move.

The rear cockpits hissed open, and two rebels jumped down onto the stage.

One was a bear of a man wearing electro-dispersion chainmail and carrying an extra-large Militia war hammer. The other, an evil-looking human armed with a large blaster with twin rails below the barrel, looked more like a conventional killer.

The beardless one shot Sanderson with an electro-dart by the look of it.

Her big bodyguard went down and twitched on the stage.

Pathetic.

In'Nalla resisted the urge to kick the useless fool. If Sanderson had gone down so easily, he could never have been much good.

"Well, gentlemen, what do you want?"

"Your resignation," said the man who'd shot Sanderson.

She switched the microphone back on. "I don't give in to demands from terrorists, or mercenaries, or whatever the hell class of scum you call yourself."

"We're not demanding anything," said the bear. It was difficult to be sure with all the bejeweled facial hair, but the man seemed to be grinning. He pointed at the crowd with the shaft of his hammer. "We don't need to. *They* will."

Now it was her turn to grin in triumph. "My people," she said into the microphone. "My brave and loyal people. I temporarily surrender myself to these killers. I will do what I can to prevent bloodshed. Please, get down from the blast shield. But do not go home. Stay here. Protect the approaches to the square. Occupy and fortify the buildings here. And above all, trust me. In'Nalla is your future."

* * * * *

Chapter Fifty:
Vol Zavage

"That filthy beast comes near my gear again, and I'll pull the plug on this op, revolution or not."

Enthree looked up from her workstation and tilted her head toward the Slern. "Do you refer to the basten goat? I made a pledge to care for him."

Zavage's kesah-kihisia was pummelled by the Slern's indignation. Meanwhile, Enthree oozed amusement—she knew damn well who the rebel hacker had been talking about.

Enthree, he was coming to realize, had many unexpected talents. Sarcasm was one of the least alarming.

"Breaker," said Zavage, "the bug's messing with your head...uh..." Zavage wasn't sure if referring to a Slern's 'head' was offensive. Too bad. Everything was offensive on this world. "I mean, messing with your *mind*. Hubert knows he's been bad."

"*Hubert?* Pah!" Breaker extended some flesh out of its shell to form a head which it promptly shook at Enthree and Zavage. "You two have been around humans too much. I can smell them on you. It's just a damned animal, you idiots. And it was nibbling my gold-sheathed, duranium-enriched core data cables. My *babies*, guys. Please, have some respect."

Fighting to keep from laughing like a human, Zavage humbly bowed his head to the little hacker.

300 | TIM C. TAYLOR

Breaker81, the Slern called itself. From its tech-filled, musty basement in one of Kaylingen's northern suburbs, the three of them were going to bring In'Nalla down.

Zavage had never encountered the race before. In appearance, Breaker81 was a cross between a scaly lizard and a mollusk, with pseudopods emerging from beneath its shell to perform functions of manipulation, locomotion, speech and eating. Its shell was painted to resemble stained wood with a cream edge in a pattern Breaker81 called Les Paul Standard, which it claimed was an ancient human cultural reference.

"Nah, you're okay, guys," said Breaker in perfect Standard. He extended a pseudopod toward Enthree. "I can forgive anything for a chance to work with *her*. You're a goddamned genius, sister. And a *moneyed* genius too. Say, the revolution'll be over by tonight. Have you any plans for after?"

"Let's concentrate on making sure the revolution turns the right way," Zavage admonished them.

Breaker had hit on a helluva topic, though. It wasn't hitting on Enthree so much as being wowed by both her hacking skills and the funds she could access to bribe the system marshal to ensure the Militia had someplace else to be today. That had taken serious money. It certainly wasn't her Militia pay.

Who was Enthree really?

"It's spreading," yelled Breaker. "Ye gods! She's done it!"

Zavage hurried over to Breaker's work pod. Even Hubert pricked up his ears in interest. The Slern said it thought better inside its shell and had stuffed most of its body inside the wood-effect carapace. Then it had extruded a single, fat pseudopod from which it had extended a half dozen fingers and stalks that each held two eyes.

Its displays showed the spread of the incriminating video footage Bronze had acquired from an insider. They had uploaded the recording to EB-Link in such a way that multiple influential groups were now sharing it like crazy, each believing it was one of their own members who had uncovered the footage they were obliged to make public.

Within a minute, even the media conglomerates were following suit.

"You're right," said Zavage. "We've done it. In'Nalla's finished."

* * * * *

Chapter Fifty-One:
Revered Leader In'Nalla

In Execution Square, the crowd stood mesmerized by the video footage on the big screen as it looped once more.

"I'm betrayed by trans-cos who are greedy and petty and led by utterly short-sighted assholes," said In'Nalla, her face red and angry. "It would be better if we had fewer companies, and they were steered by a central authority."

The citizens studiously avoided eye contact with each other, shifting their attention back and forth from the screen to their wrist slates as they scoured EB-Link, searching for someone to tell them how to interpret this.

They needed their reality defined for them.

Was the Revered Leader a traitor? A Jacobin socialist? Because that was wrong-think, wasn't it?

Or was she a victim of false news?

The battle for the truth raged on EB-Link, but it was a battle she'd always won. She *owned* reality on this world. As the REEDs liked to put it, if the Revered Leader told you two plus two equaled five, to think of any other possibility was a thought crime.

And to betray the Revered Leader was the biggest thought crime of all.

It had to have been Asher who'd taken that footage. How could she possibly have dared?

In'Nalla didn't give a shit about *why* Asher had betrayed her. It was all damage limitation now. That and…maybe she could turn this betrayal to her advantage.

First things first. Asher needed to pay. In'Nalla was about to order her sorry carcass dragged in and her secrets tortured out of her when she stopped. It was that damned Blayde Asher she would normally order to fix this sort of mess.

Damn her!

Slowly, ever so slowly, In'Nalla activated the comm link in her slate without getting more than a frown out of the killer who'd stunned Sanderson.

She tried contacting her information shapers. The first three didn't respond; they were off grid altogether. In'Nalla's heart beat faster…this had never happened before.

So, when the link to Sonep Mediaforce established, and the CEO answered, a wave of relief hit her.

"Jennling? Why are you the only media controller who's answering my calls?"

"Because, Revered Leader," said Jennling Sonep, worry so heavy in his voice that she could picture his fat hands sweating, "the others have been seized by the rebel army."

"Then you must work fast while you still can. Here's what I need you to do…"

* * * * *

Chapter Fifty-Two: General Gzeiter

"Excellent work, my friend," said Gzeiter heartedly, extending a hand to the Trucker.

The mutant transferred his cigar to his mouth so he could pump Gzeiter's hand vigorously. "Today, we will win a famous victory," he said out the side of his mouth.

His media team took images at the steps of the captured Forefront Building to show the Federation what could be achieved if the forces of resistance allied with the PHPA, even if your top military commander looked like a janitor playing dress up in a smuggler costume.

Gzeiter smiled at his ally. That's right, you dumbass fraggwort. Tell yourself you've won a great victory. Next time I see you, you'll be dead.

The combined PHPA forces and RevRec strike column had raced through the streets, never letting the civilian rabble stand firm, and pushed on to take the headquarters of the three main media-shaping corporations, ending here at the biggest of them all, Forefront Media.

They had expected a tough fight against the Militia, but other than a few brief firefights where the two sides had stumbled across each other, there had been nothing.

Casualties had been minimal.

But Gzeiter's reconnaissance teams informed him that a counter-attack was on the way.

Gzeiter took a last look at the broad street. RevRec troops were trying to fortify the approaches, as they would also be doing at the other two buildings they'd seized. They were doing a good job of it too, which was just as well as he needed them to take a heavy toll on the incoming Militia force, while suffering devastating casualties themselves.

Of more immediate importance, RevRec technicians had reconnected the Forefront Building with EB-Link. It was Gzeiter who controlled the message now. He had the best outfit of media shapers to do his bidding. At gunpoint.

And when he'd turned the population against both In'Nalla and RevRec, Gzeiter would emerge to seize the Senate Building and announce himself interim president of Eiylah-Bremah, until such time as properly constituted elections could be held.

"Good luck." He gave the Trucker a respectful nod. "I'll see you soon."

The moment he walked up the stone steps and through the reinforced bronze doors, he ordered them shut.

"I want armor plating welded across all entry points," he ordered his command team waiting for him in the marbled foyer. "All but one of our force shields are to be deployed in staggered formation behind the main entrance. The last shield is to protect the roof entrance. Mobile suppression teams, get ready for an attack coming through the walls. Indirect fire, snipers, and anti-air to the roof. Come on, people, we've planned for this. Now make it happen!"

As his team rushed to implement the plan, he keyed his comms to his propaganda and subversion commander. "Krendell, report."

"Early days, General," she replied in that smug way of hers that sounded as if she were rubbing her hands in glee. "We've recruited twenty-eight technician volunteers from the staff here, and they do appear to have the skills we need to win the information war."

"Twenty-eight? The plan called for thirty."

"Yes, sir. We press ganged thirty, but two of them contributed by sacrificing their lives to encourage the others."

Gzeiter felt a chill run up his spine. Captain Krendell studied the inner workings of the human mind—and those of most of the main Federation races—like a botanist dissecting rare plants. She understood how all the moving parts worked and how to manipulate them, but she showed no signs of possessing any human emotions herself, despite her personnel file insisting Krendell was the same species as Gzeiter.

"Very good," he said. "I'll be with you in three mikes. Gzeiter out."

* * * * *

Chapter Fifty-Three: Tavistock Fitzwilliam

From behind the half-assed cover of a few overturned cars, Fitz was watching the Panhandlers set up shop on the roof of the Forefront Building, when the news he was expecting came in.

"Trucker, Sentinel-2. Eyes on Militia column. Company sized. Light armed infantry, and we count four jury-rigged gun trucks with heavy blasters."

"This is Sentinel-4. We've eyes on another infantry column. Just coming into view. Can't tell numbers yet."

"Thank you," said Fitz. "All Sentinel callsigns, this is Trucker. Do not engage. Keep to the shadows and stand by."

Fitz keyed a second comm system, distinct from the RevRec one. "Are we winning yet?"

"We have the old witch under arrest," Lily reported, "but I don't like the crowd out there. It's a mob seething with anger. It's like a caged beast, unpredictable and dangerous."

"EB-Link is declaring a legally binding confidence vote in In'Nalla," said Zavage. "It's calling it the Court of Public Opinion. It's been made to look spontaneous, but it's actually been set up by Sonep Mediaforce who, we assume, are in In'Nalla's pocket."

"Court of Public Opinion?" Fitz queried. "What the hell does that mean?"

"I don't know," said Zavage. "We'll get back to you."

310 | TIM C. TAYLOR

"Make sure you do. I don't like the sound of it. We are redeploying early to the Horne Lane Tram Station just off Execution Square. Estimate ten mikes to get there. If you need me, I'll be at the station café, enjoying an iced tea."

"What do we do?" asked Lily. "Wait to be brought down by the mob?"

"Lily, hang tight. Strategic victory conditions for you are to let Sybutu take In'Nalla away and control her. If the situation gets too hot for you, evac and meet us at the station."

Fitz heard the rumble of engines approaching from the north and, a little quieter, the east.

"We're still on course for victory. Stay cool everyone. Fitz out." He rekeyed the RevRec channel. "All call signs. Beat feet. Avoid contact and reform at Horne Lane. Last one there buys the drinks."

Fitz and the RevRec forces abandoned the street, heading south. The Panhandlers watched them go but weren't under orders to fire on their allies who'd fought side by side with them minutes earlier.

Once they were safely out of the fire zone, Fitz stopped and sighed happily.

Didn't think we'd out double cross you, didja Gzeiter?

A few moments' later, he heard the first gunfire exchanged between the Militia and the Panhandlers.

"General Gzeiter meet Major Lyssin. Lyssin meet Gzeiter. You deserve each other."

"Trucker," called one of his RevRec aides, "it's not safe. We can't afford to get cut off."

"And I can't afford the drinks bill if we get there last. Come on, Lieutenant. Move it!"

* * * * *

Chapter Fifty-Four:
Revered Leader In'Nalla

The optics were perfect.

The two hover fliers sat there in the air, a brutal occupation force with their powerful guns sweeping the stage, itching to be freed and pour death onto the brave innocents who would not yield.

The two who had dismounted—the Viking and the killer—glanced nervously at the crowd and looked more uncomfortable with every passing second. Her bodyguard had come to and interposed himself between the two rebel would-be assassins and his ward.

Never mind that, for a team of ruthless assassins, the rebels were surprisingly eager not to hurt anyone. Never mind, too, that Sanderson, who was supposed to protect her with his life, had lasted scant seconds before being shocked unconscious. He was performing a valuable service for her now. He was demonstrating to the crowd that, despite In'Nalla carrying herself with more dignity than any of the other players on the stage, she nonetheless required protection from her opponents' crude physical threats.

And where Sanderson led, the crowd might follow.

When the big screens around the square had been hacked to loop through her unfortunate comments that seemed to reveal her as a dread Jacobin, the crowd had been stunned into silence before shifting their attention to EB-Link's group mind. Now, they were beginning to harden their opinions. Angry shouting matches were breaking out. There were several attempts to chant her name, though they quickly petered out.

Revving engines announced a new player in this act, one that would swing it decisively toward In'Nalla.

A fat-wheeled armored vehicle tried to enter from Procession Street, but the angry crowd wouldn't allow it to.

It wasn't a rebel fighting vehicle, it was the danger zone mobile news reporting studio from Sonep News, and it was going to be her key to victory in this coup attempt.

"Let it through," she told the crowd. "They're press corps. Let them through." She sneered, marveling at how the inept rebels had allowed her continued access to the mic. Quickly, she transformed the sneer into a smile, easing back into the innocent victim role she was playing.

The rebels appeared to realize their mistake. The big one with the war hammer hustled her away from the mic. She exaggerated his intervention, half falling as if she had been shoved, hard. The rebel spoke through the PA system. "You, in the armored car. No sudden moves. If you attempt to cross the blast shield, we will destroy you."

This time, In'Nalla couldn't help herself. She sneered openly. With her foes doing everything in their power to hand her victory in the battle of public perception, anyone would have gloated.

The armored wagon edged into the square and progressed inch by inch toward the stage. A hush came over the crowd when the screens blanked. Unseen, a cyber battle raged for their control. The clash was won by Sonep Media from their armored news wagon.

Seconds later, the screens came alive again with simple text.

Court of Public Opinion: Official Judgement

Do you stand with In'Nalla?

(Yes / No)

Time to decision: 58:24

As the clock ticked down, a graphic appeared below the question EB-Link was posing to its netizens.

Currently, she was losing the confidence vote with a difference of -10 percent.

But with any luck, her media forces would be rallying forces.

-8 percent.

-7.

The Court of Public Opinion was an institution that was so well entrenched by the time In'Nalla took power, she hadn't dared to interfere. She was glad now.

-6 percent.

She would win this. And her victory would be an entirely legitimate mandate. The revolution had risked all and moved too soon.

Or had it?

The balance stuck at -6 percent.

The Viking was still pulling his beard, but his friend, the killer, leered at her.

"Sanderson," she said softly, "I need to get inside the news car."

"Just try it," said the killer, aiming his blaster at her.

Sanderson sprang into action, grabbing the blaster's barrel and pushing it away.

The killer launched a rib-cracking kick at her bodyguard that threw him off and sent him rolling across the stage.

"Should have killed the bitch from the start," said the rebel, aiming at her once more and squeezing the trigger.

The final fractions of a second passed by slowly for In'Nalla, as if to punish her by drawing out the realization that it was she who had miscalculated in the end. So close. But she would die, killed by a nobody firing a generic blaster rifle.

The crowd screamed.

Which was a strange thing to be hearing when she should be dead.

She finally noticed the flexible disc Sanderson had placed over the weapon's barrel. The blaster's status lights had gone out, and the rebel was working the trigger uselessly on his dead piece of hardware.

Sanderson, meanwhile, had re-entered the fray. He had two oversized handguns aimed at the rebels on the stage.

The Viking lifted his war hammer.

"Easy, Apeman," warned Sanderson. "We're just going inside the car. Your GACs can blast us if they want to."

By 'GACs', In'Nalla assumed Sanderson was referring to the two aircraft who'd reoriented to point their nose cannons directly at him…and her standing behind him.

There was nothing she could do about them, so she unlatched a segment of the blast shield and walked through to the cheers of the crowd.

"Let me in the car," she said, and the crowd obeyed, lifting her down and allowing passage for her and her protector, Sanderson.

The crowd, she hoped, would be a better form of cover than the armor plating of the news car. If the aircraft were to attack, they would have to kill civilians before getting to her, and she didn't think they would do that. Meanwhile, from the cover of the car, she could marshal her forces to win the cyber battle for the Court of Public Opinion.

The news wagon's rear hatch opened for them. It was the only apparent means of entry. Three humans and a Zhoogene were working inside, surrounded by holographic screens. She guessed the Gliesan who'd opened the hatch was also the driver because she could see through the empty cab.

"Is the interior shielded from outside surveillance?"

"Yes, ma'am," replied the Zhoogene woman who ceased her typing and swiveled her chair around to face her elected leader. "It's one-directional too. Our privacy is locked down so tightly, we're practically in our own pocket universe, yet our signals can still get out."

"Perfect," said In'Nalla. "Leave us. Move!"

"But…" started the Zhoogene, who swiveled her chair again to face her colleagues. They were equally perplexed.

Sanderson moved in and hauled the Gliesan out.

"The Revered Leader gave you an order," he bellowed, advancing on the Zhoogene. "She thanks you for your valuable assistance—" he grabbed her by the shoulders, "—and asks that you get the fuck out of the wagon!"

The Sonep staff scrambled to get away from the growling bodyguard who shut the hatch behind them with a solid clang and a hiss of pressure seals.

As soon as they were sealed in, In'Nalla contacted Ren Kay.

"Revered Leader," said the Zhoogene, who was wearing his Militia uniform, his face heavily shadowed in shades of deep woodland moss. "You've made an interesting move. Do you think isolating yourself in that vehicle will help?"

"Isolating?" She laughed. "On the contrary, this is where I will marshal my forces of persuasion to counterattack. Starting with you. How close are you to concluding—" she glanced suspiciously at Sanderson, who was staring right at her, "—to implementing that matter we discussed?"

"Close."

"Make it closer! This is the critical moment when I stand or fall. I need it now. Within minutes, or you will abort and get the hell off my planet. Can you deliver?"

He checked something out of her sight before replying. "I concur, Revered Leader. This matter is approaching its climax, and the Blue Chamber needs to secure its assets."

"Assets! I'm not a damned *asset*. Answer me clearly, Ren Kay. Can you deliver or not?"

"Ma'am, we have been ready for some time. Given the enormity of what we're about to unleash, we've been waiting to see how the cards would fall before acting. You know how it is. Standby and check news feeds. I guarantee that, within minutes, the whole planet will be fixated on the—" he grinned, "—*matter we discussed.*"

* * * * *

Chapter Fifty-Five:
Tavistock Fitzwilliam

"I don't know what's happening in Execution Square, but I don't like it." Q'Uatiere narrowed her eyes at Fitz, clearly thinking he should be running around shooting at people and not kicking back on a chair in the tram station café. "Isn't it time to bring in Commander Slinh?"

Fitz couldn't blame her. She was only voicing the concern all his command team were feeling. Hell, that *he* was feeling too. Sybutu had just gone off grid, and that was *not* good.

"Don't let the cool jacket and cup of coffee fool you," he explained. "I'm monitoring the situation closely. Slinh's Reserve Brigade is too small to take the city. The moment her unit moves in, it will become a catalyst, one way or another. If the people are already turning against In'Nalla, armed citizens will flock to Slinh's side. If they're still undecided, Slinh's appearance will unite the people against her 'invading army,' and we will have lost. We need to give the cyber nerds a few more moments."

He took a sip of his coffee before keying in his Chimera team.

"Basement Ops, tell me some good news."

"Can't, Captain," Zavage answered. "Even with the three main media shapers offline, there's still a lot left to take the lead from Sonep News, and they're coming full force behind the tyrant now. They're claiming Vetch's team slaughtered hundreds of citizens in seizing In'Nalla. Fake footage has gone viral in the last few seconds that shows you in your Bori-Alice hat overseeing mass firing squad executions in front of the university."

"Aren't there people at the university to prove otherwise?"

"Oh, sure. But people will ignore the truth even if it slaps them in the face like a kiss from Vetch's hammer. They only hear what confirms the opinions they've already formed. This EB-Link plebiscite is going her way. Positive six percent say they stand with In'Nalla, and the number is rising fast. We've lost, Captain. Time to exfil."

"Understood. Stay on the line while I loop in the hammer lover. Vetch, any sign of Sybutu?"

"Negative. He's still inside the news wagon. I don't like to leave him, but his cover appears intact. This crowd's going to boil over any moment. Either we bring in Slinh and go for the military option, or we abort. Now."

A comm chime warned Fitz that Gzeiter was trying to raise him.

"Wait two mikes," he told his Chimera team. He reactivated his half-smoked cigar and then accepted the link to Gzeiter.

"Where the hell are you?" yelled the Panhandler general.

Fitz blew a smoke ring at the general's image on his wrist slate. The poor man had gone rather red in the face.

"Stop playing games, man." The general was controlling his anger better now. "I have the best propaganda team on the planet in the basement of Forefront Media's HQ, but the Militia attackers are jamming me, and they've cut the cable link. You have to reconnect us, or all will be lost."

"Roger that, General," Fitz replied and took a sip of coffee. "Unfortunately, we appear to be bogged down in heavy fighting. We are attempting to break out to your position."

DEPARTMENT 9 | 319

Gzeiter mashed his brows together into an angry frown. Behind Fitz, the backdrop of the Horne Street Station café should have been clear on the vid-link.

"Are you with me or not?" Gzeiter asked.

"Of course. I'm sorry to have lied, but I panicked. The truth is, you caught me on my coffee break."

"Trucker! It's vital we get our message out. The revolution cannot proceed to victory otherwise."

"Cannot proceed to *your* victory. That's what you mean."

Basement Ops sent a message that scrolled along the bottom of Fitz's slate: *New anti-In'Nalla message going viral. Unknown origin.*

Now that was interesting. It couldn't have anything to do with the general.

"I *knew* you were a problem from the start," said Gzeiter. "You're an agent provocateur. A legionary. What are you, Special Missions?"

"Oh, SpecMish have had their fingers in this world for a while now. Probably longer than you have, Panhandler. But, no, General Gzeiter. I represent the interests of the Outer Torellian Commerce Guild." He winked at his astonished command team to make it seem like a joke. Several were impressed, though, as if this admission explained a whole lot of madness.

"The damned Smugglers Guild?" Gzeiter sputtered.

"Tut-tut, Gzeiter. That's a federal speech crime, don't you know? Careless talk can be dangerous on this world."

He severed the link and rekeyed the Chimera channel.

"Basement Ops, speak to me…"

* * * * *

Chapter Fifty-Six:
Revered Leader In'Nalla

"Who do you want to run your world?" asked In'Nalla, the auto-studio in the news wagon relaying her question to the screens outside in the square and to EB-Link across the star system. "Me or off-world mercenaries with an off-world agenda?"

In'Nalla!

In'Nalla!

The chant filled the square.

Again! She moved by habit to contact Asher to fix her situation, forgetting who had betrayed her.

A screen beside her showed the Court of Public Opinion had now swung thirty percent in her favor. The two rebels on the stage had climbed back into their fliers and were about to brave the concentrated fire from thousands of angry citizens in the square. Already, a few were taking potshots from upper floors of the surrounding buildings.

The only way for her to lose now was for the fliers to completely change tactic and try to blast the armored news wagon to slag. Everything they had done had been about winning public support, and some of her most loyal supporters were clinging to the hull of the wagon as a living shield. She didn't think the GACs were a danger.

It was time to arrange the pursuit and destruction of her enemies.

Starting with Blayde Asher…

She froze momentarily.

Asher…that turncoat worm had recruited Sanderson. Was the big man part of her plot? The evidence was inconclusive. He might be entirely innocent of treachery, but that wasn't a chance she could take.

"Sanderson," she said as calmly as she could, while reaching into her jacket for the concealed needle pistol. "As soon as those fliers leave, I'm going to exit the wagon. You will leave first to check the way—"

In'Nalla never intended to complete her sentence.

She called on years of drills for this scenario to draw her weapon, flick off the safety, and aim.

Sanderson was already dodging sideways and throwing a pistol at her.

Her shot went wide, sending a double puff of smoke out of a processor stack in the bulkhead rack.

Then Sanderson's pistol barrel smacked a stinging blow against her temple that made her see flashes for a couple of seconds.

It gave him all the time he needed to launch himself across and apply a grip like a fusion-powered vise to her gun-hand wrist.

Her training emphasized shooting the bastard first. If they got a hold on you, it was game over. So, she dropped her needle pistol.

"Are you going to murder me?" she asked haughtily, still far from sure Sanderson had ever intended to betray her.

"No," he replied, patting her down for more concealed weapons. "Though it is very tempting. I don't like you, In'Nalla, but I took an oath to stay above politics."

"Oh, so you're still Legion."

"I'm on sabbatical."

She rolled her eyes. No one leaves the Legion.

"My name isn't Marc Sanderson."

"Oh, you do surprise me."

"Marc Yergin, 27th Independent Field Squadron, 141st Brigade. Nydella Sanderson, 4th battalion, 83rd Brigade. They died. So did many others, and they gave their lives for a far bigger cause than your petty world with its grubby politics. I can't murder you in cold blood, not because I can't stomach the act, but because you simply aren't important enough."

"Works well for me, Legionary. It means you will die."

"No. I'm going to walk out of here just fine."

"Delusional! Like so many others of your kind. Your only hope is to surrender to me and beg for clemency."

She knew soldiers. Had seen many of them break. Seen the calm that came over some of them when they realized they were caught in a trap they would never escape from alive. At first, she'd mistaken the man's confidence for the calmness of an imminent demise, but Sanderson really did think he'd won.

"Take a look at the screen behind you," he said.

She did.

"Oh, sweet fuck!"

The screen showed the Revered Leader of Eiylah-Bremah in her privacy bunker.

"I want a dirty bomb," she said in the recording. "Radiation. Fallout. Fear!"

Godsabove! Do I really look so unhinged?

After a brief pause, a male Zhoogene voice replied, "Not a problem. I can do that."

Another pause and then, "Wouldn't it be better to blame the bomb on the Panhandlers? You want to unite the public behind you, right? Wouldn't that be easier if you blame off-worlders?"

"You're right, damn you. Nuke that city into radioactive glass and make it look like a Panhandler atrocity. Blame them both if you can."

In'Nalla switched off all the screens.

"It looks like Department 9's changed horses," said Sanderson.

"Department 9? He said he was Blue Chamber."

"He? We *are* talking about a Zhoogene posing as Militia Lieutenant Ren Kay, right?"

In'Nalla looked away in shame. It was mortifying to see her half-crazed face calling for the mass destruction of her own citizens, but more than that, she was ashamed to have been played so easily by that damned Zhoogene.

A last spark of defiance lit her soul, and she regarded the man who called himself Sanderson. "You want Ren Kay dead as much as I do."

"That's right."

"I can't promise anything—" She had to fling her arms out suddenly when the news wagon began to rock, angry fists pounding on the outside, calling for her blood. "But I'll try to get him to reveal something about himself. Maybe you can use it to end him."

Ren Kay answered as soon as she called. He was out of his Militia uniform now, just one more unremarkable civilian in a city undergoing a revolution. "It's damned fortunate you called," he said. "I can't get a signal through to you in that wagon unless I ride your outgoing channel. Don't suppose you'd care to step outside?"

"Help me," she begged.

"No," he replied. "You've done an excellent job for us, Revered Leader, but we don't need you now."

"What do you mean? You worked for me. You committed atrocities."

"Under your orders. The evidence will clearly show you staged the Massacre of Krunacao, Revered Leader."

"Why? What could you possibly hope to gain?"

"Our agenda is to shake the Federation out of its stupidity. You should understand, In'Nalla. Societies without a challenge to face drift into dysfunction and division. They need firm leadership for their own good. That's what you were trying to do on Eiylah-Bremah, and it's what we shall succeed in doing across the Federation and beyond. The outrage citizens will feel about your actions will be one of our propaganda coups. It will help push the bleating sheep of Far Reach citizenry into calling for strong, centralized and, above all, coherent leadership. So, you see, you have succeeded in furthering your political goals, even though you won't be alive to see the benefits."

In'Nalla frowned at the man's image. He wasn't even gloating properly. He was gesturing like crazy at a workstation, setting up something, but what? Not, In'Nalla supposed, that it mattered to her anymore.

With a flourish, Ren Kay completed his workstation task and peered out of In'Nalla's wrist slate with piercing golden eyes. He was looking behind her.

"If that's your new bodyguard in there with you, say hi from me. Marc Sanderson, I believe he's calling himself. How romantic. I'm so sorry about Sergeant Sanderson's tragic demise, Sergeant Sybutu. She was your lover, I understand. But, hey, look on the bright side. You'll be joining her very soon."

* * * * *

Chapter Fifty-Seven:
Osu Sybutu

"Unlike those pansy-ass posers in Naval Intelligence, SpecMish almost never gloats or threatens," Bronze had told Sybutu back on the *Phantom*. "On the rare occasions they do, it's at the final moment before their target is eliminated."

Bronze's words rang through Sybutu's head as he looked in horror at In'Nalla's wrist slate. She was still venting her anger at Ren Kay, but the Zhoogene's threat to him had been made and sounded very final.

He worked the bolts to the hatch and shoved suddenly, with all his might, against the crush of people on the outside, fighting to get in.

He was still pushing when In'Nalla's wrist slate exploded.

The door blew open with Sybutu still hanging on. The pressure wave felt as if it were crushing his chest like an old steel can. Shrapnel fragments thudded into the light armor beneath his clothing.

The roar of the blast filled his skull, but legionary training took over, and he checked himself for injuries. It hurt to breathe. Something had pierced his leg behind his right knee. And his head throbbed. But he didn't think anything vital had been pierced.

Inside the vehicle was a different matter.

In'Nalla's arm had been blown off by the booby trap set in her wrist slate by Ren Kay. Thick blood dripped from every surface.

He checked her over. She was still alive, but only just.

Her blood-soaked eyelids flickered open, but she couldn't focus on him.

"I did what I thought was best for my people," she croaked. "Always."

He contemplated the tyrant of Eiylah-Bremah for a long moment. "I believe you."

"Thank you," she whispered.

"But that doesn't mean a damn. Pretty much every tyrant in human history believed they were doing what's right. You were nothing special."

She gave a death rattle. Then her head slumped against a rack of inert camera drones, and she was gone.

Sybutu stood by what he'd told her at the end, but he hoped she hadn't heard his final words.

He regarded her for another moment or two. Then he got his shit together. He was Sergeant Osu Sybutu, a sapper of the Legion on a temporary posting to Chimera Company. And he had a job to do.

He jumped outside the news wagon.

The crowd parted for him, giving him space.

Streaming with blood, mostly from In'Nalla, his body scorched and torn, likely made him a fearsome sight.

"Keep away!" he growled.

The crowd backed up further.

He keyed the Chimera channel on his comm set. "Fitz, Basement, Vetch, In'Nalla's dead. What's your status?"

"We're on overwatch," said Vetch. "A hundred feet above your head."

"Basement Ops here," said Enthree. "Outrage is flowing around the world. No one is going to weep for In'Nalla."

"Good work, everybody," said Fitz. "I'm calling this a victory for Chimera Company. I'll call in Commander Slinh. Now is the time for her to pick up the pieces, with a little help from Colonel Lantosh. Sybutu, seal yourself back in that wagon until we can get to you."

"Roger that," Sybutu said. "I might not be able to get a signal out, so I'll say now that Ren Kay of Department 9 knew a helluva lot about me. I think that blast was intended for me as much as for In'Nalla."

"Regrettably, I suspect you're right. Basement Ops, your new target is Kaylingen Spaceport. Sybutu! I told you to get your jack ass inside that wagon. Now!"

"Yes, sir."

Sybutu hopped inside and sealed the hatch.

He tried to remember why Fitzwilliam was in charge and what his strategic objective was, but his head was still filled with white noise.

After setting the screens to a wide-angle exterior view, he sat numbly and waited.

* * * * *

Chapter Fifty-Eight:
Izza Zan Fey

After sweeping for surveillance devices and triggering the privacy shroud, she activated the quantum link communicator.

Fitz hadn't left a message.

Not that she expected one. The deep cover protocol required that he communicate first and only when he was ready to proceed to the next stage.

So she switched on the link but didn't transmit anything. Knowing that she could if she wanted was better than nothing. It was tenuous, but she felt the two of them were connected.

She had been allowing herself to sit like this on *Phantom*'s flight deck once every four days. But a loneliness had eaten away at her all day, and she'd finally yielded to it, despite having been there the previous night.

As always, she settled into his seat, resting her heels on his customary spot on the flight console and taking solace in the majestic stars watching her through the cockpit window.

"You've been exceedingly naughty," snapped Fitz.

She almost fell out of the seat! She had never expected him to speak.

He sounded cross, but without being able to see and smell him, she wasn't sure if he was genuinely angry.

"I expect officers to show decorum aboard *Phantom*. She is *not* a clothing-optional vessel. And leaving me a message like that was outrageous." This time she could hear his grin, and she mirrored it. "The link was meant to be used for emergencies only."

"But it *was* an emergency. I have needs." She smiled. "I need you, Tavistock."

"Can't you…" He cleared his throat awkwardly. She knew what he was about to say and how difficult it was for him. "Can't you find…distractions? It's not as if you have to try hard."

She thought back to the people who'd been sharing her quarters since he'd been gone. Since he'd left her. Deep cover hadn't been her idea, she reminded herself bitterly. "No, I've tried. But it doesn't work. I wish it did, but it appears I can accept no substitutes, however unlikely that sounds when I say it out loud."

"I'm pleased that being apart isn't *too* easy," said Fitz. "Neat trick, drugging your own husband. I know it's poetic, because that's what I'd just done to the boys, but it hurt all the same. My own stupid fault, I know. But it hurt."

Izza resisted the impulse to apologize. Deep cover had been *his* idea. And when he'd told her he was having second thoughts, she'd known she had to act decisively for the both of them.

"Please tell me being separated won't have been for nothing," he said.

"It won't. Your gut instincts were right, my love. The eyes of the galaxy are upon you, not me. Activating deep cover protocol has allowed me to make excellent progress. Nyluga-Ree took the bait. I've left what you need for now at Drop Point 17."

"You are a marvel, my lady."

"I know. And here's more proof of that. I've set a low-bandwidth video mode for this connection. We can enjoy twenty minutes without depleting the q-bit store much. Are you in private?"

"We shall be undisturbed."

"Good." She activated the video link. "Tavistock! What a strange way to wear a hat."

"Would you rather I remove it?"

She ran her fingers through her head foliage and felt her eyes begin to glow.

* * * * *

Chapter Fifty-Nine:
Tavistock Fitzwilliam

Despite the band starting up with a funky up-tempo, electro-thump number, Fitz resolutely sulked in the wings of the Global Palace ballroom.

Tonight was the opening of the peace conference, just two days after In'Nalla's fall. Tomorrow, the hard business of putting this world back together would begin in earnest. Fitz had every intention of not being there with the hungover victors of the revolution.

He'd expended a lot of political capital in insisting the word 'reconciliation' not be used in the official name of the conference. To those toasting victory, that word meant firing squads and show trials, and Fitz thought Eiylah-Bremah had suffered quite enough of those, thank you.

Unfortunately, part of the cost of that bargain had been for him to make an appearance tonight and do so with hat off.

Hat off, everything off, as far as he was concerned. So, he left his shades in the pocket of the formal velvet robes they'd given him.

Everyone stared at his mutant eyes.

Well, let them. He raised his glass of wine in acknowledgement at the scandalized stares. Just so long as he kept everyone's attention on him…

"We're through, Captain," reported Sybutu over Fitz's earpiece. "Though I'd advise giving our ex-Militia troopers a crash course on basic concealment."

The waiter hovering by the opposite corridor wore a slight frown of concentration on her delightful green face. She reminded him of Izza.

But she wasn't. Fitz would happily wager a million credits that this Zhoogene was one of the Department 9 operatives working the event. They were closing in on him, and while he doubted they could decrypt his link to Sybutu, the sharp-eared Zhoogene would be able to hear his side of the conversation.

"Your complaining makes you sound like Lynx, Sergeant. And our passenger?"

"Colonel Lantosh is with us."

"Good. Standby, if you please."

Fitz marched over to a pair of women deep in discussion about ten yards away.

They looked up in surprise at his approach and then blushed a little at the unexpected attention from the hero of the moment.

"Hold that for me, will you?" Fitz thrust his glass at one of the women's hands. "Got a case of the galloping trots. Be right back."

The woman took his glass and called after him as he hurried away. "I'm sorry, I don't understand. The *trots?*"

Fitz halted. "I picked up something in the jungle. It's demanding an urgent visit to the restroom."

Leaving behind a flurry of sympathetic noises, he resisted the temptation to wink at the Zhoogene waiter and the other people he suspected were about to spring a Department 9 trap.

He bypassed the nearest restroom, favoring one instead with an exterior facing wall.

Luckily, there were no civilians inside, which made his exfil less messy.

He activated his comm. "Sybutu, begin pre-flight checks."

"But we don't know how."

"Ignore Sergeant Jack," said Lily. "We've just found the manual."

"Excellent work," said Fitz as he ditched his heavy robes and pressed the breach charge to the window. "Do the best you can. I have a suspicion we'll be making a hot exit."

He took cover in the farthest corner of the restroom.

The explosion rocked the building, spraying splintering glass onto the street twenty feet below. Using his robes as protection from the shattered portal, he lifted himself up and was halfway through, his butt wriggling for the final push, when the enemy finally made their move.

"Stay there, Fitzwilliam," shouted the Zhoogene waiter. "We want a word before you die."

Fitz looked back and saw that the Zhoogene was accompanied by one of the musicians, a young human girl. He was disappointed; he hadn't clocked that operative.

"I don't think that's appropriate," Fitz told the Department 9 waiter. "This is a gentlemen-only amenity. If you wouldn't mind leaving and coming back with a male killer to make the threats, I would feel so much more comfortable."

The Zhoogene put a bullet through the window. It passed a fraction of an inch from Fitz's face.

"Your only warning," she said. "We can kill you hard, or we can do it easy. Which is it to be?"

338 | TIM C. TAYLOR

"I'm disappointed," Fitz replied. "In Naval Intelligence, we never gave warnings."

Two suppressed blaster bolts shot out from one of the cubicles—the one with the door that had silently opened while the two women were concentrating on Fitz. The bolts burned through their necks, cutting the connection between their brains and their trigger fingers.

The two would-be assassins died messily, pumping fountains of blood over the pristine tiles of the restroom facility.

"I don't think those suppressors work," said Fitz. "My ears hurt."

"Suppressors work fine," said Bronze, walking out of the cubicle. "Your bomb was too powerful. You were only supposed to blow the window out. Typical Naval Intelligence."

Both men laughed, then got on with the business of jumping out of the building and driving to the spaceport.

* * * * *

Chapter Sixty:
Tavistock Fitzwilliam

"Let's get this bucket of rust and bolts up into the black," Fitz announced the moment he entered the flight deck. "Better strap in. There's no knowing whether this old tub has been maintained properly." He took the pilot's station and rubbed his hands with glee as he tried the controls.

Far from a rust bucket, the ship they'd stolen had been In'Nalla's luxury space yacht, a heavily customized *Hitomi*-class racer with jump capability, opulent berthing, and, from what his people had reported so far, lavishly equipped drinks cabinets.

But it was tradition for a new pilot to treat a ship with cynicism until their first shakedown flight. So rust bucket it would remain for the time being, though as he spooled the main engines and felt the ship throb with power, he didn't think he'd be calling it that for long.

"Where are we headed?" asked Lily, narrowly beating everyone to the question.

"Away is good enough for now," Fitz replied. And that might not be easy if Department 9 still retained as much influence as he suspected.

"Signal intercept," said Zavage. "Militia fighter craft have scrambled from polar airbase to the north."

"Militia, eh?" Fitz lifted off from the landing pad. "I wonder whose side they're on today?"

Not theirs, that was for sure. After In'Nalla's death, the Militia in Kaylingen had negotiated a ceasefire with Gzeiter's surviving troops, which allowed the remaining Panhandlers to leave the city unmolested. Since then, the Militia had heavily reinforced their presence in the capital but had declined to take a view on the 'internal matter' of who should rule Eiylah-Bremah, so long as they followed the requirements of federal law. The long war with RevRec was over. For now, at least.

With those fighters scrambling, though, it looked as if Chimera Company's war with Department 9 was anything but over.

Bronze looked up from the navigator's position, where Izza should rightfully be. "There are several pre-calculated courses for jumps initiated from the L5 point in Eiylah-Bremah's interaction with its primary moon."

Fitz engaged the primary drives and soared for the black. He gave Bronze a searching look. Although the man didn't have the pretty green face or the beautiful marbled eyes of the one he dearly wanted sitting beside him, he was nonetheless turning out to be an asset. "Very good. Pick one at random. L5, here we come."

"Militia fighters are ordering us to land," said Zavage.

"Tell them something suitably rude."

A holographic tactical display emerged automatically. "Belay that." The screen showed that the fighters had launched a fan of missiles. "And hold tight."

The engines roared as Fitz pushed the throttles to the stops.

More screens appeared, feeding him data that made his eyes pop.

The air was rolling freely past her bows, having been charged and deflected by a front shield projector.

The speed was on par with the atmospheric fighter craft trying to kill them, which made this one glorious racing boat.

"My goodness," he muttered in awe. "I think I'm in love."

* * * * *

Chapter Sixty-One:
Vetch Arunsen

Once, it had been a great temple.

In its heyday, the air had been pungent with lit censers, its cloisters patrolled by bloated holy priests carried on the shoulders of acolytes, who would not allow the holy feet of the priests to be sullied by contact with the stone floors. Allied groups of these elevated great ones would patrol in formation like fighter craft, trapping opponents from rival religious schools and engaging them from all sides in unrestrained theological debate.

That's what Fitz had told them when he landed on the deserted planet of Milsungamka in their stolen luxury space yacht, a ship Fitz had renamed *Ghost Shark*.

Vetch hadn't paid much attention at the time. He'd had something far more pressing on his mind.

Whatever its past glories, the temple was deserted now, just a single tower of cracked stone poking out from a mound of fine red desert sand.

With Vetch accompanying him, Fitz had climbed down into the dark bowels of the temple complex, making use of ropes and tunnel borers where the stairwells and passageways were blocked by sand or broken masonry and, in one case, by a huge mound of bones that reached the ceiling. Twists of sinew were still attached to some of the bones. Eyeballs stared from skull sockets. The place gave Vetch the creeps.

Fitz had insisted Vetch bring Lucerne with him, and after seeing this mound of death, he gripped his hammer tighter and sharpened his eyes.

A short distance farther, they'd encountered an ornate fireplace with a hearth mostly filled with sand.

"Keep watch," Fitz had ordered, "while I dig."

And so, Vetch patrolled the ancient corridor lit by a perimeter of glow globes and imagined what stories the stone walls could tell.

"Won't Nyluga-Ree kill you and take the data?" Vetch asked after a few minutes of silence, mostly to hear the comforting sound of his own voice. He didn't expect a straight answer to the question they had asked many times, but it was a matter that had been uppermost on everyone's mind since *Ghost Shark* landed. Everyone's except, apparently, Fitz's.

They were here to make a data pickup and then conduct an exchange with Nyluga-Ree, the crime boss Fitz had been running from ever since Vetch had met him.

"Oh, don't you worry," Fitz replied cheerfully, "all this talk of murder is overblown nonsense."

"Are you saying she doesn't want you dead?"

Fitz paused his digging. "The Outer Torellian Commerce Guild is like a big, happy family. We have occasional family disagreements, but we always come together. Trust me."

"*Trust me.*" Vetch laughed. "Do we have any choice?"

Fitz stood and gave him a comradely slap on the shoulder. "Good man." He held up his prize—a small metal box displaying the logo of a popular brand of fruit-flavored sweets. "When she gets her sweaty hands on this, Ree will love us. C'mon, let's get topside. She'll be waiting for us."

* * * * *

Chapter Sixty-Two:
Vetch Arunsen

"Payment, ma'am."

Fitz handed over the sweet tin to Maycey or Kaycey, the two Kayrissan bodyguards who were indistinguishable as far as Vetch was concerned. Both cat-women had sleek fur, striped in shades of bronze and verdigris, and were armed with power lances.

The Kayrissan opened the tin and sniffed its contents.

Fitz had told Vetch it contained data on the ancient mystery ship they'd chased from Rho-Torkis. Who had uncovered the info and how? He'd refused to answer. Maybe it was Kanha-Wei or, perhaps, Izza Zan Fey was still working with her estranged husband. It was difficult to be sure of anything with his new CO.

The cat-woman handed the box over to her mistress who was glaring at Fitz from her floating basket.

Unlike her svelte bodyguards, who moved with the grace of ninja ballet dancers, Nyluga-Ree looked like a fat, sweaty baby in a loin-cloth. A shocking pink baby.

Vetch had never seen a Glaenwi before, but Fitz had explained the species came from a frigid world, which meant Nyluga-Ree's people generated enormous internal body heat.

He had also said to never, ever call Nyluga-Ree a flamingo.

347

Or to stare at the array of brooding pouches that coated her belly, especially at any which were in use.

But most important of all, Fitz had warned them to remember that Nyluga-Ree was not a direct physical threat. The cat sisters were the deadliest assassins in the sector, so Fitz's Chimera Company escort of Vetch, Lily, and Darant focused on them.

Nyluga-Ree looked at Fitz the way Vetch liked to look at a glass of cold beer next to a plate of hot meat pie. "*Down* payment," she said in a voice that sounded like a pressure leak. "This is a first installment only. I require more."

"Of course," said Fitz. "But…well, I seem to have many masters and mistresses at present. There's one in particular—a rather peculiar old man—that I don't like to keep waiting. Maybe I should make him happy next."

"Lord Khallini is a force to be reckoned with," Ree conceded, "but he doesn't own you. I do."

"Own? I think that's putting it a little strongly."

"Never forget, I hold the key to your heart, human."

Fitz frowned, apparently confused "Do you mean that old green girl I used to hang around with? Hah! I think not."

"Zan Fey loves you still," Ree hissed. "And no matter what you tell yourself about her, I know she will always be a lever to control you."

"Hey, I thought we were friends now?"

Nyluga-Ree shook her body, spraying Fitz with sweat. What that meant in a Glaenwi, Vetch didn't know, but he took his cue from the Kayrissan cat-women. They appeared as calmly aloof as ever.

Vetch wanted to know what it would feel like to stroke that beautiful fur.

Laughing from deep within her belly, Ree held out a glossy pink hand whose fingers were adorned with chunky rings.

Fitz bowed before kissing the proffered hand.

"Our rift is healed," said Ree. "*Temporarily*. You may conduct your business with Lord Khallini before returning to me for further instructions."

The cool desert air shimmered. Suddenly, ten armed Zhoogenes drew back their cloaks and stepped out of nowhere, blasters at the low ready. They surrounded Fitz and his escort.

Stealth cloaks.

Vetch lifted his hammer.

Darant and Lily set their blasters free, the charge packs humming with threat.

"I remind you that I can reach you anywhere, should I choose," said Ree.

"Don't underestimate Chimera Company," announced Sybutu. He shimmered into existence atop a dune fifty feet away to one flank, aiming a tripod-mounted SFG gun at Ree. Zavage knelt beside him, ready to serve the plentiful ammo drums. Their appearance surprised the hell out of Vetch. When the two jacks had activated the stealth box they found waiting for them when they landed, they had been in a completely different position.

Different tech from that of the Zhoogenes in the stealth cloaks but similar outcome.

"We have many surprises," added Lantosh, who stayed hidden in her stealth box with Bronze, but her voice appeared to whisper through the air from every direction at once.

"I shall take your inventiveness under advisement," said Ree, who appeared delighted by this display, unlike the Kayrissans, whose fur stood on end. "You humans continue to amuse me. Such an exciting species to outwit. It is what keeps you alive. Don't ever make the mistake of becoming predictable, Fitzwilliam. The day I tire of you is the day you die."

* * * * *

Chapter Sixty-Three: Vetch Arunsen

"Hold 1 is secure, Captain. Proceeding to Hold 2."

"Copy that," Fitz responded over the intercom.

Fitz had sent everyone to scour *Ghost Shark* for any signs of Nyl-uga-Ree shenanigans. Vetch suspected the exercise was just as much about deflecting questions about why they were dealing with the crime boss. But for now, at least, he was still treating Fitz as his commanding officer.

As he was walking out of the hold, Vetch stopped and sniffed the air.

He'd been a scrawler as a kid, spray painting tags and wry commentary on public buildings. He would recognize the odor of quick dry paint anywhere. Even here.

Following his nose, he walked over to a bulkhead panel.

It looked the same as the others—dirty, bare metal. Unlike the fancier parts of *Ghost Shark*, the hold obviously hadn't warranted valet treatment.

Then his eyes took in what they were really seeing.

The panel had been *painted* to look like the others, but something about it was different.

He heard a faint noise behind him and turned to see one of Ree's cat-women swinging her power lance at his head.

Vetch ducked, but he wasn't quite fast enough. The lance struck a glancing blow on top of his head, which was bad enough, but it also set lightning bolts buzzing around the inside of his skull.

Instinctively, he flung his arms out as he fought to stay conscious, only to have them grabbed and pinned behind him.

He tried to fight free, but his head was still buzzing with static from the power lance, and his muscles were refusing to obey orders.

"We had planned on seizing one of the human females," whispered the cat-woman just behind his left ear.

"But then you volunteered yourself for the role," said her sister into his right.

Two of them! Vetch didn't think he was getting out of this.

They pushed him through the bulkhead. Vetch was too confused to be sure what was happening, but it seemed the assassins had attached an airlock to *Ghost Shark*'s hull and cut through into the hold without raising an alarm.

Together, they cycled through the airlock and into a tiny bubble-craft on the far side. It detached and sped away into space.

Leaving her sister to pilot the craft, the other Kayrissan regarded Vetch through green, slitted eyes. "Our mistress is far too indulgent with her favorite human," she said, "but even Nyluga-Ree realizes Fitzwilliam is headstrong. As her hostage, you will help bring him to heel."

"And if you don't," said the pilot, "she'll have you stuffed and mounted in her trophy room. One hundred credits says the bearded human will be a taxidermy display before the year is out."

The other sister purred as she again inspected Vetch. "Unacceptable. I counter-wager he will still be alive and have all his limbs one hundred standard days from now."

"One hundred and twenty days and two hundred credits."

"Agreed."

The Kayrissan caressed Vetch's cheek with the back of her hand. Her touch was so smooth, it made puppies and freshly changed babies feel like wire wool and sandpaper. "Don't give me cause to dislike you, human. You must stay alive for a few months. After that, you are free to die."

* * * * *

Chapter Sixty-Four: Osu Sybutu

"Captain, the cyber-attack has been cleansed," reported Enthree at her station in the cramped info-suite.

"It was intended to delay and conceal rather than destroy," added Zavage, but it was the Muryani that Fitz was frowning at. She clearly bothered the hell out of him, and Sybutu felt the same way.

Enthree noted the attention, which was interesting. Normally, she appeared oblivious to human body language. "What is it about me that worries you, Captain?"

"Partly, your sudden acquisition of advanced cyber skills," Fitz replied. "But mostly, who the hell is funding you on such a scale that you could issue that bribe back on Eiylah-Bremah?"

"We're all due some answers," said Sybutu, looking pointedly at the captain, "but our priority is to get Vetch back."

Lily raised an eyebrow. "That's the first time you've called him Vetch."

"I still think he's a fat oaf," Sybutu explained, "but he's a vital member of Chimera Company." He narrowed his eyes at Fitz. "We've left too many people behind as it is."

"Yes, of course," Fitz said. "We must rescue the princess."

Sybutu shook his head in disbelief. "Did you just call our hairy Viking a princess?"

Fitz grinned back. "If retrieving him means the inconvenience of going head to head against Nyluga-Ree, when we should really be attending to Kanha-Wei and Lord Khallini, then a callsign of Princess seems a fair price for him to pay."

"Their jump tunnel is still open," said Zavage. "*Ghost Shark* is lightning fast. I think we can still follow them into hyperspace."

"Not so directly," said Fitz, reaching for a cigar from his jacket pocket but appearing surprised when he pulled out a miniature bronze jar instead. "Ree would simply kill Vetch. No, we need an indirect approach." He grinned at his team while he stashed the jar and pulled out a cigar from another pocket. "You know, my friends, I feel that, as an interstellar civilization, we don't spend enough time with those unfortunate individuals at the fringes of society. I'm thinking particularly about elderly freakish wizards. It's time we paid a visit to Lord Khallini."

* * * * *

About Tim C. Taylor

Tim C. Taylor lives with his family in an ancient village in England. When he was an impressionable kid, between 1977 and 1978, several mind-altering things happened to him all at once: Star Wars, Dungeons & Dragons, and 2000AD comic. Consequently, he now writes science fiction novels for a living, notably in the Human Legion and Four Horsemen Universes. His latest project is an adventure serial called Chimera Company, which has been described as Warhammer 40,000 in the style of Star Wars. For a free starter library of stories from all the worlds he writes in, join the Legion at humanlegion.com.

* * * * *

Looking for the Latest in Scifi Goodness?

Come join us on the Factory Floor on Facebook!

Meet us at: https://www.facebook.com/groups/461794864654198/

* * * * *

AUTHOR' NOTE

Get More Chimera Company!

If you want to keep up with the news on the latest season, you can check out the Chimera Company page on https://humanlegion.com/, where you can also download prequels and join the Legion to get the latest skinny on my stories and learn about the Chimera Company Insiders.

There are three prequels so far, featuring the Militia, Legion, and Special Missions (with Vetch, Osu, and Bronze on the covers). You can download some for free from the Chimera Company page, and the rest by joining the Legion at humanlegion.com.

I'm going to write at least two more Chimera Company novels. I would love to write more, but for that to be a reality, the series needs to sell well. Spreading the word and leaving positive reviews are things you can do to help it succeed.

Thanks for reading.

Tim Taylor—June 2020.

* * * * *

The following is an
Excerpt from Book One of the Revelations Cycle:

Cartwright's Cavaliers

Mark Wandrey

Available Now from Seventh Seal Press

eBook, Paperback, and Audio Book

Excerpt from "Cartwight's Cavaliers:"

The last two operational tanks were trapped on their chosen path. Faced with destroyed vehicles front and back, they cut sideways to the edge of the dry river bed they'd been moving along and found several large boulders to maneuver around that allowed them to present a hull-down defensive position. Their troopers rallied on that position. It was starting to look like they'd dig in when Phoenix 1 screamed over and strafed them with dual streams of railgun rounds. A split second later, Phoenix 2 followed on a parallel path. Jim was just cheering the air attack when he saw it. The sixth damned tank, and it was a heavy.

"I got that last tank," Jim said over the command net.

"Observe and stand by," Murdock said.

"We'll have these in hand shortly," Buddha agreed, his transmission interspersed with the thudding of his CASPer firing its magnet accelerator. "We can be there in a few minutes."

Jim examined his battlespace. The tank was massive. It had to be one of the fusion-powered beasts he'd read about. Which meant shields and energy weapons. It was heading down the same gap the APC had taken, so it was heading toward Second Squad, and fast.

"Shit," he said.

"Jim," Hargrave said, "we're in position. What are you doing?"

"Leading," Jim said as he jumped out from the rock wall.

* * * * *

Get "Cartwright's Cavaliers" now at:
https://www.amazon.com/dp/B01MRZKM95

Find out more about Mark Wandrey and the Four Horsemen Universe at:

https://chriskennedypublishing.com/the-four-horsemen-books/

* * * * *

The following is an
Excerpt from Book One of the Salvage Title Trilogy:

Salvage Title

Kevin Steverson

Available Now from Theogony Books

eBook, Paperback, and Audio Book

Excerpt from "Salvage Title:"

The first thing Clip did was get power to the door and the access panel. Two of his power cells did the trick once he had them wired to the container. He then pulled out his slate and connected it. It lit up, and his fingers flew across it. It took him a few minutes to establish a link, then he programmed it to search for the combination to the access panel.

"Is it from a human ship?" Harmon asked, curious.

"I don't think so, but it doesn't matter; ones and zeros are still ones and zeros when it comes to computers. It's universal. I mean, there are some things you have to know to get other races' computers to run right, but it's not that hard," Clip said.

Harmon shook his head. *Riiigghht,* he thought. He knew better. Clip's intelligence test results were completely off the charts. Clip opted to go to work at Rinto's right after secondary school because there was nothing for him to learn at the colleges and universities on either Tretra or Joth. He could have received academic scholarships for advanced degrees on a number of nearby systems. He could have even gone all the way to Earth and attended the University of Georgia if he wanted. The problem was getting there. The schools would have provided free tuition if he could just have paid to get there.

Secondary school had been rough on Clip. He was a small guy that made excellent grades without trying. It would have been worse if Harmon hadn't let everyone know that Clip was his brother. They lived in the same foster center, so it was mostly true. The first day of school, Harmon had laid down the law—if you messed with Clip, you messed up.

At the age of fourteen, he beat three seniors senseless for attempting to put Clip in a trash container. One of them was a Yalteen, a member of a race of large humanoids from two systems over. It wasn't a fair fight—they should have brought more people with them. Harmon hated bullies.

After the suspension ended, the school's Warball coach came to see him. He started that season as a freshman and worked on using it to earn a scholarship to the academy. By the time he graduated, he was six feet two inches with two hundred and twenty pounds of muscle. He got the scholarship and a shot at going into space. It was the longest time he'd ever spent away from his foster brother, but he couldn't turn it down.

Clip stayed on Joth and went to work for Rinto. He figured it was a job that would get him access to all kinds of technical stuff, servos, motors, and maybe even some alien computers. The first week he was there, he tweaked the equipment and increased the plant's recycled steel production by 12 percent. Rinto was eternally grateful, as it put him solidly into the profit column instead of toeing the line between profit and loss. When Harmon came back to the planet after the academy, Rinto hired him on the spot on Clip's recommendation. After he saw Harmon operate the grappler and got to know him, he was glad he did.

A steady beeping brought Harmon back to the present. Clip's program had succeeded in unlocking the container. "Right on!" Clip exclaimed. He was always using expressions hundreds or more years out of style. "Let's see what we have; I hope this one isn't empty, too." Last month they'd come across a smaller vault, but it had been empty.

Harmon stepped up and wedged his hands into the small opening the door had made when it disengaged the locks. There wasn't enough power in the small cells Clip used to open it any further. He put his weight into it, and the door opened enough for them to get inside. Before they went in, Harmon placed a piece of pipe in the doorway so it couldn't close and lock on them, baking them alive before anyone realized they were missing.

Daylight shone in through the doorway, and they both froze in place; the weapons vault was full.

* * * * *

Get "Salvage Title" now at:
https://www.amazon.com/dp/B07H8Q3HBV.

Find out more about Kevin Steverson and "Salvage Title" at:
http://chriskennedypublishing.com/.

* * * * *

The following is an
Excerpt from Book One of Murphy's Lawless:

Shakes

_____

Mike Massa

Available from Beyond Terra Press

eBook and Paperback

Excerpt from "Shakes:"

"My name is Volo of the House Zobulakos," the SpinDog announced haughtily. Harry watched as his slender ally found his feet and made a show of brushing imaginary dust from his shoulder where the lance had rested.

Volo was defiant even in the face of drawn weapons; Harry had to give him points for style.

"I am here representing the esteemed friend to all Sarmatchani, my father, Arko Primus Heraklis Zobulakos. This is a mission of great importance. What honorless prole names my brother a liar and interferes with the will of the Primus? Tell me, that I might inform your chief of this insolence."

Harry tensed as two of the newcomers surged forward in angry reaction to the word "honorless," but the tall man interposed his lance, barring their way.

"Father!" the shorter one objected, throwing back her hood, revealing a sharp featured young woman. She'd drawn her blade and balefully eyed the SpinDog. "Let me teach this arrogant weakling about honor!"

"Nay, Stella," the broad-shouldered man said grimly. "Even my daughter must cleave to the law. This is a clan matter. And as to the stripling's question..."

"I, hight Yannis al-Caoimhip ex-huscarlo, Patrisero of the Herdbane, First among the Sarmatchani," he went on, fixing his eyes first on Volo and then each of the Terrans. "I name Stabilo of the Sky People a liar, a cheat, and a coward. I call his people to account. Blood or treasure. At dawn tomorrow either will suffice."

Harry didn't say a word but heard a deep sigh from Rodriguez. These were the allies he'd been sent to find, all right. Just like every other joint operation with indigs, it was SNAFU.

Murphy's Law was in still in effect.

* * * * *

Get "Shakes" now at: https://www.amazon.com/dp/B0861F23KH

Find out more about Myrphy's Lawless and Beyond Terra Press at: https://chriskennedypublishing.com/imprints-authors/beyond-terra-press/

* * * * *

Printed in Great Britain
by Amazon

29383572R00208